Unstill Life

Tales from the Valley of Fruit and Silicon circa in the Year of Our Lord 1982

Unstill Life

Tales from the Valley of Fruit and Silicon circa in the Year of Our Lord 1982

Janis G. Wick

Saen & Gelhorn Press, MMXXI
Palo Alto, California

Some stories in this volume have previously appeared elsewhere as follows:

"The Importance of Stars in the Sky." *Faces and Tongues: Poetry and Prose About People and War.* Laughing Waters Press: 1986

"The Collected Correspondence of Jo Lynne Ducket and Edward R. Beck." *Eclectic Literary Forum* 1(2): Summer 1991

"Brick Red." *San José Studies.* Fall 1991.

"What Exactly Happens as Time Goes By." *Eclectic Literary Forum* 8(3/4), 1998.

"O Come Let Us Adore." *Surreal,* accepted for publication

Cover photography:
Original "family photo" by Josue Michel at photo sharing site Unsplash.com as well as at josuemichelphotography.com.
Original "cloud" photo by Kirill Ermakov at photo sharing site Unsplash.com

Cover photo editing done by author using the free version of the photo editing app Photoscape, including custom emojis. Photoscape offers a Pro version at a modest cost for advanced users.

A nod to R.M., R.I.P.

The author acquired considerable knowledge regarding the art and "mechanics" of publishing from a YouTube video series produced by author, graphic artist and publisher, Mary Ames Mitchell, founder of Plum Tree Press.

Saen & Gelhorn Press, Palo Alto, California

Copyright © 2021 by Janis G. Wick – All rights reserved. No part of this book may be used or reproduced in any manner whatsoever without written permission from the author.

Library of Congress Control Number: 2021914615

ISBN paper: 978-1-7376121-0-0

Dedicated to the writers living and dead circa the Year of Our Lord 1982 of South America and Central America, and the Nation of Mexico and the Island Nations of the Caribbean including the Nation of Cuba. You, men and women of the pen in all these beloved places, with all your tremendously varied voices and imaginations and sensitivities and courage, you all have given me my own modest courage to tell these tales how I wished and intended to do. With this dedication, it is my hope that, though I may disappoint you, I have not grievously offended you.

Thanks go in particular to Daina Chaviano with whom I had the pleasure to dine and "dish" and share stories in the summer of 1988, La Habana, Cuba.

Ms. Chaviano, who now resides in the United States, is an award-winning writer and actress whose works in Spanish have been translated into many languages and can be discovered at www.dainachaviano.com. You might enjoy her latest, *Children of the Hurricane Goddess* or *Los Hijos de la Diosa Huracán*—a remarkable achievement of historical-futuristic archeological detective story, and that description does not begin to do it justice.

Tales of Content

Trying to Be Wiser Than a Goldfish 1

Bird Feathers 31

For Free 45

What Happened On The Bicycle Path 69

Brick Red 81

Barriers 103

What Exactly Happens … As Time Goes By 133

Getting Comfort 149

The Golden Rule 225

O Come Let Us Adore 237

A Journey, Not A Cataclysm 251

The Importance of Stars in the Sky 287

The Collected Correspondence of Jo Lynne Ducket and Edward R. Beck 308

In Memoriam 333

TRYING TO BE WISER THAN A GOLDFISH

"Margaret, wake up." Fred poked his wife.

Margaret groaned under a plush, pale blue comforter.

"Margaret, come on. Wake up."

Fred's wife sat bolt upright.

"What is it?!"

"I had a bad dream."

"A bad dream?"

"I dreamt I saw God."

"Fred, you don't believe in God." Margaret flopped back down, groaned again and pulled the comforter over her head.

"But God, Margaret, God was Bella Abzug. *Bella Abzug* for Christ's sake. I was climbing the steps to City Hall, see, and I knew I was going to see God and—"

Fred's wife laughed.

"Margaret, this is serious."

"Okay, okay," she said. She sat up next to Fred. "Maybe you could paint it. Bella Abzug, robed in white atop a marble staircase."

"Stop it," Fred said. "My painting's no joke."

"No, of course not."

"Anyway, my point is Margaret, my point is, I don't want to dream about Bella Abzug."

"No?"

"For pity's sake, Margaret, Bella Abzug's a—" He stopped. "Ballbreaker" was what he had meant to say. He started again. "Look, I want to dream about—well about ravishing Raquel Welch."

"Raquel Welch sends you?"

"Well, no. Raquel Welch bores me actually."

"Who would you like to ravish?"

"Well, um …"

"Bo Derek?"

"Margaret, no. Somebody like—well like—oh, I don't know."

"What about—"

"My God, Margaret." Fred had suddenly had a crushing thought. "I can't think of anyone I want to ravish. What's happening to me?"

"Perhaps you're maturing, honey."

"Don't get snotty, Margaret. This is a crisis."

"Fred, crises always look better in the morning. Let's get some sleep."

So Margaret slept and Fred stayed awake, gingerly considering the idea of playing with himself, something he had not done in a good many years, but which he reasoned might now get his somewhat repressed juices flowing and then abandoning the idea at the thought of his possible mortification if Margaret woke up, and then pursuing another line of musing in which he ravished his wife while she slept, which he abandoned as well because she had a court date at 9 a.m. and would probably not be too fond of impromptu sex in the middle of the night. Unsatisfied, Fred fell into a restless sleep in which he dreamt he painted Bella Abzug's head on a thirty by forty foot canvas.

At the breakfast table the next morning, Fred, wrapped in a bathrobe he had put on inside out, said to his wife, she dressed in an immaculate gray wool suit, "Margaret, I want to talk."

"Are the girls up?" she asked.

"Getting up. Now—"

"Fred, this really isn't a very good time."

"Margaret, this is important."

"Okay, okay. But can you make it quick, honey. Was it your dream?"

Margaret looked at Fred with her big brown eyes in a way that made him feel small.

"Margaret, I'm going back to work."

"You are working, Fred. Painting is working."

"Yeah, but it's kind of weird, Margaret. A strange thing for a grown man to be doing."

"Was Pablo Picasso weird?"

"No, but I'm no Pablo Picasso."

Fred was a painter, though, and they both knew it. He not only sold his paintings and for a fair amount of money, but he had received a bit of cautious critical acclaim that had reached well beyond the suburban valley in which he lived. And, of course, he worked at it, hard and every day, interrupted only by grocery shopping and tossing in another load of wash.

"Daaaaaaaad. Where are my underpants?" It was Melanie, Fred's elder daughter.

"They're in your drawer."

"No they aren't."

"Yes they are."

"No they *aren't.*"

"Then they're in Lisa's drawer."

This exchange was followed by a disgusted "Dad" and then silence.

"Fred, what is this? Painting means everything to you."

"I know, I know, but we need the money."

"We don't need the money, Fred. We're making more money than ninety percent of the people in this country."

"Daddy?" It was Lisa, Fred's younger daughter, who had tiptoed into the room.

"What is it?"

"Daddy, can Mary Ellen come over after school?" Lisa looked up with her mother's big brown eyes.

"No, honey. The house is a mess."

"My room isn't, Daddy. My room is neat. I just made my bed."

Fred knew the truth of that statement. Margaret had managed, prior to her sally into the world, to raise one daughter, Melanie, who was a hellion and whose aim in life at a mature thirteen was to become a neurosurgeon or an astronaut perhaps, and another daughter, Lisa, age eleven, who was a delicate child—she had asthma, sometimes quite badly—and who, to the amazement of everyone but most of all Margaret, wanted to cook, clean house and raise children. Margaret had often said they should have had a third who might have found some middle ground. Fred wondered, when Margaret said that, what exactly middle ground was. He needed to know—for himself.

"Okay, honey," Fred said to his daughter. "But blindfold her till she gets to your room."

"Okay, Daddy." Lisa turned to go.

"Lisa, Daddy was kidding," Fred said.

"Oh, okay. Okay, Daddy." Lisa smiled and wandered back to her bedroom.

"God," said Margaret. "She's *humoring* you. Where did she learn *that?*"

Fred shrugged and then said, "We do need money, Margaret. What about the roof?"

"Oh—yeah. I forgot."

"You would."

"Fred, that isn't fair."

"Uh oh, a fight, a fight. Can I watch? Can I?"

"May you, Melanie, and the answer is no," Fred said. "Anyway, we're not fighting."

"Just *disagreeing?"*

"Melanie, eat," Margaret said and then, "Fred, honey, why don't you do some more consulting for a bit."

It was agreed. Fred would consult with his previous business associates, and, in the process, Fred hoped that the roof, and just possibly himself, might get fixed.

It was not that Fred wanted to abandon painting. When Margaret had finished law school and had actually become a lawyer, and it looked as if he might actually become an artist, or at least a craftsman of a sort, he and Margaret had celebrated over champagne for five straight days. And then he had begun to paint, and it had absorbed him as nothing else had. He could paint right through the buzzer on the dryer, which was as loud as a civil defense siren and buzzed for ten minutes. He could paint through a rainstorm and not notice that the lights had gone out. And he didn't mind the housework even though it bored him and his friends teased him about it and the commercials on television never had a fifty-year-old man despairing over a ring around somebody's collar—a despair Fred had, in fact, experienced.

But then he had begun to dream about Bella—Bella who wore business suits and talked tough and made Fred feel like a bug. He had begun to feel, in his most private thoughts, that he had to take her on, somehow. The fact that Margaret wore business suits and was one hell of a defense attorney—she'd use arguments that left prosecutors verbally castrated—didn't disturb Fred at all. Why, he was all for her, proud of her. But Bella—Bella was after him, and a paint brush wasn't much of a defense.

After his wife and then his daughters left the house that morning, Fred washed the breakfast dishes, made the beds, with the exception of Lisa's, made a quick foray through the house to see if there were any dead plants, sick goldfish, or moldy food and then decided that the status quo, mild chaos, was quite livable. He went into the kitchen and poured himself a second cup of coffee.

This was usually Fred's favorite time of day, those minutes just before he would begin to paint. Without any clear or conscious image, he would know then exactly what he was about to do. It was a feeling, a sense of anticipation, almost a sense of danger, of risk, and nearly a sense of euphoria. He had felt such things only once before—in Vietnam, on patrol. It had sickened him then. Now he cherished it.

But this morning was different and surprisingly disappointing. He had made a call to a former business partner who had been insisting for months that Fred should investigate a small computer company for him as a possible investment. The partner was delighted. Fred wasn't, but he thought he should have been. After all, it fit in perfectly with his strategy against Bella. He had planned to put on a business suit and watch people grovel at his feet—well maybe just treat him with a little respect—well no, grovel at his feet. His lack of enthusiasm for the prospect stunned him.

In any case, he was supposed to meet the president of Iptech, the computer firm in question, at one. In the intervening hours when he might have painted, he simply sat or made half-hearted attempts at cleaning house and wondered why he didn't feel better.

He entered the front office of Iptech at precisely one and introduced himself to the receptionist. He waited for the obligatory obeisance that he believed to be his due.

"Fred White," he said.

"Rita Goldfine," the receptionist said, holding out her hand.

"Oh," he said. He shook it.

Rita wore a white T-shirt emblazoned in magenta with the words, "Jane wants equal pay, it's the Dick that doesn't." She pulled up a loose strand of hair with a long and bony, but remarkably graceful hand.

"Uh, I've come to see Mr. Porter, Ted Porter."

"He's out," she said. "But you can wait."

She smiled and the smile softened the bare bones of her thin face.

"But I had an appointment."

"You did?" Rita fumbled through a stack of crumpled papers and found what appeared to be a calendar.

"Oh, so you did." She smiled again.

"Well, is he expected back soon?"

"I doubt it," she said. "The assemblers are threatening a strike. It's kind of a crisis."

Fred nodded. "Is there a union?" he asked.

"There will be," she said, pointing to a small button on the neck of her shirt. "We're organizing."

He nodded again, and Rita smiled again. Each time she smiled, her bony face softened a bit more, and oddly, at the same time, the strength of it seemed to grow. That peculiar combination gave Rita's face an uneasy grace that left Fred thoroughly and most uncomfortably enchanted.

"Have you ever been painted?" he asked, surprising himself.

"Are you a painter?" Rita asked.

Fred nodded.

"And you'd like to paint me?"

"Yes, very much," said Fred, blushing in a way he had not in years and surprising himself once again.

Fred never saw Mr. Porter that day nor the next but he did see Rita. She came to sit for him. The morning she came, Fred was irritable and crabby with his wife and kids. It had a bit to do with the fact that Fred had been unable to "perform" the night before, something that had happened to him on occasion but that had seemed particularly devastating this time given the fact that he had believed while in the act, or while *trying* to be in the act, that Bella was watching and snickering behind a big-boned hand. His irritability had a bit to do, too, with the incipient arrival of Rita. Fred, however, with the murky insight of someone who is at best bored with his own inner machinations, attributed his less-than-sunny spirit to the considerable number of household chores that needed doing before he would let the milkman inside his house let alone an impressionable young woman.

His wife left saying she would be late. Melanie left saying she would be very late, a statement left unquestioned by her distracted father, and Lisa left saying she would be home by three to help her father start dinner.

Fred then swept accumulated muck, dirt and dust under the area rugs in each room, gathered a football (Melanie's), assorted doll clothes (Lisa's), a lavender bra (Margaret's), and a half-eaten pear (his probably) and stuffed them into the only empty orifice in the house, the electric clothes dryer. Then he got himself a second cup of coffee and watched his hand shake as he drank it.

Fred had learned through some laborious but entirely subconscious process that he really did very much want to paint Rita and that in painting her he would venture far away from the strokes of brilliant color that produced the vivid impressions of sailboats at sunset or pale green bottles on teal blue tables. He had always chosen objects for his inspiration rather than flesh, and he had refused to paint his daughters, even though they had begged him. It had troubled him and made him feel a failure in some way, but the sight of a body, a person or even a moment with a person had simply never been the source of the dreams, and sometimes the nightmares, he splashed across his canvasses. Rita, though, Rita was quite different. He wanted to paint her, and he wanted to do that so badly that the desire made him weak.

She arrived promptly at 10 a.m., exactly as she and Fred had agreed.

"I've got till one," she said as she stood on the doorstep wringing a purple cloth handbag.

Fred nodded and led her into his studio—a large, light, high-ceilinged room he had built himself at the back of his house.

"Coffee?" Fred asked.

Rita nodded. "Yes, thanks."

He brought her coffee and then asked her to sit on a straight-backed chair in the center of the large bare room.

He looked steadily at her without speaking and with eyes that saw subtle curves and shadows and colors in the woman who sat before him in faded blue jeans and a pale green T-shirt.

"You're making me nervous," said Rita.

"Am I?" he said. "Sorry. It's just that you're so—magnificent." And she was, because he saw again in the bones and thin flesh something so soft and so strong that he was nearly moved to tears.

Rita laughed. "Me? I'm Rita Goldfine—honorary wallflower of the class of '82."

"The boys must have been idiots," Fred said.

Rita laughed again and then asked, "Do you want me to take my clothes off?"

"Uh—yeah—in a minute." Fred had begun sketching. He looked up and saw Rita blushing.

"It's all right," he said. "I've done this millions of times. It's part of my work."

He stopped—because he was lying, of course—he had not painted a nude in twenty years—and because Rita seemed more uncomfortable still.

"I don't think Ted would like this," Rita said, blushing again.

"Ted? Porter? Why would he—you mean because you're missing work?"

"Well—no. Well, yes. I guess so."

Fred sketched quickly, and Rita sat and watched him. Then she began removing garments. First her T-shirt, then her jeans and then her underclothes. Finally, she undid her hair and let it fall down her back. Fred watched her and saw the flesh of her body revealed piece by piece. He was at first curious, then interested, and then amazed. Her skin was opalescent, nearly blue. Her eyes and hair were black. The contrast was breathtaking, almost frightening. Fred was not only amazed, he was aroused.

Rita looked at Fred and then away. He knew she wanted reassurance. He couldn't give it to her. He asked her to stand at a window, slightly oblique to himself. He chose the angle to diminish her in some way—so he could paint her. Otherwise, he knew he wouldn't be able. He sketched and Rita stood and neither spoke.

After an hour, he suggested coffee and brought Rita an old bathrobe.

"That was weird," said Rita. "Nice in a way, but weird. I'm not an exhibitionist."

"No, I know," said Fred. He wanted to take her hand, and he wanted to kiss it and say something to her, something about herself. But he did and said nothing. After coffee, she stood and he sketched and then it was over and she left. She was to return the next day.

After she had gone, Fred felt slightly ill—actually more than slightly—so rather than returning to the studio, he vacuumed, something he hated but that seemed to calm him. He did the edges and the curtain tops as well. Even Margaret had done so only once every six months.

Lisa and Melanie arrived at three. Mary Ellen had a cold and couldn't come over, which was of considerable relief to Fred. Mild chaos was livable but not socially acceptable. Lisa wandered into the kitchen and leafed through *Julia Child's* in hopes of finding something interesting to do with pork chops, and Melanie headed for the bathroom into which she disappeared for several hours. Fred kept Lisa company for awhile and then went in search of Melanie.

He was worried about Melanie. She moved through life like a locomotive, undaunted by those who tried to put obstacles in her way. He was worried that she, too much like himself at thirteen, might begin to leave wreckage behind.

He tapped on the bathroom door.

"It's open."

"Okay if I come in?"

"Sure thing."

The bathroom was in a state of considerable disarray. Fred removed a vial of black fluid and a make-shift Bunsen burner from the toilet seat and sat down.

"What exactly are you doing?" he asked.

Another Bunsen burner on the sink top was heating an odious-smelling fluid in a glass beaker.

"An experiment," Melanie replied.

"What experiment?"

"Can't say. It's experimental."

"Oh."

"If I do it, though, if I do it right, every asshole in that class will have to eat sh—"

"Melanie."

"Sorry, Dad…I'm the smartest person in class, you know."

"No, I didn't know. But I believe it."

Melanie poured the black liquid into the heating fluid. The mixture bubbled precariously near the top of the beaker and then settled down.

"Melanie, I want to tell you something."

"Shoot."

"You probably won't understand this, but being smart—smart in school—isn't everything. I mean—"

"You mean I need to be smart about the mushy stuff, too?"

"Well, yes."

"Well, I am, Dad. At least Billy Norden thinks so."

"Who's Billy Norden?"

"My boyfriend."

"You have a *boyfriend?*"

"Sure, why not?"

"Oh—uh, no reason. Do you get along?"

"Fine, Dad. We get along fine. He made me these Bunsen burners."

Fred nodded, thinking of the secrets and the secret lives about which he knew nothing.

At six, Margaret arrived home to a hot dinner and a very dirty bathroom. She shrugged and asked Fred with he had been painting. He hedged. "Bella Abzug," he said. Margaret laughed and then mopped up the bathroom.

Over dinner, Lisa's orange-glazed pork chops and boiled new potatoes, Bella Abzug was discussed as a possible presidential candidate. Melanie was all for it; Lisa wasn't sure; Margaret favored Gloria Steinem; and Fred said the whole idea upset his stomach. Margaret gave him a long look—which Fred didn't return.

Melanie drifted off shortly after dinner, Margaret went to her study to work, and Fred and Lisa cleared the plates and began to do the dishes.

"What do you really think of Bella, Lise?" Fred asked after he had braced himself with a cup of coffee and sat down letting Lisa dry the last of the dishes.

"I don't like her," said Lisa.

"Why not?"

"She's too loud."

"But she gets her way."

"I get my way, too," said Lisa.

"You do? Even with Donald?" Donald Dornacher was Lisa's friend. Fred knew all about him. Lisa brought him to the house almost every day.

"Yeah. He makes fun of my dolls, you know. But I told him if he didn't like them he didn't have to play with me anymore."

"And?"

"He still plays with me. He plays with my dolls, too. But I'm not supposed to tell anybody."

"Mum's the word," said Fred.

Lisa smiled shyly and kissed her dad on the cheek and said goodnight.

More secrets, Fred thought. It amazed him how his two daughters had found ways to live over which he seemed to have had no influence at all.

Fred looked for Margaret then. He found her in the living room, reading a novel. She was wrapped in a chenille bathrobe and curled up comfortably in Fred's chair. When Fred saw her, he felt guilty, though he couldn't have said why. She looked up and smiled and went back to her book. He was relieved that she didn't want to talk. He wouldn't have known what to say.

He watched his daughters' goldfish instead. They were a pair, of indeterminate sex, christened Henry VIII and Elizabeth I by Lisa, who had a fondness like her mother for the English monarchy and especially its nastier members, and then rechristened Hank and Betty by a less reverent Melanie.

Hank and Betty were subdued this evening. They swam gently through the water with their fins moving in quiet waves. Fred found the movement amazingly graceful, and this upset him. Why did Hank and Betty get to move through their small world with grace while Fred trod like a dinosaur? Why weren't they confused? Why weren't they anxiety ridden? Why didn't a thirty foot head of Bella with a bit of mustache on her lips appear in *their* dreams?

"You okay, honey?" Margaret asked.

Fred jumped. "Fine," he said. "You?"

"Oh, fine." Margaret yawned. "Come to bed?"

"No. Not now," said Fred. "I want to paint."

Margaret frowned and then shrugged and turned to go. Fred suddenly wanted to touch her, to take her in his arms, as he had done so many times and as he believed he could so easily do now. And he loved her at this moment perhaps more than he ever had. But he let her go.

And when he did, he felt a fragile thread break—a thread that had held Fred White together with a life that had been good if he had only known how to live it.

He went into his studio and turned on a small lamp with an amber shade. It cast a faint yellow glow over his sketches of Rita and made them seem, rather than newly done, as if they were remnants of the past—as if they had been saved, sequestered, hidden. And, as Fred studied the sketches, Rita seem to come alive not as the woman she was but as a descendant from that past—a great-grandchild perhaps of a woman who had lain across the sheet-strewn bed in an artist's studio and had been painted and then had lain across that same bed with the painter. It seemed so simple to Fred—nothing else need matter—the artist and his model in a high-ceilinged, well-lighted womb.

Fred painted that night—all that night—and when he heard the alarm clock sound, it was with a kind of terror that he forced himself to stop. But he did not pause to look at his canvas one last time, a canvas now filled with muted flesh tones and rose and ebony brush strokes.

Fixing coffee and pancakes and bacon calmed Fred, but when his family trooped into the kitchen and Melanie and Lisa began arguing over a particularly fat pancake and Margaret gave him a worried smile, he fled to the bathroom and stayed there until his family had left.

Rita was due at noon. She had the afternoon off. Fred had no idea how he might manage to occupy the three and a half hours until her arrival. He didn't want to paint. He didn't want to touch the canvas until she had seen it—until she knew—surely she would know then—that he loved her, that he was madly in love with her.

So Fred wandered instead through his house without seeing or noticing anything. Finally, he sat down in an armchair next to the fish tank and watched Hank and Betty swim back and forth in what now seemed less like grace and more a sort of lonely, nonsensical aquatic pacing. It terrified him.

He scoured the kitchen floor instead—on his knees with a stiff brush. He was only half done when Rita arrived. His hand shook and rattled the door knob as he closed the door behind her.

She was wearing jeans again but she had put on a white cotton shirt through which Fred could see bra straps. She was smiling and seemed sure of herself as she had not the day before.

"Coffee?" Fred asked.

Rita nodded and followed Fred into the kitchen.

"I told Ted," she said as she sat down at the breakfast table.

"You did?" said Fred. "Why?"

"Oh—well—I—I just thought I should. Anyway he thought it was a great idea. He wants to see the finished product."

"Well—that may be some time."

"Oh."

Fred poured coffee, annoyed that his hand still shook.

"What did you want to be?" he asked suddenly.

"Pardon?"

"When you were a kid. I don't imagine you dreamt of being a secretary."

Rita shrugged. "No. I—I wanted to be a person."

Fred said nothing. He didn't want to think about being a person.

They had three cups of coffee each and talked about the weather, which was mild, and the traffic, which was getting worse. Fred had no wish for further revelations except his own. Finally Rita smiled and asked, "Shouldn't we—I mean, don't you want to paint me or—"

"Uh, I have something to show you," said Fred.

"One of your paintings?" asked Rita.

"Well—yes," said Fred.

He ushered her into the studio and then simply waited. She saw the portrait at once. Her back was to Fred, and she did not move for several minutes, hours Fred thought. Then she turned. Her face was pale. "It's not me," she whispered. "It's not me. It's too—"

"Too beautiful?" Fred asked and then went on without waiting for a response. "But you are beautiful—you're extraordinary and I love you. I love you."

Rita backed away from him. He reached for her and pulled her to him.

"Let me go," she cried. He released her immediately.

"You don't understand. Ted—Ted and I ..."

She didn't finish. She fled the room and then the house. The front door slammed behind her.

Then a second door slammed, and it was this bang that woke Fred from a momentary but entirely welcome stupor. *Someone else was in the house.*

Fred searched. Melanie's door was closed tight and locked.

"Melanie?"

"Go f--- yourself."

"Melanie, let me in."

"We're not coming out 'til Mom gets home."

"Who's we?"

"Go away, Daddy," Lisa said.

Fred let himself sink back into the stupor. He sat at the kitchen table and studied the grains of formica. The phone rang. It was Margaret.

"Fred, honey, one of my clients—remember Frieda Locklane—80-years-old?"

"No—yes. What about her?"

"She's in trouble. She hit her husband over the head with a princess phone. He's in the hospital. She's in jail. I've got to help, okay?"

Fred didn't answer. He was imagining himself as the victim.

"Fred, honey? Okay?"

"Yes, sure. We'll manage."

Fred walked back to the bedrooms and knocked on Melanie's door.

"Mom's going to be late."

Melanie opened the door. She was fighting back tears. "I *am* smart, you know, you jerk, you—you—I'm *really, really, really* smart and I'm going to be *somebody.*" She slammed the door in Fred's face.

Fred wandered into the living room and sat and calmly watched the fish. Their slow, graceful movement through the water began to hypnotize him, and he suddenly longed to be in the cool water where bubbles gently rose to the surface and everything seemed endlessly peaceful. But then he began to wonder if Hank and Betty knew that they were caged—forever—and if they cared, and then he decided he would buy them a sunken city.

"A sunken city," he said. "You'd like that. You could swim around it and through it. It'll be fun. You'll see."

Hank and Betty ignored him and each other and suddenly Fred was sure, very sure, that Hank and Betty were both profoundly and obscenely stupid.

"Daaaaaaaad."

It was Melanie's cry, and it wasn't a cry of anger. Fred ran. The door was open to Melanie's room, and he saw at once what had made his very angry daughter cry out to him for help.

Lisa sat crouched and gasping for breath at the end of Melanie's bed. She was having as asthma attack, a bad one it appeared.

"Get the inhaler," Fred shouted.

Melanie ran from the room and returned with the small plastic tube screwed into the lid of a vial of medicine.

Fred held Lisa in his arms and tried to calm her. She sucked in a gulp of the medicated air, coughed and wheezed and began to suck again. But Fred took the vial away from her. It was potent and effective but a little was enough and too much dangerous. Lisa wheezed and coughed and then threw up.

"I can't breathe," she gasped and then she started crying which only served to complicate and worsen her struggle for air.

"Maybe we should call the doctor, Daddy," Melanie said, near tears.

"Yes, do that, do that."

Lisa continued to gulp and wheeze and beg her father to do something. He held her and prayed, to no one in particular and to everyone in general. He had no idea what to do. Margaret had handled these crises in the past. He had stood by helpless. He was still helpless.

Melanie returned with instructions, and Fred allowed Lisa more frequent breaths of the acrid vapors from the vial while he stroked her forehead and her back and murmured that he loved her and that she would be okay, the former of which he was quite sure and the latter of which he was not sure at all.

But in time, Lisa's breathing did ease although she continued to wheeze with an audible and disconcerting whistle.

Melanie, who had thought to call the doctor and had then proceeded to clean up Lisa's vomit and tidy the room and who had remained surprisingly calm during the worst of it, now began to cry.

"Melanie—" Fred began.

"You did good, Dad. But that doesn't make up for it."

With that, she left the room.

Lisa curled more deeply into her father's arms and held on tightly to his hand. With his fingertips, Fred stroked her forehead again, and her nose and her cheeks and her arms, arms that he found surprisingly small and delicate. And he began to marvel at the child who was his daughter, just as he had when she had first been born. And he wanted to protect that body, which was still was very small, and protect it in a way he had never felt before, as if it were he who had given birth to her and nursed her when she was a baby. And he sat with her, she clutching his hand even as she fell asleep, and he listening to her labored breaths and the night sounds of the house, the beams creaking as they cooled and the furnace starting up.

Close to midnight he left Lisa to look in on Melanie. She was still up, sitting at her desk in a plaid flannel robe she had bought in the boy's department at Sears, against Fred's better judgment.

"What are you doing?" Fred asked.

"Writing in my diary," said Melanie. "And you can't read it so don't even ask." She slammed it shut.

"I don't think I'd want to read it," Fred said.

"Not tonight, you wouldn't."

"Melanie, I'm sorry. I—I—well, things happen when you're an adult—it's different—you can't possibly understand."

"Bullshit. I understand plenty. But I won't tell Mom if that's what you're worried about.

"No you won't. I will. But that's not the point. If you understand so much then do you understand that people make mistakes sometimes—bad mistakes—that hurt people—and that they wish they could take back in the worst way?"

"Well—yeah. You mean like when I laughed at Lisa's poem that wasn't supposed to be funny?"

"Something like that."

Melanie nodded and then said, "So—so it was a mistake. You're not going to divorce Mom and leave us?"

That was it, he thought. It wasn't just betrayal, but abandonment as well.

"No," he said. "Never. We're all gonna stay in this house and work things out."

He said it with more conviction than he had thought possible and was surprised and heartened by it.

"And you'll take care of us?"

"Yes, every day—as long as you want."

Melanie nodded again. "You scared me, Daddy. I don't like you very much."

"That's okay," said Fred, thinking it wasn't okay—at all. "I don't like myself very much."

Melanie said goodnight and let her father kiss her on the cheek. Fred returned to Lisa's room where he found her sound asleep and still whistling although more faintly. He left her door open so that he could hear her breathing and then he began to roam the house and, not aimlessly as he had done in the past in search of something to do, but rather with a purpose although not an entirely conscious one.

He found a wool scarf of Melanie's stuffed into the corner of the living room couch and rescued it and folded it and pressed it with his fingers. Then he put it to his cheek and smelled at once the fragrance of his daughter—not a sweet, cloying smell, but rather a faint scent of sweat and young flesh. He put the scarf around his neck and went to check on Lisa. He heard the noisy but now regular breaths of his daughter as he stood at the door and watched her in the dim light thrown into the room from the hallway. Then he saw a slip of Lisa's lying on a chair by her bed, and he crossed to the chair and picked it up and smelled that, too. It was the same. The smell of youth, he thought.

He found himself finally in Margaret's study, formerly the den. He sat down at her desk and studied the doodles she had made in the corners of her desk blotter. They were angular, geometric, precise drawings made over and over again. Fred looked at the patterns and wondered if he knew anything, anything at all, about the woman with whom he had lived for twenty years.

Then he saw Margaret's sweater, and, of course, he smelled that, too, and breathed in the fragrance that he had thought was of youth but which he knew then was the fragrance of the three women with whom he lived and whom he loved and knowing that made him cry—

because he had simply never noticed before nor cared to notice nor had time to notice. And he decided that he wouldn't have traded that knowledge for anything in the world.

He waited up for Margaret in the living room, with the scarf still wrapped around his neck. He sat and watched Hank and Betty. He decided that he liked them just as they were and that he was glad he wasn't one of them. He wanted to talk to Margaret, not to confess, just to tell her what he knew. She was the only person he wanted to talk to and he wanted to talk to her very badly. But he fell sleep instead.

Margaret woke him up at 6 a.m.

"Are you all right, honey?" she asked, looking pale and tired.

"I love you, you know," Fred said.

"I know," she said and sighed. "Come to bed?"

"You go on," he said. "I have something to do."

He'd just remembered Rita. Margaret nodded again and shrugged and left him.

Fred went into the kitchen and got a carving knife and then he went into his studio and looked at the portrait of Rita. It was exactly as he had suspected. It was not she and it was so much not she that it was nearly unforgivable. He took the carving knife and rent apart the canvas until it lay in shreds at his feet. Then he simply stood and looked at the bits of rose and black and ivory shreds on the studio floor.

In the silence, he heard a sigh. He thought it was Margaret's or maybe his. He turned and saw Melanie and Lisa at the door to his studio.

"You should tell her," Melanie said.

"Your mother?" he asked.

"No, that woman," she said.

He nodded.

"What are you going to paint now, Daddy?" Lisa asked.

"I think I'll draw first," said Fred.

"Well, what are you going to draw?"

"You."

Lisa smiled shyly.

"Me, too?" Melanie asked.

"You, too," Fred said.

"Hot damn," said Melanie.

His two daughters stood in the doorway, beaming at him. He didn't think he deserved it.

"Go on," he said. "Get breakfast started."

"Right, Dad," Melanie said.

"Okay, Daddy," Lisa said.

His daughters ate breakfast and left. Margaret slept until noon and Fred began his drawing—of the three women with whom he lived and whom he loved and whom he believed he could draw and maybe someday even paint. But something held him up, stopped the flow of his charcoal pencil, and he knew what it was.

He left his studio and went into the kitchen. He closed the doors and phoned Rita. When she answered, he simply apologized. He didn't offer explanations or excuses. She didn't ask for any. He told her he'd destroyed the canvas. All she said was "Good" and "Goodbye".

After he hung up, he made a pot of coffee and said his own goodbye to Rita in the quiet of his kitchen. When he returned to his drawing, his pencil flowed easily across the small pad.

At noon, Margaret came into his studio.

"Something new?" she asked.

"Well, for me," he said. Then he shook his head and said, "But it's really so old I just didn't notice."

He showed her the drawing, and he believed that she understood because she smiled and took his hand and kissed it.

Shortly after noon, Fred and Margaret headed for the bedroom. Once there, Fred began caressing Margaret's thigh on the plush, pale blue comforter. Bella appeared and hovered a few feet above the bed, but she didn't linger. She simply smiled and faded away. Fred believed he would miss her.

.

BIRD FEATHERS

A shopping mall is not a pretty sight. Five hundred tubs of artificial ivy, fountains crafted after the Milpitas sewage disposal plant, 750 pea-brained teenagers smoking cigarettes and listening to 750 Sony Walkman radios, and various stores specializing in foul-smelling hypoallergenic beauty products, chocolate that comes two thousand calories to the ounce, and kitchenware shaped like chickens and cows plus enough women's clothing to put a 200 dollar dress in every closet in China is not what God had in mind when he said, "Be fruitful and multiply."

These were the thoughts of Olivia Masterson as she pushed through the plate glass and chrome doors of Macy's on a Saturday in May in pursuit of a wedding gift for her niece. But as Olivia walked down the aisle between Women's Wear and Perfumes, her thoughts were suddenly replaced by a very precise, very vivid vision of Women's Wear, Perfumes, and the seven hundred and fifty teenagers being vaporized in one poof—a surgical nuclear attack perhaps. And at the moment that the vision was at its most intense, Olivia felt a pleasure unlike anything she had experienced in her life.

Then she saw a child in a stroller. How could I? she thought. Olivia sprung, as was her wont and lifelong habit, into her most common and cherished feeling—guilt. It was as familiar and necessary to her as a drink is to a drunk.

A nuclear attack? Olivia headed for the escalator. A nuclear attack? Why, she hated nuclear weapons. She hated weapons of any sort. It was true, of course, that she harbored very private and very evil thoughts about Central and South American dictators, the CIA, evangelical snake oil salesmen, bigots, and the manufacturers of stereo boom bases. And these thoughts were plenty evil. But, again, they were only thoughts and private thoughts at that.

At the top of the escalator, Olivia found herself in Linens. Her plan was to buy towels for her niece, the fourth niece or nephew to get married in a year and most likely the fourth soon to be separated or divorced. Olivia, despite a reasonable cash flow, was not willing to spend her husband's hard-earned money on another marriage that was in the process of disintegration at the altar. And she wouldn't have the towels monogrammed either—thus avoiding any further unrest when the actual split came.

Now towels are generally neutral territory in most people's lives—unless, of course, they're monogrammed. Not so with Olivia. Towels come in two types, the traditional looped arrangements similar to terry cloth and the snazzy velour kinds with a velvety sheen. Olivia loved the velours, and she had, in fact, bought some. Olivia's husband of forty-five years had refused to use them, however. "They don't absorb," he had said fretfully. So Olivia put the ones she had bought in the guest bedroom and got her husband "looped" towels.

A small matter in an otherwise pleasant marriage? Not so, although Olivia wouldn't have ordinarily admitted it. But today a screw had loosened itself in her otherwise well-sealed emotional casing, and so, when she saw towels in every imaginable color and size stacked on shelves and in cubicles and especially when she saw the velour ones, rather than thinking about what colors would go well in her niece's fashionably pastel bathroom, she began to feel resentful—resentful not only of the towels she couldn't or wouldn't buy, but of the white water rapids trip her husband had vetoed, and the lithograph of a languid nude, also vetoed, and the part-time job in a group of subversive suburban mothers, which she had never even brought up to be vetoed, and the countless other things that began to look a lot less like compromise and a great deal more like surrender.

"Shit," said Olivia aloud and then she looked around to see who had used such offensive language. She saw a woman, her age or perhaps older, dressed in magenta who had a remarkable necklace of multicolored bird feathers strung around her neck. The woman had turned from a stack of towels (velour) and had seemed to smile at the word. It couldn't have been she, thought Olivia. And then she saw a much younger woman stooped over a pile of towels (looped) that she'd apparently toppled, and Olivia decided that it was she who had befouled the air with the rude word.

How did we raise such uncouth children? Olivia thought. She hoped by fixing her mind on the sins of youth that she would deflect her thoughts from the equally unpleasant but profoundly more painful recognition of her personal decampment and retreat.

She had half a mind to buy the velour towels, and in *magenta,* and the *big* ones—the three-by-eight-foot bath towels—and keep them all to herself.

But she didn't. She bought white velour towels for her niece and nephew-in-law, in hopes that he too wasn't obsessed with absorption.

And she felt calm then, at least until she was on her way to the rest room when she was suddenly grabbed by a pain in her chest, and she gasped and walked unsteadily into the pink Women's Lounge and once inside doubled over and nearly cried out. She knew the pain wasn't a heart attack. It wasn't her lungs failing her either.

"Don't you see?" she suddenly wanted to ask, and she wanted to ask it of her husband. "Don't you see what I've given up, dear?" And she would have said "dear" because she loved him more than anything on earth. And she would have said, "They were little things, of course—at the time not all that important—but it mattered, I guess." And, yes, she would have said "I guess," too, to take the sting out of it somehow.

And so she sat on a chair and rubbed her chest and breathed deeply as her doctor had recommended if she were overly excited. And she gained control because Olivia always gained control.

Then, to satisfy needs that could not and would not be met, Olivia decided to buy herself something. She went to Lingerie and looked very carefully and very particularly, this slightly drooping, slightly pudgy sixty-five-year-old woman, at every slinky, lacy, beribboned black satin nightgown on the racks and then chose three to try on.

As she gathered them together to go to the fitting room, she saw the lady in magenta standing next to a rack of lavender bikini underpants. The lady smiled at Olivia once again. Olivia started with recognition though she didn't know the lady at all. Surely she didn't know her, not someone like this. The lady's dress reached to her ankles and she wore gaucho boots underneath. Olivia imagined that the lady's hair might have reached to her ankles as well although she had it piled at the back of her head in swirls of gray streaked with black. Olivia stared for a moment. She couldn't help herself. There were so many colors in the necklace of bird feathers. It was so *rich* in some way, so alive, so, well, unexpected, *daring* even. And then she looked into the woman's eyes. They were alive too and multicolored, changing from gray to hazel to purple to deep brown to green and to fluorescent blue even as the lady held her head perfectly still.

It was too much for Olivia. She broke away from the gaze and asked a salesgirl, whose eyes were as dull as dust, if she might try on the gowns. The girl gave Olivia a wide open gape of befuddlement and asked, "You want to try them *on?"* and asked it as if Olivia's request were a hieroglyph, the meaning of which would take years to sort out.

"Yes," said Olivia, "I want to try them *on*."

The hieroglyph was decoded instantly. The girl looked Olivia up and down and, with a smile spread with the contempt youth reserve for those over twenty-five, said, "Please come this way."

Olivia was left in a four-by-six foot carpeted box with three mirrors, a stool, and a sign threatening life imprisonment to shoplifters. She struggled out of her clothes with difficulty because she was trying to avoid wrenching her sore back where a disc had eroded and had left the nerves constantly inflamed. She had not missed the salesgirl's smile, and she noticed as she undressed that her hands were shaking. And when she noticed this, the screw in her casing fell plumb out.

Olivia began talking to herself as she slid the first of the three nightgowns over her wrinkled body. Does she think I'm dried up? And old prune? Or just ugly, just offensively ugly, because I'm not twenty-five and she won't be either forever and she doesn't want to be reminded of that. Is it some sort of depravity that my womb still goes warm when Peter touches me? Is that a sin? An offense to nature?

"Is it? Is it?" Olivia began to ask aloud.

"Pardon?" asked the salesgirl, who had apparently been standing just outside the fitting-room door.

Olivia took a look at her trembling, aging body in triplicate, and she thought suddenly that she looked almost svelte and not bad at all, and she opened the fitting room door and said into a face not yet, and perhaps never to be, lined by any sort of insight or profound thought, "I like sex. Did you know that? I'm orgasmic. Have been all my life."

The salesgirl backed away slowly, as if confronted by a rabid dog, and then ran. Olivia burst out laughing and decided on the spot that she'd buy the nightgown with the most dramatic décolletage of the three. Then she looked at the price—seventy-five dollars.

Oh I can't, she thought. There are so many people in need. She started crying, then stopped. She tried to gain control by blowing her nose and willing the screw back in, though it wouldn't engage. She put her seersucker suit on, tidied her hair, freshened her lipstick, and then walked out of the fitting room, right past the salesgirl, right out of Lingerie, and right out of Macy's all together, leaving the nightgowns behind.

Since she had bought what she had come to buy, the linens for her niece, there was no need to stay in the shopping mall another minute. But she stayed, and she believed it was because she saw a sign advertising a sale on teakettles in the window of a kitchen shop. Olivia needed to buy a teakettle since she had burned the bottom out of her previous one by boiling it dry. So she headed directly into the kitchen shop and, because buying something she needed, that was in fact essential to the household, was an act of purely rational behavior, it calmed her as nothing else could have.

But once inside she felt a bit of confusion as she realized that she would have to decide between four shapes of teakettles in bright red, blue and yellow and three shapes of teakettles in orange, beige and rust, plus copper kettles and tin kettles and a bizarre item in cast iron, none of which she wanted but one of which she felt obligated to buy because the price was so low. She worked her way around twelve other women who were also in hot pursuit of a cheap teakettle in a store with a floor space of ten by forty feet. Olivia found the shape she wanted but not the color and then she found the color she wanted but not the shape. She kept looking. She got elbowed in the ribs. Someone dropped a teakettle on her foot. In desperation, she approached another dull-eyed, somnolent salesgirl and asked if the store might have the teakettle she desired "in back."

"What's out is what we got," drawled the girl.

"But I wonder," asked Olivia, "if there might be some in those boxes? See—there." Olivia pointed to a stack of boxes that did, indeed, appear to contain teakettles since they were labeled as such.

The girl shrugged. Olivia wanted that teakettle. She *needed* that teakettle. Screws popped loose all over her now precariously unsealed casing.

"Could you perhaps check?" Olivia asked.

"I can't leave my post." The girl shrugged again.

"Your *post?*"

The girl shrugged once more. It was the final shrug that did it. Or maybe it was the velour towels, the salesgirl in Lingerie *and* the final shrug that did it.

"You ought to be fired," Olivia said. "You, you, you—"

"Now wait a minute," snarled the salesgirl.

"No. You wait a minute. You just listen to me. In some parts of the world you'd be in *prison.*"

"Listen, lady—"

"Five to ten in San Quentin. A little genuine suffering and hardship would do you a world of good, you little twit."

"Help," wailed the salesgirl.

Olivia took a deep breath and prepared to continue.

"What seems to be the problem here?" asked a young woman. A small white name tag labeled her a sales manager.

Olivia stopped herself. "Why teakettles," she said politely, and then she explained her dilemma, which no longer held much interest for her.

"Well, I'm sure we have just what you want," replied the sales manager. "Let's take a look."

She took Olivia's arm and guided her through shelves of red, blue, yellow and green storage baskets, picnic plates, napkins, table mats, coffee mugs and potholders.

"What's all this about prison?" the sales manager asked laughing with a light patronizing lilt.

"I just got out," Olivia said.

"Of *prison*?"

A final screw fell out of Olivia's casing.

"Yes, *prison*," she said. "I did fifteen years for crimes against the state."

"The state?" Another hieroglyph to be sorted out.

"Yes, the state. I threw a grenade at an army recruitment office."

The sales manager stepped back a hefty three-foot step, but another young woman, an unlikely consumer of chic kitchen items with her shredded jeans, shredded running shoes and a machine-embroidered blouse from Mexico, stepped forward. "You fought against the *state?*" she asked.

"Yes," said Olivia.

"You don't look like the—" The young woman stopped herself, but not in time.

"Oh yeah?" said Olivia. "Oh *yeah?*" she said again. The sales manager and the young woman reared back and prepared to go for help. But Olivia sagged suddenly.

"A home-made grenade," she said to no one. "The apricot jam made a real mess." Better that, she had thought, than the idea of an eighteen-year-old boy ending up ... Olivia had not gone to jail afterwards, though. She had home and freshened up before Peter had returned from work. She had had two grenades to spare—grape jelly and liver pâté. Peter never knew a thing.

Olivia turned and walked calmly past the startled women, out of the store, across the mall, into Macy's, and then directly into the pink-tiled, pink-papered, pink-painted Women's Lounge where she sat down on a pink upholstered chair and collapsed.

The lady in magenta approached her and touched her shoulder.

Olivia looked up and said, "I'm not dead, you know. We're not dead." She began crying.

The woman nodded as if she understood.

"We're alive," sobbed Olivia, "We're alive."

The woman nodded again and took Olivia's hand. The woman's own hand was long and bony, lined and veined, but very elegant and ringed with one bright opal. Olivia held onto the elegant hand, which felt warm and strong against her own. She wanted to touch the bird feathers, too, to run her hands down the soft fibers of each and every one of them, and she wanted to look into the woman's eyes and see all the colors. But she didn't dare. Instead she searched in her purse for a handkerchief.

"It's like this," she said, sniffling and choking, "like this—my husband never understood that it was the little things that mattered. You know, the little things—like the time—oh God, so many times. But they mattered because nothing else mattered—because I didn't have anything that really mattered …"

She sobbed while the woman held on tight to her hand.

"Kids, you know, kids are great. I like mine—love them—but it isn't enough—it was never enough—I thought it was. It wasn't … Don't they know—don't they know I had my dreams—I had dreams. I did. I *did*. You know—you'll get a laugh out of this—but I wanted to join Castro in '56—I did—and go to the mountains and be a nurse or something—a rebel—and help—be useful." Olivia laughed a bitter laugh. "Ridiculous, huh?"

The woman in feathers shook her head no and smoothed Olivia's seersucker suit as Olivia sobbed.

"And now," Olivia said, "And now, it is over? Is it all over? Do I *still* have to do what's expected of me? Am I supposed to be a nun of some sort?"

The woman shook her head vigorously and the bird feathers flashed in the light. No, it seemed she meant, an emphatic no.

"And do I quit? Do I stop dreaming? I'm not dead, don't you see? Don't they see? I'm not dead. I want to live."

The woman kissed Olivia's cheek as if to let her know that she was very much alive. And then the woman moistened a paper towel and sponged Olivia's flushed face.

Olivia closed her eyes and rested her head against the back of the chair and let herself be cared for. She began to feel the spray from the white water rapids and the bob of the boat as it dipped and swayed, and she felt the sun in her hair and a brisk wind at her back. And suddenly she wanted to thank the woman, to embrace her, and she opened her eyes, but the woman was gone.

Olivia blew her nose, re-applied her lipstick, straightened her hair, and picked up the sack with the white velour towels in it. Then she went to Linens and bought magenta velour towels and then she went to Lingerie and bought a black nightgown and meanwhile she thought she just might join the suburban subversives. But she knew none of that was enough.

As she walked out of the mammoth shopping mall, leaving behind the brittle ivy and the shops and stores and the 750 teenagers who would be sixty-five someday, she felt uneasy, as if something were now expected of her. She stopped only once on her way out, at a jewelry shop. She saw a pair of large, gaudy earrings in the window and went inside to get a closer look. She held one to her ear and saw opalescent blues and greens and purples and grays and browns in the ceramic feathers of a peacock dangling from a single gold loop. And she saw then the same colors in her eyes, eyes she'd always believed were gray. So she bought the earrings and wore them home.

FOR FREE

Gus pulls his black-and-white up to the curb and stares at the store. He's pissed off. Peculiar things piss him off. What's a beat-up vacuum cleaner shop doing in a classy town like this? Do people who drive Porsches buy their vacuum cleaners in a tiny old house on the only ugly strip of asphalt for ten square miles, the strip with gas stations, all-night coffee shops, dead-beat bars, and auto parts dealers? Do they? No. They don't even want to drive on the strip. They'd rather stay in their nice big fake Spanish haciendas and watch their neighbors jog their flab off. Besides which they wait for sales on Hoovers at the Palo Verde Shopping Mall, where you pay too much, to Gus's mind, for something that's marked down fifty percent. And do the guys in the bars, gas stations and auto parts stores buy vacuum cleaners? They don't even vacuum. So who is buying the vacuum cleaners?

And this crumby little store, Vac-n-Sew they call it (pitiful name), doesn't just sell vacuum cleaners. Oh no. It sells sewing machines, carpets and DMSO. Everybody thinks DMSO will cure what ails your houseplant and heal in-grown toenails in the bargain, but it happens to be illegal. And so where do they put everything, huh? It's a little house. You couldn't get a rag rug in there if you tried. So maybe he hasn't been inside. But he knows. Yeah, he knows.

And as if that weren't bad enough, Vac-n-Sew isn't the only beat up vacuum cleaner shop around. Not by a long shot. On that same strip of asphalt that heads south, hooking up one boring town after another, there are fifteen storefronts selling vacuum cleaners. Fifteen! In five miles! How do they all stay in business, huh? Well, they don't, Gus figures.

So fine. Gus gets out of his car and walks across the parking lot. The air stinks, has for days. Maybe it's the smog. Doesn't smell like smog, though. Smells like—well, hell—Gus doesn't know. But it gives him the creeps. He takes a look in a window of Vac-n-Sew. The damn thing looks deserted. The door's open though. So he goes inside with his hand on the butt of his gun, just resting there, just in case, no big deal.

"Hello."

Gus spins around. A woman, thirty maybe, with fuzzy hair and too much weight on her, smiles at him.

"Uh—" he says and stops. Damn.

"May I help you?"

"No, uh—" He should have planned, had a story. He takes a look around the place. Maybe he'll see something—the mistake, the thing they forgot to hide. The place smells like an attic and looks like an attic. There's dust on everything—old vacuum cleaners, old sewing machines and rolls of green indoor-outdoor carpeting, the kind that's supposed to look like a lawn.

"I want some DMSO," he says.

"For your rear-end?"

"Huh?"

"Your butt. Nevermind. I thought cops had sore butts."

The woman shrugs and then smiles. She sits down on an orange crate that looks as if it might split. Gus feels for his rump—which is sore, sorer than heck—and then whips his hand away. He didn't mean to do that. The bitch is laughing. Jewish, he thinks. Maybe it's commies.

See, if these little stores aren't making a business off vacuum cleaners, which any moron would know they aren't, then they must be up to something and they're probably all in it together. They're dealing dope maybe; worse maybe, they're a mafia front for prostitution, gambling, loan sharking, and dope. So maybe the only people caught with drugs are fools sucking on joints at rock concerts, and so maybe the hookers are free-lance and their business pretty much hit or miss, and, okay, there's plenty of gambling and for high stakes, but what there is is done at the stockbrokers, and, of course, everybody borrows money up to their receding hairlines, but they do it at the bank. So maybe all this is so.

So okay, he has another idea. Better. The businesses are run by subversives. They're moving into suburbia. Gus has heard about it—somewhere—hasn't he? So maybe he has been on the force fifteen years and that'd make anybody a little jumpy. People pullin' guns on you, seeing men in business suits beat up ninety-pound hookers and like it. So maybe everybody starts to look bad to you. But every now and then somebody who looks bad is bad.

"DMSO works," says the woman. "You know I'm not supposed to sell it for that and I know I'm not supposed to sell it for that, but it works." She shrugs and smiles again. Smiles a lot, this woman.

"Yeah?" he asks. He can't help himself. It's getting so he can barely sit. He's tried cushions, massage, exercise, aspirin. Nothing works.

"Un huh," says the woman.

"How much?"

"I'll give you a sample. See how you like it."

"Okay," he says. What the hell.

The woman disappears behind a door covered with a curtain at the back of the store. Gus walks around. He sees a stack of *Valley Times Tribunes*, third section, the ladies' page—gossip, fashions, advice columns. The top paper is opened to "Tania's Tough Talk." So she reads that! Now we're getting somewhere. Tania herself is a little pinko, if you want Gus's opinion. Okay, he reads it, sometimes, yeah. It's pinko but it's kind of interesting. Gus takes a look at the top paper.

This time, guy writes in, it's his first anniversary. Bought his wife a diamond ring. The wife bought him a tie. Is that fair? How much can she love him if she thinks he's only worth a tie? Loves her though. Signed "Disappointed."

Tania writes back:

"Dear Disappointed: Your problem is not the tie, buster. It's bellyaching. She remembered, didn't she? So it's only a tie. Big deal. Maybe she thought it fit your personality. Wake up, buster. People are dying in Lebanon, Afghanistan, Central America. You go to bed at night with a good chance of waking up alive, some people don't. You got food to eat, a lot of people don't. My advice: Don't be puny. Love that gal and treasure every good minute. There's a lot of pain in the world—you may run into some of it yourself, but you can always put that tie on and say, 'Somebody cares.' That's life, buster. It's a big world. Try to be big in it."

Gus laughs. Can't help himself. The pinko's right, damn her.

"What's funny?" The woman's come back with a brown bottle.

"Nothing," he says. Damn, he's supposed to ask the questions.

"Sell many vacuum cleaners?" he asks. Good. Conversational he's being, not too obvious.

"None of your business," she says.

Aha! He leaves Vac-n-Sew and climbs in the black-and-white. He's smiling now. On to something. Hell, she gave the stuff away free and she reads Tania and then that bit about "It's none of your business." In Gus's opinion, people who act like they're hiding something usually are. But, damn. The woman was nice. First person to be nice in ... Gus pulls down the visor and checks his calendar. First person to be nice in twenty-six days. But she's got an angle, too. They all do.

**

Gus rolls down the window and peels off down the strip. Air stinks worse than ever. Definitely not the smog. He knows the smell, though. He's sure he knows it. Can't place it though. Anyway, he's lost his smile.

He gets a call. Domestic problem, in the hills—big houses, big views. Damn. Someday he'll get killed because some guy's wife is cheating on him. He gets to the house—big house, long uphill driveway in, some fake New England thing, brand new, on a brown hill with two oaks. Gus knocks. Nobody answers. He hears shouts—a man's, then screaming—a woman's. Gus tries the door. It's open. His chest feels like it's gonna burst, his heart's pumping so hard. He'll die of a goddamned heart attack if he doesn't get shot first. Sees the couple; they're in a stand off with carving knives. The husband sees Gus and says, "Get the fuck outta here."

Gus says, "Now hold on. Let's just put those things down a minute."

Wife says, "Screw you."

Husband says to Gus, "You're next."

Wife says to husband, "You're first."

Husband says, "You're dead, you bitch. So's Pierre, if I find him."

Pierre? Gus thinks.

Husband comes at wife and she backs away screaming, "What's it to you. You haven't got it up in ten years!"

Gus pulls his gun. "I'll shoot your fucking heads off if you don't drop those knives now." He's not supposed to do that. So what.

The wife and husband stop and stare.

"I think he means it, honey," the wife says.

"Neanderthal," the husband says.

They drop the knives. Gus gives them a lecture. They got everything. Look at the house. Gus looks at the house. Wood paneling, new furniture and lots of it, big windows, big deck, view of the bay, swimming pool, tennis court. Oughta be ashamed of yourselves, Gus says. The wife looks ashamed. The husband looks bored.

Gus leaves. He'll be back. Next time there'll probably be blood—hope it isn't his. Rolls his window up going back down the hill. Keeps the smell out. Shit though, it's in the car, too. Maybe he stinks.

Gus checks in at the station and then goes home to his girl friend, Carol. She's fixed tacos, his favorite. He can't eat. The world is a dangerous place, he tells Carol, and nine out of ten people ought to be locked up. He asks her if she would massage his butt. She says she isn't "in the mood." That wasn't what he meant. He grabs a six pack of beer from the fridge and stomps outside and sits down in the dirt. Everybody's got an angle.

Three beers later Carol comes out to the back porch to ask him what's really wrong. Carol is sweet, nice. That's why he liked her. He'd never have to arrest her. But maybe too nice. Derelicts disgust her. Doesn't she realize how decent a derelict can seem in comparison to ... What would she think ... Jesus.

Gus says, "Nothing much," and goes inside and rubs some DMSO on his butt. Then he crawls into bed. Carol still isn't in the mood so he goes to sleep.

Gus goes back to Vac-n-Sew the next day. So okay, he goes at the end of his shift which means he can hang around if he wants to, which he doesn't, and he goes back to Vac-n-Sew instead of some other place like Electro-Luxury or Vacs-n-Saxs, and so maybe he should be checking out the whole bunch of them.

Maybe so. But what about being thorough, huh? And anyway, it's been a bad day. What's new?

Captain says this morning, more traffic tickets. So he tickets everybody who's speeding and that's everybody, because the whole town's a thirty-five mile an hour zone if it isn't twenty-five and nobody can stand going that slow. Then a drunk in a Porsche broadsides a guy in a pickup truck. Nobody's hurt but the drunk says he's sober as the day he was born, takes Gus aside, and offers him "a little something" to "look the other way." Gus says no deal and takes the guy in and figures he, Gus, is a jerk because this guy will be out in an hour and make another million and Gus'll still be working for twenty-six thousand a year plus pension.

And then he's sure he's a jerk when a sixteen-year-old kid on angel dust decides to tear up a discount record store. Kid goes after Wayne Newton, smashes to pieces every Wayne Newton album in the store. That's fine with Gus. What isn't fine are the blows Gus takes to his cheek and ribs when he tries to stop the kid. Gus and five of his buddies clobber the kid. It takes that many cops. Well, maybe not that many. Hard to tell when the adrenaline shoots in.

And his butt's still sore and the air still stinks and DMSO is crap. He should tell her.

Vac-n-Sew still looks deserted and it's still dusty. Gus goes in and looks around. No sign of the woman. Nothing to see except the latest *Valley Times Tribune* opened to the third section.

Lady, well young lady, twenty-five, writes in. Her boyfriend dumped her. Now she's found somebody new but she scared to "commit" herself. She doesn't want to get hurt again. What should she do? Signed, "Wary."

"Dear Wary, FDR said we have nothing to fear but fear itself. This, of course, is hogwash. A gal on the breadlines in 1931 wasn't afraid of fear. She was afraid of starving to death, which, in her case, was immanent. In your case, it isn't. Maybe your boyfriend was rotten. I've known some who were 99% rotten, and I could name a few in higher office where finding 1% of goodness is a sorry task. But most of us are in the 10-20% rotten range, and you'd be surprised how easy it is to love someone even upwards of 50% and you'd be even more surprised at how often he can love you back. I'd stick my money back in the bank if I were you."

Maybe a 75 percenter? 80? Upwards of 90? Maybe he'll write Tania and ask, damn her.

"Hello." It's the woman.

"It didn't work," he says.

The woman shrugs and sits down on the orange crate. It buckles under her like a squashed tomato. She has plenty of weight on her, that's for sure. She's big—not fat—big—big breasts, big thighs, hefty but soft, too. Damn, she looks soft … soft, like he could just sink into her, just sink right in…just let her swallow him up … wouldn't that be ...

"Sometimes it works," says the woman, "and sometimes it doesn't. By the way, what happened to your cheek?"

"Huh?" He didn't hear. He's dizzy, thought he'd fallen right into the woman. Could of sworn he had.

"Your cheek. It looks like a hot-air balloon," she says.

He feels for his cheek. Jesus. He'd forgotten.

"I got hit," he says.

"Too bad." The woman shakes her head.

No questions, that's interesting.

"Want some tea?" she asks. "I've just brewed some."

Tea? God. He needs scotch.

"Sure," he says.

"What's your name anyway?" she wants to know.

"Me?" he says.

"See anybody else?"

He's turning red. He can feel it. Damn Jew, damn dyke, damn subversive.

"Gus," he says. "What's yours?"

"Phoebe, Phoebe Rosenblum."

Aha! That's better. He's on the right track.

"Sit down," she says. He sits on a spare orange crate.

Phoebe goes behind the curtained door and comes back with two tea cups. She sips her tea. Gus drinks his in one gulp and sniffs the leaves at the bottom. Smells nice. Smells good. First thing to smell good in he doesn't know how many days.

"You read 'Tania's Tough Talk,' huh?" he asks.

"Yes I do," she says.

"Like her? Like what she says?"

She nods. "I think she makes sense."

"Think she's some kind of subversive maybe?"

The woman shrugs. Doesn't even flinch. Looks right at him. Damn, he'll try again.

"What if she's a communist?"

"It wouldn't matter to me. She still makes sense."

"Wouldn't matter?"

Gus sits straight up and howls. He's smashed his tailbone into the orange crate.

"Still hurts, huh?" she asks. "I've got other remedies."

"I bet you have," he says.

"No, I do. There's an herbal tea—Chinese. You rub the wet leaves into the sore spot. It's an anesthetic."

He looks at her hands. They're big too and soft too. Maybe she would rub the leaves on his butt? Maybe onto his whole body? His neck's sore, too, and his shoulders and his stomach and—

"Gotta go," he says. She wants him to take the tea leaves. Gives them to him for free. Damn.

He tries the tea leaves that night. They *are* Chinese, Red Chinese. They smell nice though. He tells Carol he's making tea, gives her some and then goes into the john, sits down on the toilet and rubs the leaves on his butt. He's sees Phoebe's hands while he's rubbing. He gets a hard-on. Damn. He picks up *Time Magazine* off the back seat of the toilet, opens to a photograph of an emaciated bleach-blond model and keeps rubbing. The picture doesn't help get his mind off Phoebe. See, he likes women like—oh boy, imagine all that flesh, imagine just getting to touch it or ...

At 7 a.m. he decides to get a hold on himself. He goes directly to Electro-Luxury, another dinky little shop four blocks from Vac-n-Sew. He asks the man behind the counter, who's big too, but fat also, what he thinks of his competition. Does he know her?

"Course," sneers the man. "She's my cousin. And she ain't no competition."

A family of subversives? Maybe it's genetic, like being rich.

"Phoebe done anything wrong?" the fat guy asks. "I wouldn't put it past her."

"No," says Gus. "Just a general investigation."

That sounds stupid, Jesus.

The guy nods.

"You read 'Tania's Tough Talk'?" Gus asks.

"Nah, she writes shit."

"How do you know it's shit if you don't read it?" See, he's not so stupid.

"Listen, buster—excuse me, but I got work to do."

Gus looks around. No customers.

"So who owns the other shops?"

"Vacs-n-Saxs, Econo-Vac, Vac-&-Vacation?"

Gus nods.

"Family."

"Family?"

"Listen, fella, you got a search warrant or something?"

"Not yet," Gus says.

"What do you mean, not yet? "

Either this guy's stupid or he's hiding something. Gus has a hunch he's got something to hide. They all do. He leaves.

"WHAT THE HELL DO YOU MEAN, NOT YET," the guy shouts after him.

At a stoplight Gus spots a guy running out of a Quick-Stop store and he whacks his steering wheel right, floors the accelerator and peels off after the guy. He pins him in a driveway in no time and jumps from the car with his gun pulled. The guy stops, turns toward Gus and reaches in his jacket.

Gus pulls the trigger and waits for the guy to fall. The guy doesn't fall. Didn't Gus shoot? He thought he did. He's sure he did. He didn't. Jesus. The guy's got something in his hand—not a gun. He drops a package of Hostess Twinkies.

"I—I—I—w—w—was hungry. H—h—haven't eaten all day," guy says. He sticks his hands in the air. His arms look like dead tree limbs.

"Take it and get the hell out of here," Gus says. Growls it like he was some goddamned animal. He sticks his gun in his holster.

The guy looks at Gus while he reaches for the package. He grabs at it and misses and then grabs it and holds on. Gus wishes he'd kept his gun out. The guy walks past Gus and out of the alley but he turns back and says, "I ain't sorry. I gotta eat."

Gus lets him go. He doesn't even file a report. Why bother? He doesn't even drive back to the Quick-Stop store. Why bother? He goes straight to Phoebe's.

He's pissed again. Maybe more pissed than he's ever been in his life. Who do you trust, huh? Who's guilty? Who's really guilty? Phoebe, for sure. He should have known it. Nice people always have an angle. He'll find evidence, arrest her, send her to prison. So maybe she's the only person to be nice to him in—what was it? He checks his calendar. Yeah, twenty-eight days. So what. She has an angle. Everybody does and everybody who has an angle is guilty as hell.

He wants to break down the door to Vac-n-Sew. He opens it instead but slams it so hard behind himself that Phoebe comes right out from behind the curtained doorway.

"What you got behind there, huh? Weapons, huh? Sending them south I suppose? To those Marxist greasers?"

"Gus—what—"

He pushes her aside and feels the flesh give. God no, it's so soft. Forget it. He heads for the door and rips back the curtain and stands and stares. God damn.

There are books from the bottom of the floor to the top of the ceiling, some on bookshelves, some not, and more stacks of *Valley Times Tribunes*, third section. On the wall, there's a photograph of some African woman with twenty necklaces under her chin right next to a photograph of a Shell gas station on the strip and there's some old religious painting of Mother Mary holding the baby Jesus right next to some weird jungle scene with monkeys and oranges. And plus, there's all kinds of other stuff. Jogging shoes (jogging shoes?), a cracked mirror on a stand, a table with a typewriter and stacks of yellow pads and crushed papers lying all over the floor, a little kitchen in an alcove with copper pots hanging from the ceiling and a stack of orange and yellow and blue dishes on the counter, a bed with maybe a dozen pillows in all different colors, and a table next to the bed with a roach clip lying in plain view, for God's sake, and other stuff.

It's cozy. Nice and cozy. The bed looks plenty cozy, and soft. Damn. So he goes in even though he'd rather be facing some nut with a sawed-off shotgun.

"Want some tea?" Phoebe asks.

"Answers," he says.

"What do you mean Marxist greasers? What's—"

"I'll ask the questions," he says.

"Okay, okay."

They sit down at the table, and Gus lays out his evidence nice and slow. He's got time. No need to hurry now. All that stuff about giving things away free and liking Tania and having Red Chinese tea and the whole family network.

Phoebe starts to laugh.

"So that's how come Herschel—"

"Herschel?" Gus tenses. Puts his hand on the butt of his gun. Can't help himself. Herschel? And what's so funny?

"My cousin. He thought you were my spy."

She laughs again.

Gus feels his face heat up.

"You got some explaining to do," he says. "And you better do it fast. So tell me what you're really up to."

"I'm up to selling vacuum cleaners," she says and then she sighs, so deep it looks as if her body might melt. He doesn't want her body to melt. He wants to hold onto it. Does he? Damn, he does.

"You gotta do better than that," he snarls. Still sounds like an animal. Jesus.

"You're a fool," Phoebe says. "You don't deserve better. Get out."

He doesn't want to get out. He wants to stay right there, maybe crawl into that bed, maybe crawl into it with Phoebe, but anyway stay right there and forget about whatever the hell Phoebe is doing and just let her do it and let everybody else do whatever the hell they want to do and do to each other, and anyway just stay in that nice warm room and why not because he feels horrible and if Phoebe is a subversive, she's a nice subversive and there aren't many like her around.

But Phoebe doesn't look like she'd have him even if he wanted her. Figures. The world's totally screwed up. So is he.

So he goes home to Carol. First thing he asks her, "Do you love me?" If she doesn't, he doesn't know what he'll do.

"Of course I do, honey," she says. It isn't what he wants. It's not enough, not nearly enough, of what he wants.

So he drives down main street in his black-and-white the next morning and sees two kids hanging around on a corner near a jewelry store. Store's been robbed ten times in the last year. He pulls up to the curb, gets out and tells the kids to beat it. One takes off like he's got a fire up his ass but the other stays put and says, "Fuck you, man."

The kid's small and skinny. Gus beats him up. It's easy. When Gus gets a hold on himself, he stops to take a look. The kid's a mess. Gus calls an ambulance and follows it to the hospital. The kid won't die, but he's got gashes on his face that'll take a team of plastic surgeons to fix. Gus sits down in the hall outside Emergency and shakes for thirty minutes. A nurse brings him a cup of coffee. He can't believe it. Why is she being nice?

Gus goes back to the station. There were witnesses and a photographer from the *Valley Times Tribune*. He's got pictures. It'll be in the afternoon paper. Gus is called into the captain's office. The captain's got gray hair that he has trimmed at a beauty parlor. Looks likes a senator. "Take a day or two off and let the shit settle," he says.

Gus isn't happy. No. He wants to get fired. Hell, he should get fired. He should be punished. Stopped. He takes off for Phoebe's in his own red Camaro. But he's still got his uniform on. He's furious—with Phoebe. Being nice, just to confuse him. He reaches for his gun. It's there—good. He'll need it.

He gets to Phoebe's, goes in the front door and sees her reading the afternoon paper. There's some light coming in the window. Makes her hair shine. Damn, he doesn't want to shoot her. Phoebe sees him and smiles and then frowns. She invites him back behind the curtained door. Tells him to take a seat—on the bed. The bed? Why the hell not. Nothing makes sense.

The bed is soft. Phoebe sits down next to him. Her thigh's right up against his. He keeps his hands in his lap. He doesn't want to make a wrong move. But Phoebe knows what to do. She takes one of them and holds it in her own. Shit, he's gonna cry. No, wait a minute. Yes, he's gonna. No, he already is. He wants to explain.

"I—," is all he can say.

"Forget it," Phoebe says.

She pulls his hand up to her breast. God, is that nice. He can feel a hard nipple right through her blouse. So okay. He'll forget it. He'll make love to her.

It's better than he thought it would be. He gets lost in Phoebe's flesh. Doesn't mind a bit. Just gets lost, maybe for hours.

Was it good for her he wants to know after it's over and they're sitting at the table drinking Red Chinese tea.

"Oh, yes," she says.

"I beat up a kid today."

"I know," she says. "The paper."

He groans.

"The victim," he says, "left with a face only a mother could love."

"Don't do that."

Gus starts to sweat. He can feel it creep down his armpits. He probably stinks, too.

 "You made a bad mistake—"

"That's one way of putting it."

"How would you put it?"

"Felonious assault," he says.

"You're a victim too, Gus."

"Victim? What the hell—" Jesus, he is! He knows it, knows it for sure, even though he doesn't know what he means. He's the one who's got the gun and the eighteen-inch leather-covered stick. The sweat's trickling down his pant legs. Forget it.

"What do you do—really?" Gus asks. "You don't sell vacuum cleaners."

"Not many," Phoebe says. "I write 'Tania's Tough Talk'."

"You're Tania!? In the newspaper?"

Phoebe nods.

"Damn," he says. He's happy all of a sudden. "So what are you doing here? You got money, don't you?"

Phoebe sighs. "Some money," she says. "I'm here to teach my family a lesson."

Grandpa Rosenblum opened a vacuum cleaner store, Phoebe says, first one in town, and then, after a few years, he opened a bunch, one for each of his sons. He didn't set them up as one business, though. He set them up not three blocks from each other and in competition with each other. Then he sat back and watched his sons try to do each other in.

Phoebe was one of the grandchildren. Vac-n-Sew was to be hers, but she didn't want it. She was sick of seeing baseball games at family picnics turn into grudge fights and nine-year-old nephews being hired out as informants. One niece held her aunt's teeth hostage until the aunt provided annual sales figures.

The family put pressure on Phoebe, too, in a way only the family knew how—extortion, and since Phoebe didn't know what she really wanted to do, she took over Vac-n-Sew and tried to ruin it. She wrote letters, too, angry letters—to the *Valley Times Tribune*—so many, the editor finally offered her a column. The family doesn't know about Tania, but they know about Vac-n-Sew. They hate Phoebe, but they pretend they don't.

"Vac-n-Sew's nearly bankrupt," Phoebe says finally, "and nobody's learned a thing."

"What'll you do when it's gone?" Gus asks.

Phoebe shrugs.

So okay, he loves her. It's that simple. But it makes him feel lousy. She's spent her life in the back of this store and he's spent it in a squad car and they both feel like shit and what can he do about it. Nothing. He can't even tell her he loves her. He can't even think it. (It'd mean he'd have to trust her. Not possible.)

His legs are too heavy to move. But he's gotta leave. He's just gotta. So he kisses Phoebe good-bye. She smells good—sweaty and musty.

But outside, it stinks. And now he starts to place the smell. Maybe the dog he picked up on the freeway couple weeks back, still alive, bloody all over. Or maybe the kid today. When Gus leaned over him to see how bad off he was. No. That's nuts. He wouldn't still be smelling the dog, and he beat up the kid after he started smelling the smell.

He goes home. God, even Carol smells the smell and smells it on him. She tells him to take a bath. So he takes a bath and scrubs himself but he still smells.

Next day, he goes in to work. Why not? The captain doesn't mind, just says "Keep a low profile." He types reports, but then a call comes in and there's nobody to take it. Some guy's been seen in Elm Park with a gun, a guy in a business suit. Elm Park's in downtown and maybe it has a nice name and a nice green lawn, but the only people in the park are drunks, derelicts and dope addicts. Gus takes the call.

When he gets to the park, he sees the man right away. The guy's sitting on a green bench feeding pigeons. Gus walks up to him, keeping his hand near his holster. The guy looks prosperous at first, the business suit plus a nice head of gray hair, but up close Gus can see he's dirty and down on his luck. The suit's worn through, his shoes are muddy, and he hasn't shaved in a couple of days.

"Hey, buddy," Gus says. "Gotta frisk you."

"Sure, sure," the guy says, "I've got my driver's license." He reaches inside his suit jacket. And when he does, Gus smells blood—fresh blood—the blood he's smelled for days and he knows he should get his gun out and fast and he knows he should shoot because he sees the flash of chrome. But all he can smell is the blood and all he can see are the sad little stubs of whiskers on the guy's face. So the guy shoots Gus in the gut. And Gus smells his own blood.

Well he survived. That surprised him. The guy who shot him is locked up in County Psychiatric. Funny, the guy remembers shooting Gus but doesn't remember running to call the paramedics and trying to keep Gus from going into shock. Must be split personality or something. Gus checked in on the kid while he was in the hospital. Has a nice family. Gus didn't talk to them, though.

Now he's resting up at Phoebe's. He and Carol said good-bye. It was his fault, not hers. Phoebe's working on a novel. Gus is vacuuming and dusting a bit. The *Valley Times Tribune* has Tania's column today.

Guy writes in, says he's a cop but he hates it. Nobody likes him. No wonder, he destroyed a human face. He doesn't like himself much either, well not at all. Not only that, he's forgotten how to be a cop. He got shot cause he looked at some guy's whiskers instead of what the guy's hands were doing. Cop says he wants to quit but he feels like a deserter. Who'll stop the crime? Signed "A 99 percenter"

Tania writes back, "Dear a 99 percenter: One percent isn't zero and whiskers aren't such a bad thing to notice. My advice: Wake up, ditch the self-pity, and take a look around you. There's more than one way to cook a goose, bake a turkey, fry catfish, or pay off a debt. Here's a suggestion: there's a lot of people who have dusty houses and no dough. A cheap vacuum cleaner might help. And the customers would probably be nice. Give it some thought. Give it a try. And then get back to me."

WHAT HAPPENED ON THE BICYCLE PATH

The two young women were seen on a Tuesday afternoon in May on the bicycle path that winds through Bol Park. Jimmy Taylor, who was riding his tricycle along the path, giggled when he saw them and then rode on. Brent Stoppard, jogging past, took a long look and muttered "perverts," and Susan Anderson, who was pushing her two-year-old in a stroller and holding her four-year-old by the hand, gasped and abruptly turned away, shielding the eyes of her four-year-old, who had turned back to stare.

It was Susan Anderson who called Althea Johnson, the Setton girl's neighbor, to pass on what had happened. Althea couldn't believe it though she knew that Susan was no careless gossip. But Lisa Setton and Meg Brown? They were honor students and well-mannered young ladies.

When Althea hung up the phone, she immediately decided to prune the roses in her front yard. Under a straw hat, she snipped off suckers and wilted blooms and kept an eye out. It was only after she had snipped off more than she might have wished that she caught a glimpse of Lisa through the living room window of the Setton home. Discouraged, she went inside in hopes that someone might call with more information.

* * *

Tuesday evening, Alice Smythe, the Reverend Smythe's wife, received a call from Althea, who was seeking advice. Should she or should she not tell Nancy Setton, Lisa's mother, what had happened on the bicycle path. Alice Smythe cautioned Althea to proceed with care and said she would consult her husband and call Althea back. The Reverend Smythe was not at home, but Floyd Sanders, the principal of Gunn High School, was visiting. He had come by to drop off used clothing for the church collection for refugees from El Salvador. After only a moment's hesitation, Alice confided in Floyd.

"Hmm," he said calmly, sipping the lemonade Alice had given him and wishing for something stronger. "The parents have a right to know, of course. She's underage."

"That's what I thought," Alice said.

"It isn't easy these days," Floyd continued. "There's different ideas about the rights of children nowadays, at least the rights of teenagers anyway."

Alice picked through the clothing Floyd had brought. "These are lovely," she said. "Almost too nice. Are you sure you want to give them to the refugees?"

"Oh well, if there's anything you want to sell at the garage sale, go ahead, but it's the least I can do for those poor people."

Floyd sipped his lemonade again and wished he had a cigarette.

"Funny," he said, "Lisa Setton's such a beauty. Kind we used to call peaches and cream. It doesn't figure."

Alice Smythe looked into the mirror over the mahogany hutch and patted her hair. Her face suddenly looked to her—well—old.

* * *

In the early evening, Althea Johnson went out to weed the beds of petunias and impatiens that bordered her front lawn. The plants were doing well this year and were covered with copious blooms. It had been warm all spring.

Althea glanced over at the Setton house. She could see Nancy Setton in the kitchen and her husband just behind her. Though the windows were open, Althea couldn't make out what was being said. Suddenly she saw Tom, Lisa's older brother, stomp out the front door, get into his red Triumph and drive off, burning rubber and spewing gravel as he went. Did they already know? Althea wondered. How heartbreaking it will be for them.

Althea saw a snail nibbling away on a white blossom. She knocked it off with her foot and stomped on it, crushing the shell and the body underneath the heel of her shoe.

* * *

Brent Stoppard visited his psychiatrist at nine a.m. Wednesday morning. He talked, as he usually did, about his eighteen-year-old girlfriend by whom he felt misunderstood. Brent was twenty years her senior but did not feel this accounted for the degree of misunderstanding he was currently experiencing. Brent's psychiatrist listened and nodded sympathetically, but Brent had a queasy feeling that his psychiatrist was bored. So Brent told him what had happened Tuesday afternoon on the bicycle path.

His psychiatrist leaned back in his leather chair, checked the clock and said, "Hmm."

"They were *French* kissing," Brent said with disgust.

"Were they?" said the psychiatrist.

Brent nodded earnestly.

"What I'm wondering, though," said the psychiatrist, sitting up so suddenly that his feet hit the floor with a thud, "is why *you* are so concerned."

* * *

At noon on Wednesday, Susan Anderson went shopping at the All American Market to pick up disposable diapers for her two-year-old, cookies for her four-year-old and a six-pack of beer for her husband. She slid back the door on a refrigerated glass case and reached in for a six-pack of *Dos Equis*. Was that what Mel had wanted? Or was it *Corona* or was—

"Hello, Sue," Reverend Smythe said. He reached past her and pulled out a six-pack of *San Miguel.*

"Hello, Reverend. I suppose you've heard."

"Heard?" asked the Reverend. He plopped the six-pack into the bottom of his shopping cart.

"About what happened on the bicycle path."

"Um, yes," the Reverend said. "Springtime."

"Pardon?" Susan said.

"Springtime," the Reverend said. "Everybody falls in love. It's nice." The Reverend smiled, to himself.

"Yes, but *Reverend —*"

"I remember when you and Mel used to spend quite a bit of time on that bicycle path."

"But that's *different.*"

* * *

At two o'clock, Sylvia Thorton sat at her desk in front of her junior English class while her students wrote extemporaneous essays on "Passion and Responsibility." Sylvia had encouraged them to think beyond the obvious—to think of the passion of politics, music, and poetry.

Sylvia was worried about two of her junior students—Lisa Setton and Meg Brown. Floyd Sanders had told Sylvia early that morning what had happened. "I thought of you first, of course," Sanders had said. Sylvia had nodded. She was the obvious choice. Her sexual preference was hardly a secret, not after a school board fight and nine months in the county court system trying to hold onto her job. And Sanders had been no friend. So it was encouraging, if not downright amazing, that he had come to her. "I'll try to talk with them today," she had said.

By now, of course, everyone in the school knew, but Meg and Lisa seemed unaffected, detached even, and that was a bad sign. It would be better, Sylvia thought, if they were angry or defiant or upset, tearful even.

But still, Sylvia had long suspected there was something between the two of them. They were inseparable, oblivious to the male attention that came their way, and a lot came their way. They did everything together—soccer, the French Club, the Drama Club. Two weeks ago, the junior class had gone to see a performance of *The Crucible*. Both girls had seemed deeply affected by it as if they had understood something as a pair that the other students had not. And on the bus ride back, the way ... well, it was plain enough.

Sylvia shifted on her wooden chair. One cheek of her buttocks had gone to sleep. She got up and walked down an aisle between rows of desks and up another until she stood just behind Meg and Lisa. Lisa's black hair hung loosely down her back. Meg's brown hair curled at the nape of her neck. Sylvia suddenly wanted to stroke the soft hair, to mother the two young women, to save them.

She walked back to her desk and sat down. She thought with bitterness about her own teenage years—the lies, the guilt, the confusion, the furtive moments, and what had come after wasn't much better. Lisa and Meg were going to need to band together with others, like themselves.

When the class was over Sylvia called out to the two girls and asked them to stay behind. "I thought you might want to chat," she said. "A sympathetic ear?" The two girls stared back at her. Was it disgust she saw in those eyes? It wasn't detachment.

* * *

At four o'clock on Wednesday afternoon Nancy Setton sat in her living room with the drapes drawn and the phone off the hook. She was alone. Hal had gone to work, an act of desertion she did not think she could forgive. Tom had gone to school though he thought the family should have left town. He had gone only because he had spring football practice and couldn't miss it.

After Susan Anderson had called and told Nancy, with perhaps just a little too much alarm and too much relish as well, what had happened on the bicycle path, Nancy had gone upstairs to talk with Lisa. Lisa was calmly studying at her desk. Nancy had sat down on the bed, which was covered with a pale pink satin comforter. She remembered when she and a ten-year-old Lisa had decorated the room and gone shopping for checked chintz to match the comforter and to cover the chairs and the dressing table. Nancy wondered if the room no longer pleased Lisa, if she had grown out of it or past it.

"How's Meg?" Nancy asked.

"Fine," Lisa said, turning from her desk. "Why?"

"No reason ... You spend a lot of time together."

"What's that supposed to mean?"

Nancy told her. She repeated what Susan Anderson had said, omitting the exclamations and predictions of disaster. Lisa's face hardened into a mask. "Leave me alone," she said, slamming open a book.

"Is it true?" Nancy asked.

"Yes, it's true. So what?"

"So plenty. Explain. I don't understand."

"Leave me alone!"

"But I'm your mother, Lisa."

Through clenched teeth Lisa said again, "Just—leave—me—alone."

When Nancy returned to the living room, she found Hal and Tom in the middle of an argument.

"She's a dyke," Tom said.

"Hold on a minute," Hal said, "We don't know all the facts."

"We know all the facts," Nancy said. She turned and went into the kitchen and started scrubbing dirt off spud potatoes.

"What do you mean?" Hal said to her back.

"I mean it happened," Nancy said.

"Jesus," Tom said, "how am I gonna face the team?"

"I think that would be the least of our worries," Nancy said quietly. She grabbed a handful of fresh green beans and began snapping them in two.

"*Mom*—" Tom began. Hal interrupted him and dragged him into the living room.

Now, twenty-four hours later, Nancy sat in the darkened living room and wondered where it was that she had made her mistake. Had she nursed Lisa for too long? Had she not nursed her long enough? Should she not have nursed her at all? Was it letting Meg and Lisa lie naked on a blanket when they were babies, or letting them swim together in the plastic pool? Maybe it was soccer. Had Nancy sent some hidden message about men, hidden not only to Lisa but to Nancy herself? Was it society? Had Lisa been *influenced?*

* * *

What actually happened ...

Lisa Setton and Meg Brown walked home from school together on the bicycle path through Bol Park. It was warm and still, and bees buzzed in and out of poppies and alyssum. Lisa felt hot and dizzy. Her blouse, heavy with sweat, clung to her back. Meg looked cool, though a fine dew glazed her forehead and her upper lip. Neither spoke.

Lisa was waiting for a sign. She had been waiting all year. She had waited and wondered about all the unacknowledged signs that she feared were not really signs but merely reflections of her own desperate hope. Two weeks ago, though, she had begun to believe in that hope. In the bus on their way to see a performance of *The Crucible*, Lisa and Meg had sat side by side, and, when the bus had careened around a corner, Lisa had felt Meg's thigh fall against her own and then rest there, warm and alive, all the way to the City. On the ride back Meg had leaned against Lisa's shoulder and then curled up against her and dozed. Signs.

Lisa struggled to slow her breathing and to resist the warmth rising in waves through her body. Two riders came up the path on bicycles. She and Meg stepped off into the grass and waited for the bicycles to pass by. Meg kicked dirt loose and looked off to the hills. Lisa watched the riders disappear.

"Meg?" Lisa said.

Meg turned and blurted out, "I think I love you. I'm sorry. I can't help it. I'm sorry. I've felt this way for a long time. I can't help it and I can't stop it. You don't have to be friends with me anymore if you don't want to but—"

"Me too," Lisa said.

"You too? You mean really?"

Lisa nodded.

"Can I kiss you?" Meg asked.

Lisa nodded again and felt Meg's cool soft lips press against her own. Lisa touched Meg's cheek and the curls of her short, buoyant hair.

"I don't know what to do," she said.

"I love you," Meg said. She pressed her lips against Lisa's again, and her mouth radiated heat this time. The two sank down into the cool coarse grass and lay back against its cushion. Meg grinned. Lisa laughed. The sun beat down over their heads. A blue jay fluttered its wings and scolded them in an elm tree overhead. "I'm happy," Lisa said, "I'm so happy."

BRICK RED

When Helen arrived at the party, an hour late on purpose, she saw Sutton right off. He was standing by a floor-to-ceiling window surrounded by party-goers. The sunlight streaming in behind him made the black silk of his Armani suit shimmer and the white silk of his Armani shirt glow against his dark skin and dark hair. Though the temperature in the room must have been over ninety and though the armpits and backs of many party-goers' shirts and dresses were stained with sweat, Sutton looked cool and dry.

Helen edged up on the admirers to catch something of what Sutton was saying, but he wasn't saying anything. Everybody else was talking to him. They interrupted each other and talked over each other in a rabid eagerness to catch Sutton's ear. Helen was amused. As secretary to the professors of the Industrial Psychology Department, she was having the rare opportunity of watching her bosses, beings generally not plagued by low self-esteem, suddenly metamorphose into sycophants.

Helen was handed a drink, and she eased herself away from the frantic crowd and sat down on a sofa near another floor-to-ceiling window. The limitless vista the window was meant to provide of the valley below was obscured by dirt brown smog that had spread across the sky like a huge smudge. The valley itself, once blanketed with fruit orchards, nurseries, small vegetable farms, and horse stables, now grew computer chips, toxic chemicals, hamburger stands and freeways faster than it had ever grown an apricot.

Helen took another look at Sutton. He was the kind of guy, she imagined, who believed that dioxin and cholesterol-rich burgers represented progress and the American way whereas avocados and petunias simply didn't.

David Sutton was an industrialist from the East who was reputedly in possession of enormous and growing wealth despite the apparent demise of heavy industry. He was also, allegedly, in possession of a number of women. Apparently lots of money and Armani suits made him as appealing to models and movie actresses as he was to Industrial Psychology professors. Or maybe, Helen thought, they all appreciated the *real* David Sutton, the inner man. In any case, Sutton, real or otherwise, had come to the smog-smudged valley for in depth study of the silicon chip and the secret to its wildly successful manufacture. No unions, Taiwan, Helen mumbled.

The man himself still wasn't saying anything. He didn't even smile. Helen figured he had the routine down pat—stay aloof, allow the masses to grovel. She peeled her sweat-soaked blouse from her back and wondered how Sutton, standing in a silk suit in full sunlight, managed not to sweat.

Helen got up in search of another drink. Dr. Portner, the host and chair of the department, was manning the wet bar. He had been given the chairmanship based on his discovery that lavender paint was a subliminal incentive for office workers.

"Talk to him," Portner hissed at Helen. "Be *friendly.* He seems to be bored."

The *he* was understood. Sutton was now alone, standing by a window not ten feet from the wet bar. What was meant by "friendly" was also understood. Portner grabbed Helen's elbow in a crab-like grip and dragged her towards Sutton.

"Why David, you know Helen. She's our secretary."

Helen thought she should ask for cash in advance.

"Secretary?" Sutton asked, blinking.

"Yes, *secretary,*" Helen said.

"It's lonely," he said.

Helen didn't know if that were a statement, a question, or a joke. Portner handed Sutton a drink and then disappeared. Sutton took the glass, but his hand was shaking so badly that the drink sloshed over the side.

"I'll have a sip," Helen said. Sutton didn't look aloof anymore, grateful was more like it. It reminded Helen of when Nortie Hubber had asked her to dance at high school graduation. He had waited until midnight but he had still asked, and he was the only one who did.

"Get me out of here," Sutton gasped. Though it made no sense to Helen, she understood that Sutton felt the way she'd felt at seventeen standing against the gymnasium wall in her ill-fitting taffeta. But she didn't know why he felt like that. *Everybody* wanted Sutton to dance. She said sure anyway and took hold of his elbow to guide him out of the room. But he jumped at her touch and seemed to curl up, like a sea anemone, sort of folding into himself. They made it out the front door with Helen whispering words of encouragement.

"Where's your car?" she asked.

"Somebody br-br-ought me," he murmured.

"Somebody brought—"

Sutton's entire body suddenly seemed to be seized by a fierce tremor.

"Okay," Helen said. "Okay. It doesn't matter. I'll drive."

Sutton gave her his address, and Helen headed south on the freeway.

"God, it's hot," she said.

"Hot?"

"The weather," she said. "You know, the temperature."

"Oh yes, hot," he said. He stuffed his hands into the pockets of his suit jacket.

"It'll cool off," she said. "It always does. The fog comes in sooner or later."

"Fog?" he asked.

"Uh, fog, you know, sort of like clouds, only lower." Helen felt as if she were speaking to someone who not only was not completely conversant with the English language but was not especially familiar with the planet as a whole.

"Yes, fog," Sutton said with a sigh.

When they arrived at the house, Helen stopped in the driveway and asked, "Are you sure this is it? Five, three, zero?"

"Yes, yes," Sutton said. He had already begun to climb out.

Helen couldn't believe it. The house was an old orchard shack, a wood frame and plaster cubicle with steps up to a small, enclosed porch. An ancient palm drooped over a few overgrown rose bushes in the front yard.

A tiny woman, as ancient as the palm tree, stepped out on the porch. She wore a faded but starched cotton dress and black shoes that laced up to her ankles.

"Hello, David," the lady said softly. "Not much fun?"

"Uh, no," said Sutton as he walked past her. "Oh—uh—Helen here b—b—brought me ..." He flung a shaky hand in Helen's direction and went into the house.

The woman smiled. "Come in and have some iced tea, dear."

"Thank you," Helen said, "I will." Her clothes were drenched and her throat was dry, now that she took the time to notice, but also, she had to admit, she wanted to see inside. She had a notion that if she went in, somehow the woman would explain everything and she and Helen could get Sutton back to himself—whoever that was.

The house was clean and neat and furnished simply, but it was not plain. A couch and over-stuffed chair were covered in a bright blue fabric and a hand-stitched quilted pad covered a rocker's cane bottom seat. On the mantle an orchard smoke pot repainted fire engine red and a basket of fresh fruit had been placed opposite each other.

Above the fireplace hung an oil painting. In it thick bold brush strokes of red, orange, yellow, green and blue oils brought a modest bedroom to life. On an iron bedstead lay a mattress spread with white sheets and a red coverlet. Sunlight entering the room through shuttered windows softly lit a night table on which two books lay next to a small sculpture of a nude woman and a pale blue bottle of water. The wall above the bed was covered with oil paintings. And all of it, the table, chairs and bed seemed to float above a brick red tile floor.

Sutton sat on the couch like a stone. Sweat dripped from his forehead onto his Armani jacket.

"I'm Penelope," said the woman. "You can call me Penny." She held out a small, gnarled hand. Helen's hand was damp and sticky, but Penny didn't seem to notice or pretended that she hadn't. She turned instead to Sutton and asked, "Would you like some lemonade?"

After a few seconds, in which Sutton seemed to have heard nothing, he gave an almost imperceptible nod.

"Fine, come along Helen," Penny said and then added in a whisper, "He needs a breather, I think."

Helen sat in a corner of the kitchen and sipped iced tea. Penny had drawn the shades, and the room felt cool and clean.

"Are you David's, uh, Mr. Sutton's mother?" Helen asked.

"Oh, call him David," Penny said. "He certainly won't mind. No, I'm not. I'm his housekeeper. Well, his parents' housekeeper. I came out West to cook and clean for him and keep him company."

"Is he troubled?" Helen asked. A stupid question. Penny ignored it.

"It was so nice of you to bring him home," Penny said. "I can't think why he didn't call me."

Penny had brought him to the party? He didn't drive?

"Oh, it was no trouble," Helen said, though it was a twenty-mile trip out of her way.

"I'll take David his lemonade," Penny said.

Helen followed her into the living room where they found Sutton curled up on the couch. He was shaking violently as if he had caught a bad chill.

"Would you like a blanket?" Penny asked.

"I"ll get it," Helen said, in need of a breather herself.

When she found Sutton's bedroom, she was sure that it was his because this room *was* plain. The furniture was metal and bare, the carpet a drab institutional green and the walls and dresser-tops stripped of anything personal or human. The only exceptions to the barren asceticism were a few drawings which lay on Sutton's bed next to a worn gray blanket. Helen looked at one, a stark but intricate pen and ink drawing of a tract house—gingerbread eaves, well-tended lawn, absolutely pristine and unremarkable, except for one torn tennis shoe lying at the edge of the driveway. The torn shoe was riveting. Nothing else mattered.

Helen felt as if she shouldn't be looking at the drawing, as if she were a voyeur of sorts, but there was something in it that made her want to keep looking, but then again there was something in it that made her want to stop. She grabbed the blanket and rushed back into the living room where things seemed saner though Sutton looked as if he had curled deeper into himself. Penny took the blanket and draped it over him without touching him.

"I'm sorry," Helen said. "I've really got to go."

"Oh, of course," Penny said. She walked with Helen out onto the porch. Sutton didn't budge.

"He *is* troubled," Penny said, stepping down onto the front path. "That's perfectly obvious. But he's a wonderful person, you know. I don't suppose you can see that."

It wasn't until much later in the evening that Helen herself felt a chill that set her bones rattling against each other. She had sat down with a glass of wine and a manuscript to proof but found that she couldn't dislodge the memory of the tennis shoe. It's a self-portrait, she had thought suddenly, and, though the thought didn't make any sense, she immediately began to feel cold—as if she were freezing from the inside out, first in the marrow, then the bones, then muscles, fat and skin. She had felt such a chill many times before, of course, when she'd suddenly realize that the layer of cynicism she used as a buffer against life was permeable.

Helen didn't expect to hear from Sutton after the party, and she figured it was just as well. Who needed that kind of trouble?

Five days later, she was walking down a hallway at the university when Sutton suddenly stepped through a door and looked directly at her and smiled. His smile startled her. His eyes startled her more. They looked as if they had witnessed something in life that had given Sutton a bad fright.

The smile was brief. Sutton bent and studied the tops of his shoes and said, "Would you—w-w-would you ..."

"Yes?" she asked.

"Uh, I'm late," he said and walked off. Helen turned to watch him go. He walked like an industrialist then, steady, sure, determined.

"An odd bird," Professor Portner said. Helen jumped. "You know where he does his *research?"*

Helen shook her head no.

"At the Ford plant, on the line. Dexter Webb, the plant manager out there told me. He couldn't believe it."

"What's wrong with studying an assembly line?"

"He isn't studying it, Helen. He's *working* on it. The guy's cuckoo. I mean, for him—well that'd be like me deciding to be a secretary." Portner laughed.

Helen spent the afternoon planning a homicide but decided in the end that Portner wasn't worth the death penalty.

Penny phoned later that evening. "David would like you to come to dinner."

"David? Why didn't he—"

"Don't feel you have to," Penny said in a whisper, "but it would please him a great deal."

Helen suddenly realized homicide wasn't the only thing she had been considering all afternoon. She imagined Camelot with a seismic fissure. She imagined Tara with locked wings and men in Confederate white suits.

"Sure," she said. "Thank you."

Helen's hands were shaking as badly as Sutton's by the time she got to his house. She arrived in linen and silk. Sutton waited on the porch in jeans and a polo shirt. Helen felt as if she'd spent a lifetime overdressing or underdressing for dinner parties at which everyone else knew precisely what to wear without ever having to ask.

"Hello," she said. Sutton's entire body was caught up in a slight but noticeable tremor. What was also noticeable to Helen was that he *had* a body, a flesh and blood body over which the flesh was nicely spread.

"Thank you," David said, studying the tips of his tennis shoes.

"Thank *you,*" Helen said.

Apparently that was enough conversation for David. He turned and entered the house letting the screen door slam behind him. Helen thought it might have been better to spend the evening plotting Portner's assassination. But Penny opened the screen door and said, "Come in, come in."

David had disappeared into his bedroom behind a closed door. Helen sipped white wine in the cool clean kitchen while Penny cut up apricots, melons and plums for a summer fruit salad. Above the refrigerator, Helen saw a photograph framed in ornate silver and took it down to have a look at it. The frame was tarnished and the photograph mottled with spots and fingerprints. An infant, perhaps two years old, stared out as if into a void. For Helen, there was no mistaking the eyes.

"My God," she whispered.

"I know," Penny said. "But look again."

The photograph had been taken in the child's room. There were toy fire engines, toy service stations, an electric train, building blocks, and metal pots and pans. But the room was strangely bare—no carpet, blinds instead of drapes, a plain bedspread thrown over a bed with no pillow.

"It's so—cold," Helen said.

"Exactly," Penny said. "Mr. Sutton, David's father, was fond of saying, 'There are no pillows in the *real* world,' though he permitted himself a good many comforts of his own."

"What about David's mother?"

"Well, comfort was important to her, too, and an infant was simply a nuisance. She hired a nurse to take care of him. The nurse didn't believe in pillows either

"But you were with him then, weren't you?" Helen asked. "He had you." Helen wanted a silver lining for David, a sliver of redemption.

"Yes, I was there," Penny said, "but I was the housekeeper. The Suttons wouldn't let me touch him."

"But—," Helen began. She still had to know one thing.

"Oh, honey, that's enough for now. Go see, David. He really did want you to come, even if he can't say so."

The door to David's room was ajar. Helen could see him hunched over a pad, drawing with one hand and running the fingers of the other through his hair as if he were trying to smooth it and yet leaving it more unkempt each time he did it. Helen wanted simply to watch, but she felt again as if she were a voyeur and knocked on the open door instead.

"Oh Penny, I can't get it right."

"No David, it's Helen."

David turned slowly and looked at her and blinked as if he'd seen a vision he was trying to clear.

"Oh Helen. Helen," he said. He turned back to his table and drew the lid over the drawing pad very slowly.

"Please don't," Helen said. "Couldn't I see it?"

"Oh no," he said, "it's not finished." He held his hands flat against the cover of the pad.

"Are there any that are finished? May I see those?"

"Well, yes. Well, no. I mean they're finished, but—"His hands began to tremble so badly that they rattled the paper on the pad, and his face worked as if the muscles of it were waging a war against each other. Helen immediately regretted having asked, but David said, "Well, yes then. If you would like to."

He walked across his bare room and opened a closet door. Inside, the shelves and racks were stuffed with belongings—clothes, shoes, ties, a red blanket, books, a small sculpture of a nude, bottles of green and blue glass, and canvases and empty frames haphazardly stacked against each other. David ignored it all and made his way to the back to a deep shelf on which a sheaf of papers lay two feet high. He lifted up the entire pile up and carried it to his bed.

"These are finished," he said. "I'll just—I'll just—" He fled the room on wobbly legs.

The drawings, all wrought in pen and ink, were intricate, precise but strangely barren. There were drawings of men and women bent over assembly line belts, of parks where old people fed pigeons, young mothers rocked babies in strollers, and teenagers embraced, and of fast-food restaurants, supermarkets and service stations.

The drawings made a stark record of the people and places Helen knew well and had come to ignore, but they did more than that. Each drew her eye to one detail—beneath the Formica tables, the families of four and the Styrofoam detritus of a busy fast-food restaurant, a knit baby bonnet lay in a pool of spilt Coca Cola and globs of thickening catsup; in a manicured, well-swept park, an old man had taken an elegant pose on a freshly painted park bench though cracked nails that had curled into the parchment flesh of his toes had broken through the stitching of his once elegant wing tips; as the last man riveted the last bolt and the gleaming white car rolled gently off the line and the wide flat belt dipped to turn under and begin its inexorable circle again, a pair of wire-rimmed glasses were caught between smooth rubber and smooth metal, one lens shattering into a starburst.

Helen was weeping, but she sensed that David had returned to the room and tried to stop.

"Oh, don't," he said. He sat down next to her but just far enough away so that their bodies didn't touch. "So you looked at them then," he said.

When Helen nodded, David leaned over and kissed her cheek. "You smell so nice," he whispered.

Helen turned and kissed him back. She felt his cool, dry lips withdraw immediately.

"No!" he said. "No."

Helen scrambled to her feet.

"No," he said again. He wasn't stuttering and he wasn't trembling. He sat absolutely still, absolutely frozen, like cool dead marble.

Helen ran from the room and from the house. She drove home and stayed there for five days. The phone rang on and off. She didn't answer it. There were knocks on her door. She didn't answer those either. The only thing she looked at with any interest was a photograph of herself at five. By the time the photograph had been taken, Helen's father had already disappeared and with him he had taken her wife's interest in life and in Helen. At five, Helen hadn't looked into the camera as if into a void. She had looked into it with eyes that were already dead. Helen didn't want line drawings and marble sculptures.

On the fifth day, the phone rang and she answered it.

"David wants to see you," Penny said.

"No," Helen said.

"Honey, he wants to see you very badly."

"Then I want to hear it from him."

Helen thought the phone had been dropped or was merely being held. All she heard was an eerie silence that seemed to have some life to it.

"David?" she asked.

"Helen—I—would—very—much—like—to—see—you—I—"

"Okay, David," Helen said. It was all she had wanted.

"—realize—that—it—would—be—more—proper—for—me—to—come—to—you—but—since—"

"David, I said okay."

"—I—don't—drive—at—the—moment—I—was—hoping—that—you—would—come—to—see—me."

"Yes, David. I will. Now?"

"Thank you," he said.

Helen washed her hair for the first time in five days and changed her clothes and drove south for ten miles to the orchard shack.

"Have a seat, honey. I'll get you some tea," Penny said as she ushered Helen into the living room. Helen sat down on the bright blue sofa and looked at the painting above the fireplace. She wished that it were possible to be in that lush world of red, blue and green oils and sunlight, bottles, and books. Then suddenly she realized that she *had* been in it.

Penny returned with iced tea for both of them. "I know I haven't answered all your questions," she said. "David is a very private person, Helen. I wish he knew how to tell you himself so that—"

"I know," Helen said quickly. "I know it isn't fair, but I feel I'm in so— *deep.*" Despite five days in a stupor, Helen had not realized just how deep until that moment. Falling through the seismic crack in Camelot terrified her; the descent, though, was somehow familiar.

Penny sighed. "David was considered a very fortunate man, Helen. He went to the right schools and did well. He went into business and made more money than his father ever had, and what his father had made was considerable. David had his choice of women and his choice of famous friends, but he was frozen out somehow ... or maybe by that time, he had frozen himself out."

"But what *happened?* I mean, how did he get here?"

"He made a routine visit to a plant one day and saw a familiar sight—an assembly line and his employees along either side of it. I think it looked too familiar to him that day. He wouldn't leave the line. In the end, they had to carry him off in restraints, and his father had him locked up in what amounted to a very expensive prison. I got him out by offering to take him away and take care of him. The Suttons let me, I suppose, because he was more than a nuisance by then."

"But he's *working* on an assembly line, why would he do that?" Helen asked.

"I don't know," Penny said. "I know so little. Just what I see. David doesn't talk to me either, you know. He doesn't talk to anyone."

Penny smiled. "David's waiting for you in the garden, honey. Go on out back and have some tea with him. I'll be in the kitchen if you need me."

David sat in jeans and a T-shirt in a worn wicker chair. He would have looked very handsome if it hadn't been for his arms that he held rigidly by his sides and his eyes that seemed to stare straight out into the apricot orchard without seeing. Helen sat down a foot away from him and said hello.

"You mustn't love me," he said.

"Why not?" she asked, realizing suddenly not only that she *did* love him but that she'd already made many assumptions about why he could never love her, none of which had anything to do with seismic fissures or Confederate white suits. All of it was temporary, she had thought, the orchard shack and the assembly line. David would return to himself, and he would never love her then. She was an employee.

"There's nothing to love," he said. "I'm not a person."

Though it wasn't the answer she had expected, she understood immediately when she heard it.

"You're the tennis shoe on the lawn, the eyeglasses caught in the line?"

"No, just the line—the pulleys and the belts, moving around and around the edges of things, sometimes crushing them." He spoke almost normally now, without stutters or hesitation.

"But the drawings—you wanted somebody to notice? So you could stop?"

"Yes, I wanted somebody to notice. You did."

"And did you stop?" Helen asked.

"When I touched you," he said. "I felt as if I'd finally gotten into the middle."

Helen wasn't about to risk another attempt to cross the fissure. She looked out into the orchard of fruit-laden trees. The grove was an endangered species that would soon be subdivided. And though the sky seemed clear and blue, she knew that between her and the heavens lay an invisible smudge of airborne waste. Still, she wasn't prepared to lose interest, not yet anyway.

"The painting over the fireplace," she said, "that's yours, isn't it?"

David began to tremble. His head shook and he could not bring his hands to a rest.

"And it's your bedroom?"

David shook more violently but managed a wobbly nod.

"Was your bedroom like that once?"

Suddenly David stopped shaking altogether.

"Please—come—with—me—Helen—if—you—would—like to."

Helen followed David into the institutional gloom of the gray-green bedroom. David went to a corner and pulled back the bare carpet. Beneath it was a worn hardwood floor painted brick red.

"When I first came," he said, "I had a dream—about the floor. I liked it. The color."

"Why didn't you pull up the carpet?" Helen asked.

"Oh, I couldn't, I couldn't do that. No." David said. "So I—so I—painted it—like a wish." He smiled at the patch of brick red wood.

"It's a lovely color," Penny said from the doorway. "Perhaps we should take up the carpet."

David looked from the brick red wood to the institutional green carpet and back again.

"Would you like that, Helen?" he asked.

"Yes, I would."

David knelt down and pulled the carpet back an inch or two more and then peaked underneath it.

"Do you think it's brick red all across the room?" he asked.

"Be my guess," Penny said.

"Helen?"

Rather than answering, Helen knelt down by David and began pulling the carpet up. It was tacked down in spots and glued down in others. Penny got paint thinner and a hammer, and Helen and David set to work softening glue and prying up carpet tacks. When they had lifted the last corner, they were dripping with sweat and out of breath. They rolled the gray-green carpet up tight and carried it out to the backyard.

"I'd bury it, or burn it," Helen said.

David laughed—for the first time, in Helen's memory anyway.

When they returned to the bedroom, Penny had a pitcher of lemonade waiting. Helen and Penny sat on the chairs covered with Naugahyde and David sat on the bed with the metal frame. The brick red floor seemed to glow beneath their feet.

"To a lovely color," Penny said, lifting her glass.

"I like it," David said.

"So do I," Helen said.

The smudge in the sky didn't matter so much to her at that moment. When she looked at the brick red floor she felt as if it might be possible to see through the smudge in the sky to something clean and clear beyond.

"Don't you see, David?" she said. "You *are* a person."

He looked at her then as if she had just said that gold could mined in an asphalt parking lot.

"No, David. Listen to me. Belts and pulleys didn't make those drawings. It wasn't a machine that painted a picture so—full of life, so full of *your* life. David, a machine can't ..."

"Can't what?" he asked.

"Nothing ... nothing, never mind."

"Can't what?"

"Love someone."

"I see," David said.

They both studied the patch of brick red wood.

BARRIERS

One night when Fred Hubberman was having an otherwise pleasant few hours of insomnia, traffic barriers crept into his mind. Traffic barriers had not been a conscious subject of contemplation for him until that night, but subconsciously they had been working their way into his brain for months. Every time he took a turn off a main drag to avoid traffic in Palo Verde, there in front of him, blocking his way, was a traffic barrier. Sometimes it was a railroad tie cemented into the street, sometimes mounds of concrete or a fence, sometimes decorative boulders, sometimes truncated telephone poles. And when he was out to visit a friend not five blocks away, he found himself in a maze that required endless turns and backtracking.

Would there be an end to it? Fred wondered, in the darkness of his empty house. Or was the potential limitless? Could every street be blocked or blocked in a new and improved way? Could traffic be infinitely redirected? Would the town simply reject traffic entirely? Would it wall itself off, perhaps, from all communication? What, in effect, were the broader implications of a town obsessed with blocking traffic?

Fred sighed and wished that Mary Margaret, his wife, deceased for ten years, were still alive. She would have made sense of it. When she was alive, Fred had taken care of the hardware store, the grocery shopping and the gardening, and Mary Margaret had taken care of the world. And, because she had been strong-willed and opinionated, she either got her way or dismissed her adversaries with a sniff of her aristocratic nose. If Fred had been perplexed or troubled by a neighborhood's outrage at the suggestion that ten units of low-cost housing be built in the middle of it, Mary Margaret had answered, "They've all got hearts the size of peas and constitutions as strong as overcooked spaghetti. Don't worry, honey. We'll beat 'em down." And beat 'em down she had. And Fred had gone back to counting his stocks of nails, bolts and hammers from ten p.m. until four a.m.

But Mary Margaret was dead and Palo Verde was obsessed with traffic barriers and Fred had no one to turn to. He rolled over in the big, high double bed he and Mary Margaret had shared for thirty years and tried to sleep. But he couldn't, and this time the insomnia wasn't pleasant. The bed seemed too big and cold even, and the house empty like a hollow egg. Mary Margaret had been the best thing that had ever happened to Fred and she was dead and he was too old to have a second chance even if he wanted one which he didn't.

In the morning, Fred drove his '52 Buick Super through the leaf-strewn streets of Palo Verde on a route he had carefully selected for its lack of traffic barriers. Fred was almost as fond of the Buick Super as he had been of Mary Margaret. He could have traded it in on a newer model; he could have bought a Porsche if he'd wanted one. But it would have been an extravagance. Extravagance upset

Fred. It made him uneasy. You were supposed to work for what you got, and, if you got more than enough, you were supposed to pass some on to somebody else. There was only so much to go around, after all.

When Fred arrived at his store, he took his time opening up. He brewed coffee, dusted off the counter tops, straightened the rakes into a neat row, and checked the bins of nails to make sure there was an adequate supply of each length and width. None of Fred's customers, what remained of them, expected him to open up on time anyway, and none of them wanted to hurry him either. They were the downtown residents who lived in old hotels and didn't own cars and needed a hardware store within walking distance. In any case, they came less for the hardware and more for company, a cup of freshly brewed Maxwell House coffee, and an easy chair to sit and drink it in.

Fred walked to the front of his store, sighed, pulled up the shades one by one, unlocked the door, and flipped the "Sorry, We're Closed" sign to the "We're Open" sign.

Florence Greenway was Fred's first customer. She was a widow of two years whose husband had been a customer of Fred's. She wanted a packet of thumb tacks. Fred knew Florence could have bought thumb tacks most anywhere, and he was pleased that she had chosen Hubberman's Hardware.

"How are you today, Mrs. Greenway?" Fred asked as he handed Florence her tacks.

"Fine. I'm just fine. I do think I'll sit down for a minute. It's a long walk, and it seemed longer today."

Florence sat down and Fred offered her a cup of coffee. He stayed behind the counter, tidying up things that didn't need to be tidied up.

"I'd be pleased to drop you home," Fred said, "if you don't feel like walking back."

"Oh my, dear no. I've got to keep these old sticks of mine oiled." Florence laughed. Fred looked at the old sticks out of the corner of his eye and thought they looked very nicely oiled.

"Oh, I didn't meant to suggest—" he began.

"Oh no," Florence said. "Besides, they've got the street all torn up. They've been making an awful racket since early this morning."

"Probably resurfacing," said Fred. He placed a rubber stamp two inches to the left of where it had been and straightened the credit card stamping machine square with the counter top.

"No, I don't think so," said Florence. "I think it's one of those barriers they're putting in. They've got chunks of telephone poles out there."

Fred hands froze on the credit card stamping machine. "A traffic barrier?" he asked.

"Yes. That's it. I think they're blocking off the street."

"Flo—Mrs. Greenway, does that disturb you at all?"

"Disturb me? The traffic barrier?" Florence looked up, and Fred nodded, met her eyes and then looked away. He felt a flush rising in his cheeks.

"Well, as you know, I don't drive," she said. "I'd hardly be aware of traffic barriers if it weren't for the City Council meetings. It's all they ever discuss at the meetings anymore. It's damn dull." Florence sniffed.

Fred laughed. He liked Florence's sniff.

"Oh, forgive me," said Florence, her pink cheeks deepening to red.

"Why nothing to forgive, Mrs. Greenway. I've been known to use a strong word or two myself sometimes, when the situation called for it."

Florence smiled and set her coffee cup on the counter and said, "I should be going. I'm sure you have work to do."

"Well, yes," said Fred, who had very little to do. "But I've got time. Have another cup before you go."

And Florence said she'd have half a cup and did, and Fred asked her what she made of it—the proliferation of traffic barriers. She said it troubled her in the "broader sense," which pleased Fred because that was exactly how it troubled him, but neither one of them could put their finger on exactly what the "broader sense" was. Another customer came in at that point so Florence suggested that perhaps they should discuss the "broader sense" over dinner, at her house, that evening. Fred thought that was a very good idea and said he would be pleased to accept.

The customer who had come in was Old Mr. Ballard, a carpenter by profession and an inhabitant of the Presidential Arms Residential Hotel. And he *was* old, maybe ninety-six, maybe older. He couldn't remember. Nobody else could either.

"WHAT CAN I DO FOR YOU?" Fred shouted at Old Mr. Ballard. Ballard was hard of hearing, blind in one eye, and he walked with a cane. And he may have been old but he wasn't senile. His mind was as sharp as it had been when he led a strike in '37 of construction workers and sat in jail for two months for his efforts.

"I NEED DYNAMITE," Ballard shouted back.

"DYNAMITE?" Fred asked.

"YEAH, DYNAMITE," Ballard said. "I'm gonna blow up North Valley Development Company and J.G. Winston with it."

Fred laughed. Old Mr. Ballard didn't. North Valley Development Company was notorious. So was J.G. Winston, its president and a standard bearer in the community for "chic." The town loved him. His daughter was a debutante. His son was a high school football star. The City Council gave him building permits whenever he asked and he asked often.

"NOW BALLARD," Fred shouted. "WHAT'S HAPPENED?"

"EH?" said Ballard.

"I SAID, WHAT'S HAPPENED?"

"WINSTON'S EVICTING US."

"EVICTING YOU?"

"EVICTING US. YEAH. ISN'T THAT WHAT I SAID? GONNA TEAR DOWN THE ARMS AND BUILD CONDOMINIUMS."

North Valley Development Company's favorite developments were condominiums that sold for a half-million dollars each, built on the sites of old apartment buildings that no longer met earthquake codes and were in danger of being condemned.

"HE CAN'T DO THAT," Fred shouted. He was astounded and dismayed. Half his customers lived at the Presidential Arms.

"HE'S DOING IT," Ballard shouted. "UNLESS I GET THE DYNAMITE."

"I DON'T HAVE ANY DYNAMITE."

"THEN GIVE ME A LANTERN AND A FLASHLIGHT IN CASE THEY TURN OFF THE JUICE. WE'RE STAYING PUT."

Fred sold Old Mr. Ballard a lantern and a flashlight and offered him the use of his camp stove and a sleeping bag.

Ballard said no thanks and hobbled out, pounding his cane on the store floor like a jack-hammer. As he left, he shouted back at Fred, "AND I DON'T LIKE THEM DAMN PURPLE SHADES EITHER."

Fred agreed with Ballard about the maroon shades that now adorned the front windows of Hubberman's Hardware. For forty years, the shades had been green. Now they were maroon—to match the shades of the video rental shop and the gelato ice cream parlor between which Hubberman's was now sandwiched. The City Council had insisted on it—uniform shades, uniform awnings, so as to enhance the general atmosphere of "chic" that the town was vigorously cultivating.

The new awning and the new shades had cost Fred quite a bit of money but had done nothing for his business. The patrons of the video shop and the gelato ice cream parlor, who did own cars and who were particular about their movies and their ice cream, didn't shop at Hubberman's. They went to discount hardware stores in the shopping malls.

Fred didn't have his heart in his work that day. He closed at 4 p.m. sharp and headed for University Avenue. He drew his overcoat tight around his neck. It was autumn and the sky was darkening early and the air had a nip in it in late afternoon. Fred walked four blocks to the See's Candy Shop to buy Florence a box of chocolate creams. He had expected to see Mildred Stone behind the counter, back stiff, bosom thrust out like a shelf. He even asked for her. A teenage girl whose nails were covered with fluorescent purple polish had never heard of Mildred Stone.

Mildred Stone was, in fact, dead. Fred had found her himself, in a bare room with grease spots on the walls, at the Presidential Arms Hotel. After forty years of selling See's chocolates and secretly handing out caramels and mints to any child who came in and cooking batches of home-made divinity fudge for the high school bazaar, Mildred Stone had died childless, penniless and alone. When Fred had found her, her body had already begun to decompose.

On the walk back to his car, Fred saw Old Mr. Ballard hobbling down the street, huddled against the cold autumn in a frayed overcoat. Then he saw a young couple, arm in arm, wearing sweaters tied around their necks. The girl had hair the color of honey and soft creamy skin. The boy had bright white even teeth and a disarming smile. They both looked to Fred so fresh and clean and perfect that he imagined them newly minted. Old Ballard walked right by them, but they didn't notice him.

Fred's legs began to feel stiff. The walk back to his car seemed longer than usual.

At home he shaved and showered and picked a bouquet of autumn daisies from his garden. The garden was showing signs of fall. Fred had pulled up the summer beds that had turned brown. The leaves were beginning to drop, and the hedge had stopped putting out new shoots. But Fred wasn't thinking about autumn as he dressed for dinner, nor was he thinking about Mildred Stone nor traffic barriers nor newly minted people. He was thinking about Florence Greenway and aftershave. He wondered if Florence, a fine lady, a graduate of Stanford University, a retired school teacher, would prefer aftershave on a man or not. Mary Margaret had loathed it. But Fred had purchased a bottle two days after Florence and he had first had a brief chat. Perhaps Florence's husband had used aftershave, though, and it would sadden her to smell it on another man. Or maybe it would bring back warm memories and in this way be of benefit to Fred. But what if Florence were allergic to it and sneezed all through dinner?

Fred knew exactly where Florence lived. He had admired her house before he had begun to admire her. The house and garden were neat as a pin. It was indisputably a house in which the resident took considerable pride. Not a weed was to be seen nor a chip of peeling paint.

Fred turned onto Florence's street and nearly ran into five steel posts cemented into the middle of the pavement.

"Confound it," he cursed quietly.

He drove around the block and found railroad ties blocking his way. He made a U-turn and tried a street parallel to the street on which Florence lived. It was one-way the wrong way. He passed it up for the next and drove until he approached Florence's house from 180 degrees in the opposite direction. A concrete slab three feet high blocked his way. He made left turns, he made right turns, he said "Confound it," again and then again. He felt blood rushing to his face. He considered driving out to the main drag and calling Florence to tell her that she was marooned. But he wanted to have dinner, and with Florence.

In desperation he parked and walked into Florence's neighborhood. There were cars on the street. It amazed and upset him. He stood before Florence's house and wiped his perspiring brow with a fresh handkerchief and took a few deep breaths. He rang the doorbell when he felt sufficiently calm. Florence answered it herself.

He thought she had never looked finer. She wore a sky blue dress patterned with small white flowers. He saw only a hint of make-up and decided he'd been right about passing up the aftershave.

"You look very lovely," he said, handing her the flowers and candy. She blushed and asked him to come in.

"You have a very nice house," he said as he came into the living room. And he meant it. A fire burned steadily in a large fireplace, illuminating a room with many books and photographs and paintings.

"Please sit down," Florence said. "Would you like a sherry?"

"Yes, thank you," said Fred.

"If you don't mind my saying—or perhaps I shouldn't," Florence said.

"No, please go on," said Fred.

"Are you all right? You look a bit shaken. Should I offer you something stronger?"

"No, no. I'm fine," Fred said, sinking down into a soft sofa. "It's just that I had a devil of a time getting here. I had to *walk* in."

"Walk in?"

"Yes, I parked on Kingsley. It's the traffic barriers, Mrs. Greenway. I believe you're entirely blocked off."

"Oh dear no. Really?" Florence laughed suddenly and kept laughing. She laughed so much that tears began to form in her eyes.

Fred stared at her, startled by her laughter.

"Oh forgive me," she said, chuckling still. "It's just that I knew they'd do it one day. I thought they'd wall themselves off, but it seems they've walled me off."

"Mrs. Greenway, I'm sorry, but I don't think it's funny. Your—friends. How will they visit? Your children? And if you needed an ambulance or the police? Think of the implications."

"You're right, of course," Florence said as she stood up and used a poker to stir up the fire. She turned to face Fred. "It's a very troubled world," she began, "and there are a great many things to worry about. Our town worries about traffic barriers and *only* traffic barriers. Half our city budget goes for traffic barriers. There are plenty of serious implications in that."

"Half the city budget?" Fred asked.

"Nearly," Florence sighed. "They just don't see."

"See?" Fred asked.

Florence sat down, stuck out her feet and crossed them at the ankles.

"Remember when they wanted to institutionalize Patrick?" she asked.

Fred nodded.

"They wanted to put him away, you know," Florence said. "They wanted the police or a social worker to do something. Nothing cruel. Nothing drastic. Just solve the problem. They didn't want to have to look at him and be reminded. They didn't see, they don't see, and they don't want to see."

Fred remembered Patrick, who had sat on a bench on University Avenue every day for twelve years and talked quite cheerfully to non-existent friends and who had gone home at night to the Presidential Arms and cooked his own supper and then had gone peacefully to sleep.

"I remember," Fred said.

"Of course you do," Florence said. "You don't forget a thing like *that*," she added with a sniff.

Fred didn't want to talk about Patrick. He liked Florence Greenway so much at that moment that he didn't want to talk about the Presidential Arms or Old Mr. Ballard either; he wanted to cross the room and kiss Florence. At the thought, blood rushed up his neck and into his cheeks.

"Is it too warm for you?" she asked.

"Why no," said Fred. "It's just fine."

"Shall we eat and work out a plan of attack. I've made veal in lemon sauce and creamed leeks. We'll have wine."

"Plan of attack?" Fred asked.

"To free me," Florence said with a broad smile.

"Oh yes," Fred said. "I'd like nothing better."

Over dinner, Fred told Florence about the Presidential Arms. She was appalled. Friends of hers lived at the Arms. But she was not surprised. Fred suggested a midnight excursion to demolish the traffic barriers and North Valley Development Company. Florence laughed and suggested a visit to the City Council.

They sat in Florence's cozy dining room and ate veal and sipped wine and talked about Fred's garden and Florence's garden and his hardware store and the school she used to teach at. And around towards midnight, Fred, who usually began his nightly insomnia at 10 p.m., realized suddenly that he'd kept Florence up entirely too late and, in doing so, had been very rude. But Florence, who looked as fresh and cheerful at midnight as she had at 6 p.m., brushed away Fred's apology with a sniff and said he "shouldn't be a stranger," and Fred said, "No, of course not. I mean we do have to plan our strategy," and Florence said, "Yes, indeed."

Fred shook her hand good-bye and wondered on the walk back to his car, as he pulled his coat tight against the chill night air, if he should have kissed Florence and then was sure he should have and cursed himself for not having had the courage. But the evening, in any case, couldn't have been more pleasant. It had been a long time since Fred had dined out and in such good company. He drove home dodging traffic barriers and enjoying the anticipation of a few quiet hours taking stock of his store.

But once again, after he'd settled down into bed in the house that seemed much too quiet to him now, his insomnia was interrupted by the thought of traffic barriers, and North Valley Development Company as well. It wasn't, however, the specter of a marooned Mrs. Greenway or a homeless Mr. Ballard that drove him out of bed at three a.m. for a cup of warm milk (Mary Margaret had sworn by warm milk and railed against the heavy consumption of tranquilizers in its stead). No, it was not a specter that disturbed Fred. It was a thought, the thought that traffic barriers and North Valley Development Company, while just possibly the ruin of Palo Verde, might also be the best things that had happened to Fred in the last ten years having, in a sense, been responsible for bringing him and Florence into closer communication. Fred believed that this thought was perverse, and it made his stomach churn as he tried to digest the very large meal and the several glasses of wine he had consumed at Mrs. Greenway's.

When Fred gave up on insomnia and decided to sleep, his dreams were equally perverse, as he himself believed even as he dreamt them. He dreamt he was snuggling up to a nice warm body, and it wasn't Mary Margaret's. It was Florence's, and it was naked. He awoke with a start at seven a.m. and immediately switched on the light and groped for the framed photograph of Mary Margaret that stood on his bedside stand.

"I'm sorry," he said, near tears. "I'm so sorry."

"Don't be an idiot. It's about time," Mary Margaret sniffed, or so Fred thought.

Fred stared into Mary Margaret's eyes. There was no mistaking her meaning. Fred felt sad—and relieved.

On the way to Hubberman's that morning, Fred shivered as the Buick Super made its way through a morning of heavy overcast. Fred decided he'd drive past Mrs. Greenway's house, just to take a quick look and know that she was inside, safe and sound and warm.

He'd forgotten about the barriers. He remembered a block away and said, "Confound it," and made a hasty U-turn.

At Hubberman's, after he had made coffee and drawn up the shades, he sat behind the counter among boxes of invoices and receipts and returned merchandise—a hammer with a crack, a rake that had fallen apart on first use, a set of dishes that had bubbles under the glaze—and he began to write his speech for the City Council, which was to meet that night. It wasn't easy. His hand shook as he did it. He was sure Florence would find it "heated". He began to look for ways to subdue the heat.

"What I fail to see ... " he wrote. "What I simply cannot understand ... " he wrote, hearing his voice rising in his own head, "is why a citizen, a fine citizen, a citizen of this town for more years than any of you on this Council, should be imprisoned ..." He underlined imprisoned, "<u>imprisoned</u> in her own house and another fine citizen, perhaps the oldest in this town, should be shoved out into the street ..." He underlined street. Then he stopped.

It was all wrong. He was exaggerating. "Inflammatory," Florence would say. Why was he so angry, he wondered. It was a simple matter of requesting some restraint, some reason.

Fred heard sirens and jumped up immediately. His hardware store was in an old building on an old block, and a fire anywhere on the block meant a fire in his store. He rushed out the front door but saw only police cars, no fire engines, and they passed the block and sped down University Avenue. Fred waited until the pounding of his heart subsided and then he locked the front door and walked the half block to University Avenue.

Fred looked up the street and saw three police cars, their red lights flashing, pulled up in front of The Presidential Arms along with two windowless paddy wagons. He walked the block and a half to the hotel and stood in a crowd of onlookers and watched what they watched. What they all watched were twenty or so white-haired, stoop-shouldered senior citizens being ushered, gently to be sure, into the back seats of police cars and into the back doors of paddy wagons by Palo Verde policemen. Fred looked around for J.G. Winston but didn't see him. Being a cautious man, Fred did nothing and would have done nothing if it hadn't been that he saw Old Mr. Ballard, shouting a storm of obscenities and struggling with a strength that belied his years, being dragged out the front door of the Presidential Arms and then being cold-cocked by one of Palo Verde's finest. Fred burst through the crowd with a strength and agility he hadn't known he still possessed. With a leap, he tackled the policeman. But no sooner had Fred grabbed the arm that had done the cold-cocking than his own arms were grabbed and one was jerked up behind his back. The pain stopped him in his tracks. He was dragged towards the curb and the waiting paddy wagon.

"This is an outrage!" Fred yelled.

One of the cops who held his arm in a grip turned Fred around to face him.

"Mr. Hubberman!" the cop said.

"Officer Daniels!" Fred said.

Officer Tim Daniels patrolled the neighborhood of Hubberman's Hardware Store. Officer Daniels often came into the hardware store for a quick cup of coffee. Officer Daniels had caught a thief making off with all of Fred's cash one day a few years back.

Officer Daniels loosened his grip on Fred's arm.

"This is an outrage," Fred said. "Do you know what you're doing?"

"I'm following orders," Daniels replied, with less conviction that he might have.

"Orders?" Fred said.

"Look, Mr. Hubberman, just forget about this. You just go on along now. This isn't any of your business, and I've got work to do."

Fred left but not before he'd muttered, "Work, ha!" and sniffed in the finest manner of Mary Margaret and Florence Greenway. He was so angry that he was unsteady on his feet as he walked the block and a half back to Hubberman's Hardware Store. He had two things on his mind and two things only, a phone call to Florence Greenway and a trip to the city jail to bail out Old Mr. Ballard. He went inside, drew the shades, flipped the "We're Open" sign to the "Sorry, We're Closed" sign and called Florence Greenway.

"Flo," he said, "I mean, Mrs. Greenway—" Florence Greenway interrupted him.

"Have the goodness to call me Flo. I don't like formality between friends."

"Fine, Flo, fine," said Fred, taking no notice of the fact that Flo considered him a friend. He launched right into a recounting of the events on University Avenue, speaking so fast he found himself out of breath.

Flo interrupted him again. "Now just slow down, Fred Hubberman. Slow down and *breathe.*"

Fred took a deep breath, but it didn't do any good. "They evicted them. They *arrested* them."

"Fred dear, come over. Have a cup of tea. We'll sort this thing out."

That helped more than the deep breath. A lot more.

Fred left his store and climbed in his Buick. It was slow starting. It caught and died and caught and died and finally caught again. The afternoon had turned cold, not like fall, more like mid-winter. The sky was so gray Fred couldn't spot the position of the sun let alone see it.

He drove straight to Flo's. That is, when he hit a one-way street going the wrong direction, he went the wrong direction and blasted his horn at on-coming motorists who swerved out of his way. And when he came upon a traffic barrier, he drove up on the sidewalk and right around it, taking the branches off a few city-owned bushes, until he could get back into the street. He scattered bicyclists, kids with balls, and joggers as he went.

On his way, he passed J.G. Winston's house, a large old house built like a hacienda with a clay tile roof, arched walkways, wide green lawns, bougainvillea spread across the terra cotta walls, and a fountain with a fine spray of water near the front drive. This house gave no sense of having been newly minted. It had a feel of history, a sense of having been well built, at a time when craftsmanship had meant something. Craftsmanship had meant something to Old Mister Ballard. In 1928, Old Mister Ballard had helped build this house. He had constructed and carved and polished every smooth, shiny hardwood surface in the house.

In 1975, J.G. Winston and his family had moved in. In 1976, Fred and Mary Margaret had been invited to pay a visit. Much of the shiny, smooth hardwood surface had been painted over—"to lighten up the place" J.G. Winston's wife, an interior decorator, had said.

Fred floored the accelerator and careened past J.G. Winston's house and around five railroad ties. He parked directly in front of Flo's and went right up the steps and buzzed the doorbell until Flo answered.

When Flo opened the door, he wanted to rush into her arms. He might have even cried. But he did neither. He started to speak but Flo held up a hand.

"Don't say a word," she said. "Take a sip of this first."

Fred took a finely cut, crystal sherry glass in his hand and followed Flo into her living room. A fire was burning, and the room was warm. Fred sipped what he thought was sherry and then drank the glassful in one gulp. It was whiskey.

"Thank you," said Fred, sitting down in the easy chair Flo offered him.

"It helps," said Flo who sat across from him on the edge of a sofa. "I had a shot myself just a minute ago."

Fred leaned back in the chair and sighed and hung his head and shook it slowly back and forth. The bravado on his trip over had left him.

"Now's not the time to give up," said Flo.

Fred felt ill, the way he had when he was a child, when he'd been so upset he had started to feel queasy and faint, the way he had the first months after Mary Margaret's death when he had forgotten for a moment and had seen a dress he had thought she'd like and had planned to tell her about it until he had suddenly remembered.

"Lord," he said.

"Now Fred," Flo said, "J.G. Winston's money can't buy him everything."

"What do you suggest?" Fred asked.

"The City Council", said Flo. "I suggest we denounce the creep."

Fred laughed in spite of himself. "Will that help?"

"It may help. It's a start. The first salvo. Now let's see ... " Flo stood up and stoked the fire. "We denounce him. We start a campaign. We organize a defense fund for Ballard. We run Winston out of town."

Fred laughed again.

"What?" asked Flo, turning to look at him in surprise.

"It's just, it's just—" Fred didn't finish. It was just that Flo was ready for a fight, and Fred hadn't seen a woman ready for a good fight in a long time. He'd forgotten how nice it was to see.

"What about traffic barriers?" he asked instead of explaining.

"No need to forget them. Now there's a context. Now there's a perspective. A broader sense of the thing. Right here and on University Avenue. It's perfect, Fred. It couldn't be more perfect."

Flo looked as if she had just witnessed a live birth.

Fred showed her his speech. He was sure she'd disapprove. By the time he'd finished writing it, he'd been irate and he'd held back nothing as he'd written.

Flo loved it. "Perfect," she said. "Let's have some dinner and get over there early. I want a good seat."

Flo had made pot roast, and she wolfed down two portions of it, one of which would have been large enough to keep a sixteen-year-old football player sated for a week. Fred took nibbles and wished he had a bottle of antacid.

They arrived early at the City Hall. At the door, Fred and Flo were handed a flyer decrying the proliferation of traffic barriers by a man in a business suit.

"This'll help," said Flo.

Fred wasn't sure. The words printed on the flyer reflected nothing of the broader sense. The words were irate, but they spoke only of the annoyance, the inconvenience, and the need for people to keep themselves and their children out of the middle of the street.

In the Council chamber itself, Fred and Flo sat down on plushly covered benches in the middle of the room and waited. Fred looked around the huge, high-ceilinged, cold room and felt small, as if he'd suddenly shrunk. He saw faces in that room that he recognized and many that he didn't. Florence patted his hand. He smiled at her. He thought he should be reassuring. He didn't feel like being reassuring. He wanted to go home.

Then he heard a voice he recognized, directly behind his head.

"God, this day's been a ballbreaker," J.G. Winston sighed.

"I can imagine," said another.

"I begged them. I *pleaded* with them. You know this was the last thing I would have wanted."

"I don't get it," said the other. "Unless they were just all too senile to understand."

"I don't know," Winston sighed again. "It breaks my heart to see something like this happen. It's not as if we didn't offer them an alternative. There was the retirement home. I don't understand it either, but it's been a hell of a stress on me, to say nothing of the family. I've got to get Helen and the kids away for awhile, maybe the south of France, Puerto Vallarta, I don't know."

J.G. Winston sighed for a final time.

Fred wanted to turn around and punch him in the nose. Fred had never punched anyone in the nose in his life, but he wanted to punch J.G. Winston in the nose. He looked at Flo. Flo looked back at him.

"Let's move," she whispered.

Just then the Council members filed in. The council persons sat down one by one at a huge dais that could have easily served the Supreme Court of the United States. Flo got up and approached the dais to request that both she and Fred be allowed to speak.

Fred didn't want to speak. The imposing dais, the microphones, and the two-story high ceilings that gave an echo to every sound were not things with which Fred was familiar or comfortable. Fred suspected, despite his nerves, that the chamber was intentionally designed to intimidate and silence all but the most foolhardy, arrogant or fanatic. When Fred realized that, he regained a bit of his composure and the small beginnings of determination. Flo returned her seat, and he patted her hand and smiled with a reassurance that was genuine.

The proposal before the City Council asked that all further construction of traffic barriers be delayed until a thorough study of traffic patterns and safety be completed. The first speaker spoke in opposition. He had three children. One of them, while on her bike, had been hit by a speeding car. She was not seriously injured, but she was shaken up and had since been afraid to bicycle anywhere in town.

Officer Tim Daniels, looking immaculate and well rested after an afternoon of mass arrests, then spoke and said that the child in question had run a stop light and that the driver was not at fault. Officer Daniels was followed by J.G. Winston who spoke in favor of a ban on barriers, mentioning not only that he had children but he kept them well in tow and the previous speaker should do the same, but also that he believed traffic barriers were a hindrance for shoppers and thus were bad for downtown business, although that was certainly of secondary concern. He stopped to clear his throat. Fred, who had sat stiffly and silently through it all, leaned over and whispered to Florence, "Hold me down, Flo. Hold me down." Flo looked at him in alarm and then rested her hand on his right forearm. It kept Fred in his seat, but it didn't keep him from letting out a loud raspberry in the middle of J.G. Winston's next sentence which began, "I am a reasonable man—" The crowd laughed. The laughter didn't cheer up Fred.

Others spoke one after another, for and against the proposal, in surprisingly equal numbers, as Fred and Flo waited to be called. The vitriol from speakers on both sides soon reached the point that the Council was forced to threaten to clear the chambers.

Then Fred's name was called. He got up and went to the microphone. His knees were knocking against each other, but not from fear, rather from a kind of exhilaration, an overflow of adrenaline, from the knowledge that he was about to do something precipitous, maybe even dangerous, and he was still going to do it.

"Fred Hubberman," he said into the microphone so loudly that there was a loud, high-pitched whine followed by laughter. Fred stood back from the microphone a step and went on.

"I have lived in Palo Verde for sixty-nine years," he said. "I have seen a good many changes and most of them weren't good. I'm not against progress. I'm against stupidity and selfishness. We've spent one and one-half hours debating traffic barriers. I came to speak about traffic barriers. To say that the City won't live or die by them. To plead for compromise and reason. Mrs. Florence Greenway, a resident of this town for as long as I, is a prisoner in her own home, blocked off from visitors, ambulances, and police cars by railroad ties and concrete at every corner. This is certainly not reasonable."

Fred was interrupted by loud applause from barrier opponents.

"I'd suggest you wait until I've finished," he went on, warming to his subject now, anticipating a reaction but not sure exactly what it would be.

"Nor is it reasonable not to afford neighborhoods relief from excessive traffic."

Another round of applause, although less enthusiastic, from the barrier proponents.

"But now," Fred said, "I'm of a mind that the residents of this town don't deserve a reasonable solution. Don't deserve a reasonable community. Because I believe this town is unreasonable, that it has lost its *mind.*"

Fred paused. His mouth was dry. He noticed a pitcher of water next to the dais and poured himself a glass and drank it. The crowd was silent. The City Council members leaned forward waiting for Fred's next words. One might have even been suspicious that Fred took the pause not just to whet his whistle but to let his words sink in, create an unease, that Fred knew exactly what he was doing.

"This afternoon," he said, "arrests were made." A murmur began in the crowd. The City Council members shifted in their seats. "Today, the people who built this community, who built your schools, who taught you to read, who planted the first trees and paved the first streets, these people were put in *jail* today, put in jail because they are too poor and too old—"

"Mr. Hubberman, uh—" the mayor began.

Fred didn't stop.

"These people are in jail for having had the *stupidity* to believe in hard work, only to end up—"

"Mr. Hubberman, Fred," the mayor said. "Fred, I'm sorry but this isn't on the agenda."

"I don't *care* if it isn't on the agenda. I—"

"Fred," the mayor said, "you are out of order."

"This *town* is out of order!" Fred yelled. "We're talking about traffic barriers and people are in jail. They're—"

Fred felt a tug on his arm. It was Flo beside him. She leaned towards the microphone and spoke. "Mr. Mayor, might we put the subject *on* the agenda?"

"Yes, yes, of course," said the mayor. "Just see the city clerk next week. Of course you can—"

"Next week?!" Fred yelled so loudly that the microphone squawked and echoes bounced back and forth and up and down from wall to wall and ceiling to floor.

"Fred," Flo whispered. "Fred."

Fred looked at her. Her eyes were rimmed with tears. "Next week," she said.

Fred turned away from the microphone and followed Flo out of the hall, past the now silent crowd. A handful of those inside joined Fred and Flo in the street and offered their sympathy and support. Fred was not comforted. He didn't know if Flo was either. Six or seven people out of a crowd of three hundred wasn't comforting.

"We've been silenced," Fred said as he and Flo sat in his Buick Super with the motor running waiting for the heater to warm up. The sky was a dark gray gloom. The stars and moon were obscured by a high heavy fog.

"It's only the first battle," Flo said. "Those people need the blinders peeled off their eyes, and we're gonna do it."

Flo said the words Fred expected to hear and would have expected to hear if it had been Mary Margaret sitting next to him. But the words didn't stir him. He looked up at a large elm lit by a street lamp and gazed at its bare branches to which only a few lifeless leaves still clung.

"I don't know—" he said.

"Oh Fred. It's not the end. Why there's—"

"Let's go bail out Mr. Ballard."

They went to the jail. They could not bail out Mr. Ballard. They sat for an hour and forty-five minutes in a bare room that smelled strongly of stale urine and tobacco smoke only to be hold that bail hadn't been set. It was suggested that they come back the next day.

Flo urged Fred to come back the next day. Fred said he'd stay there the whole night if that was what it was going to take. He wasn't going to let Old Mr. Ballard sit in a cold cell without a blanket or warm clothing or a hot cup of coffee. Fred wasn't ready for another battle. He was beyond all that. He wasn't going to fight. He was going to sit, just stay put, until somebody paid attention to him. The jailers ignored him.

It was only when Flo said she was getting faint from the odor and chill in the bare room that Fred agreed to take her home. She said she wanted to go *his* home. It was two a.m. Friday morning. Fred agreed.

Fred's house wasn't as cheerful and warm as Flo's. Things had gotten worn since Mary Margaret's death, and Fred hadn't bothered to replace them, but Flo didn't seem to mind. She built a fire and lit it while Fred made coffee and spiked it with whiskey.

So they had a night cap and sat in front of the fire until it burnt down to a deep red glow. Then Flo said, "This isn't a night you should spend by yourself, Fred Hubberman." She blushed as she said it. Fred blushed too. But he got up and took her hand and guided her up the stairs to his bedroom.

At the door, Flo suddenly seemed shy. She stood in the doorway, not moving in, not moving out. Fred crossed the room and switched on a lamp on the night stand. Next to the lamp stood the black and white photograph of Mary Margaret. Fred looked at it and then looked back across the room at Flo and said, "Come in."

Flo came in. She took Fred's hand in her own and kissed it and then she smiled and then she kissed his lips. Her kiss was sweet and cool. Fred kissed her back. They shared the big high double bed, and they shared each other.

Fred sat up in bed the next morning and looked over at Flo. She was sleeping soundly and breathing with a soft purr. He felt a fierce tenderness for her and was suddenly astonished at his good fortune. He couldn't quite believe that a second fine woman had entered his life. He turned away and looked at the photograph of Mary Margaret. He wanted to apologize, but he heard her sniff and realized that no apology was necessary.

He got dressed and went downstairs to prepare a substantial breakfast for Flo. He looked out the kitchen window at the quiet street and saw a city pick-up truck drive by with a load of railroad ties. It was then that he felt a threat to his second chance at happiness. It was then that he feared for people like himself and Florence and Old Mister Ballard, for the people who seemed to be disappearing behind all those architecturally-approved, environmentally-safe barriers.

WHAT EXACTLY HAPPENS ... AS TIME GOES BY

Sundays through Saturdays

At Nordstrom Department Store, well-dressed shoppers browse to background music provided by piano players in tuxedos. The music is meant to soothe and reassure, to suggest that Nordstrom has everything and can handle anything, don't worry.

Monday ll:05 a.m.

Michael Martinelli saw the woman for the first time when he was halfway through "Malagueña." She was standing at the perfume counter staring directly at him. There was nothing particularly remarkable about her carefully coiffed gray hair and carefully tailored suit. She was just another shopper, but her look seemed to suggest recognition—no, not recognition, *knowledge*. Michael fumbled a measure of "Malagueña," cursed, recovered himself and looked up. The woman was gone.

The next song on Michael's play list was "Moon River." He hated it. It was the dullest song known to mankind in his opinion. He hated "Tie a Yellow Ribbon," too. There were a lot of unforgivable songs in the world, and he had to play them all.

Michael didn't think he could play "Moon River" or anything else, not after the look the woman had given him. It had humiliated him. She knew, he was sure, that playing the piano weekdays at the base of the first floor escalator in Nordstrom was not how he had meant to spend his life. He did play "Moon River," and with every note he wished the composer dead. Another shopper walked by and cooed, "Lovely, just lovely." She left an overpowering odor of sickeningly sweet perfume in her wake. A music lover, hah! Michael thought.

"Thank you. I mean, thank you for playing it. I mean, it's just that it reminded me of Havana." The woman from the perfume counter looked at Michael through sea green eyes, the most beautiful eyes he had ever seen. When he met their gaze, the woman blushed, looked away towards the shoe department, and then back.

"Well, thank you," she said again. She walked away without another word.

Michael's fingers were rubbery. He played "Feelings" with such a muddled tempo, a crowd in Las Vegas would have thought it intentional and wonderful.

Charlotte Reynolds looked around the perfume counter at Nordstrom in search of a scent that had no resemblance to roses or violets, scents she found stuffy and old-lady-like. She listened to strains of familiar songs to which she couldn't put names, but she thought that the piano player was playing very nicely.

Charlotte had been Mrs. Roland Reynolds for more than forty years, but now Roland was dead. She had a date that evening with as nice a man as she could have hoped to meet, but she didn't want to go. She sniffed scents that were meant to hint at tropical jungles, English castles, Southern flowers, and sex. Then she heard the strains of a song she could put a name to, and her hands froze on a bottle of *Tiempo*. "Malagueña" was the name of the song.

Charlotte was jolted back more than thirty-five years to Havana and to Andres. She felt dizzy. She let go of the bottle of *Tiempo* and grabbed onto the cool counter top. The temperature in the store seemed to her excessively hot despite a continual blast of frigid air blowing down from the vent directly above her head. She took a quick look at the piano player. That was when she got her second jolt. He was dark-haired, dark-skinned and had a jet black mustache. And he was staring at her with the same look Andres had given her thirty-five years before, a look that had always been a challenge. It was too much.

Charlotte fled to the shoe department. She was too old for any more challenges. In Shoes, she convinced herself that she was being ridiculous, and, to prove it, she decided to speak to the piano player. He was probably a perfectly normal person. She walked up and stood beside the Steinway. The piano player looked up at her, and she saw the challenge in his eyes again. She couldn't meet it. She didn't understand it. She thanked him and then fled.

Tuesday 10:05 a.m.

Wasn't it noon yet? Michael wondered as he played "New York, New York" like a funeral march. He couldn't bear to look at his watch. If it wasn't noon, he didn't think he could go on. He looked at his watch. He wanted to take a hatchet to the Steinway.

Michael's right hand listlessly plucked out the melody. He wasn't just upset about the music. He was upset about the woman and Havana. Not upset exactly, shaken was more like it. It gave him a jolt just to think about it, her mentioning Havana, because Havana in the winters of '56, '57, and '58 had been the happiest times of his life, an escape from the gray snow and slush of Manhattan, from the year-long routine of four hours of music classes and four hours of practice a day. Havana had been three weeks of sleeping late and spending his days in the sun and sand and his nights tagging along with his parents to the casinos, where nobody cared how old he was as long as he was an American.

Michael finished "New York, New York" with a flourish that was meant to be played *con brio* but which he managed *adagio di molto*. Would he ever see the woman again? Yes, she was just riding up the escalator. He'd nearly missed her. He started ten measures into "Malagueña." The woman was about to disappear into Level Two, but she turned and stared at him until her sea green eyes disappeared, then her shoulders, her breasts, her legs and her ankles.

Charlotte's heart pounded as she walked in the glass-walled entrance of Nordstrom. She had left home to shop for a scent and had arrived at Nordstrom with the sure knowledge that she was doing nothing of the sort. She went to the perfume counter anyway. She sniffed Chanel, Opium, Passion, Georgio and Franco. Then she sniffed *Tiempo*. She'd buy it, or maybe she'd sniff a few more. She was stalling for time. She heard the strains of a song she couldn't put a name to. She was waiting for the song she could put a name to.

Charlotte had gone out on her date. The gentleman had bored her. That wasn't so bad. It was better than what she'd felt when she'd seen Andres in Havana five months before after forty years of total silence. She had heard some time back how he might be reached and had written to him after Roland's death, on a whim she had told herself. Amazingly, to her, he had answered. He was delighted with her letter and invited her to visit. She had made arrangements immediately. She had also made the usual mistake, imagining him still to be the dark reticent lover with a secret urgent life. He was nothing of the sort, of course. He was a balding bureaucrat, a sub-minister of education, with a salt-and-pepper mustache and a wife and four children. He had a quiet dry charm that had come from the weathering effects of forty years of reality on the intensity and ideals of his youth.

Charlotte gave up on scents and headed for the escalator. The nameless song seemed to absorb the piano player totally. Charlotte stepped on the escalator and went up, and it was only then that she heard "Malagueña" enticing her back. She turned and looked at the piano player, who seemed reticent now, no longer challenging her, almost unable to meet her eyes. Did he, too, have a secret urgent life?

Charlotte was to have another date with Ernest, the gentleman who bored her. He was a successful lawyer and a well-read man, but he was very dull. Charlotte tried on silk dresses in front of three mirrors she couldn't avoid looking into. When she had had the courage to remark to Andres on the change in him, he had smiled and said, "I think life is sort of like a pumice stone. At best it wears away our sharp edges. At worst it begins to erode what's underneath." In that moment, Charlotte had not been sure if the pumice stone had treated Andres well or badly, but, as she lifted a silk dress over her head and let it fall, all that she could see of herself was erosion. She wasn't the soft, pale-skinned beauty of forty years ago, and Andres had not made the mistake of expecting her to be. Her skin was crinkly, her hips had spread, and her breasts hung low.

Michael played "Blue Moon," "It Had to Be You," and "Night and Day" with hands he had difficulty controlling. Another heavily-perfumed shopper walked by, leaned over and said, "Beautiful, could you perhaps play 'Copacabana'?" Barry Manilow, Jesus, Michael mumbled. He didn't want to play Barry Manilow; he wanted to play Beethoven. He wanted to prove himself to the woman. But he knew that the senior manager of Nordstrom would never let him get away with it. So he'd play *Rhapsody in Blue* complete with cadenzas. It would display his virtuosity but keep the senior manager off his back, maybe.

As Michael played the opening trill and chromatic scale, he began to feel the excitement and ease with which his hands moved up and down the keyboard. He was back again sitting on the Carnegie Hall stage, the piano in front of him, and an audience of one thousand, there for the piano competition. He had been nervous, nearly ill with fright, but his hands had never been steadier; he had never played better. For the first time in forty years what Michael Martinelli had meant to do with his life was exactly what he was doing.

"Stop this instant!" a voice hissed in his ear. "What the hell do you think you're doing?" It was the senior manager.

"I—" Michael began.

"Forget it, not here. See me in my office in thirty minutes."

The manager walked away. Michael sat at the Steinway with his hands in his lap. It was noon. He should eat. He didn't want to eat. He stared at his hands, at his long slender fingers that could reach beyond an octave.

"You're a pianist. I didn't realize." The woman spoke the words in a whisper. Michael looked up at her. She smiled tentatively. He didn't notice her skin or her hips or her sagging breasts. He was falling in love.

"I'm nothing," he said. "I'm a piano player."

The woman smiled again. Michael could see an edge of sadness around her eyes and lips, but the smile made him happy nonetheless. He didn't want the woman to leave, but he couldn't think of anything more to say. He watched her walk away.

"You're beautiful," was what he would have liked to have said.

At 12:30 p.m. the senior manager told Michael that Nordstrom Department Store was not Davies Symphony Hall and that the shoppers at Nordstrom needed to be soothed not startled, and that, if Michael didn't stick to the play list, his services would no longer be required. Understood?

Wednesday 11:30 a.m.

Charlotte Reynolds returned to Nordstrom for the third day in a row with the intention of buying accessories to complement the silk dress she had bought. She went immediately to Jewelry, which was on the first floor and which provided an unobscured view of the Steinway. She looked in the locked cabinets that displayed gold jewelry. She wondered if Ernest, her date, liked gold jewelry.

Probably fine gold jewelry, nothing flashy. She wondered if all that remained for her were gentlemen who preferred nothing flashy.

In Havana, Andres had gotten old and paunchy. "I wouldn't even sleep in my back yard now," he had said, speaking of his months in the *Sierra Maestra*. But what else had Andres said when they'd sat in his garden on bent metal chairs drinking rum and coke and swatting at mosquitoes? He had deftly evaded most of Charlotte's questions, but he had said something of substance anyway. Yes, he had said, "We created a cemetery, Charlotte, and then we tried to build something new and good on top of it. Getting up in the morning and brushing my teeth and having my first cup of coffee of the day still seems like a miracle to me sometimes. And that miracle is the only antidote, *Carlota,* the only redemption, for having hurt you, for having killed—at least for me."

Charlotte fingered a piece of fake gold jewelry, a bracelet. Andres had hated gold jewelry, fine or flashy, it hadn't mattered. He had hated the gold jewelry that the *Yanqui* women wore, that they flaunted in front of cooks and maids and chauffeurs and people starving in the streets. Charlotte had never worn gold jewelry in Havana, but Andres had seemed to hate her anyway despite the passion he felt for her.

Where was the music? Where was the young piano player with the secret urgent life? A saleswoman asked Charlotte if she needed help. Charlotte started but recovered quickly and asked to try on a gold chain. As she was fastening it at the back of her neck, she heard another song she could put a name to, "As Time Goes By." She suffered another jolt and fled to Shoes to try to clear her head.

"As Time Goes By" was one of Michael's favorites because, like "Malagueña," it reminded him of Havana, especially of Havana in '58 when there'd been plenty of intrigue and danger and romance, when he had been old enough to feel or sense it but too young to fear it. In Havana in '58 he'd not only tagged along behind his parents to the casino, but he'd actually sat on the stage and played "Malagueña" for fun. The audience had loved it and loved him, and the band leader's girl friend had enticed him into a hallway and drawn his head into her breasts and then between her naked thighs. He'd decided that he was finally living despite the gunfire just outside.

Michael saw the woman in Jewelry. He wanted to keep playing "As Time Goes By" again, but he didn't dare risk it. He played "Night and Day." It was the next thing on his play list, and he liked it anyway. It didn't remind him of anything. It was just a good song, and, because it was, he began to play well.

He had played extremely well the year he turned fourteen, the year the family did not go to Havana for Christmas because the city was under siege and nearly ready to fall into the hands of young men Michael's parents considered barbarians. It was the year that he went to Carnegie Hall instead, because his parents thought he was ready, because his teacher thought he was ready, because his manager thought he was ready, no matter that he himself did not think he was ready. He had been nervous, but he had played extremely well. Not well enough, though. He hadn't even placed.

"You mustn't say you aren't a pianist. You mustn't say that. You are."

Michael looked up. The woman was standing quite near him, so close that he could smell a faint scent of her. Her sea green eyes were rimmed with tears.

"You're beautiful," he said. His fingers were absolutely steady, but his foot wobbled on the pedal.

"Oh, gracious no. No, I'm not," the woman said.

"You shouldn't say that," Michael said. "You are— beautiful." He had never said that to a woman and meant it.

"May I watch you play?" the woman asked. "It won't make you nervous?"

"No," Michael said, a lie, but he wanted the woman to watch, even if he'd feel as he'd felt on the Carnegie Hall stage.

Charlotte stood at the pianist's side, leaning against the escalator railing for support. She listened to him play "As Time Goes By" again. Why was life so ridiculous was what she wondered as she watched the pianist play. Why did hearing a song, just a few measures of a song, make one remember, no, make one feel as one had so many years ago, as if there had been no maturing, no seasoning, no pumice stone, as if she were still that twenty-five-year-old woman who'd met secretly too many times with Andres not to know what his secret urgent life was? She had failed him, not met his challenge, because it meant lying to her husband, to whom she had lied many times, but the lie Andres wanted told would have destroyed her husband.

The pianist was looking directly at Charlotte as he played "Malagueña." He was looking at her as if they were in each other's arms, whirling across a ballroom floor or a wide veranda. Charlotte let herself be swept away by the swell of the music. She could feel the humid salt air against her skin and the heat of a body pressed against hers. When the song ended, she leaned close to the pianist, so close that she nearly touched his skin with her lips. "A good song may be the antidote," she said, "possibly even redemption."

Friday at Nordstrom Department Store

Michael Martinelli was very nervous. He lay the single long-stemmed red rose in the music rack of the Steinway and sat down to play. He played "Copacabana" and kept an eye out. She wasn't in Jewelry. Maybe Shoes. He played "You Light Up My Life" and thought, not with this song. And he played "I Gotta Be Me" and thought, what a pity when you could be someone else. Browsing shoppers smiled and nodded at him. He ignored them. Was she upstairs maybe? No, she was in Hats.

He stopped midway through "I Gotta Be Me." The abrupt pause startled a jewelry-laden shopper, who looked sharply at him and walked on. Michael began again the opening trill and chromatic scale. He was nervous but he was absolutely steady. He hit the octaves of the opening theme, and the chords in A flat sent out the bluesy rich tones he had always loved. Did the woman love them, too? He thought she might. He could not look at her.

Charlotte Reynolds entered Nordstrom for the fifth day in a row with the intention of buying absolutely nothing. She had nearly exhausted the possible offerings on the first floor. Gold jewelry was not redemption nor was *Tiempo*. The only department remaining to her was Hats, which was satisfactory since it, too, provided an unobscured view of the Steinway grand.

Charlotte picked up a broad-brimmed peach-colored hat with a band of white satin. She chose peach because that was the color of the silk dress she was wearing, a soft, maybe even sensuous, color.

The piano player was playing a song she could not, and didn't care, to put a name to. She wondered if yesterday had been a dream, a mirage maybe. She wondered if she should accept Ernest's invitation to a chamber orchestra recital that evening. And then she heard it, that unsettling trill and the swift scale that rose steeply only to fall into a string of seductive notes.

Michael was flying through the chords *tempo giusto.* The fingers that sounded the notes *fortissimo* felt as light as down to him. He was soaring with the music up and around and inside of it. A few shoppers stopped to watch. Michael sensed their presence. None of them cooed or smiled. They seemed to be listening. He slipped into *pianissimo* with ease and delicacy. Just then the senior manager's voice boomed out. *"You're fired!"*

The manager was hissed to silence by the shoppers, among them, Michael could tell though he had not looked, the woman with the sea green eyes. Michael played on.

The shoppers were rapt despite the fact that they could not purchase what Michael offered. The senior manager departed in a huff.

Charlotte stood to one side, afraid to stand too close to the piano player, who was exposing his secret life with urgency, with fingers that raced over the keys, that raced to that moment when the jazz-driven notes slowed suddenly and softly into the swell of the *Andante,* and Charlotte's heart lifted with it. She stood and let herself be filled with sound that didn't bore or even remind, that simply was.

Michael thought he might lose his nerve as he returned to the opening theme. But his audience had grown and he was no longer fourteen and he would not disappoint them. His fingers, those fingers that had held so much promise, sent sounds that resonated through his audience, and through Shoes, Hats, Jewelry, Perfumes, Men's Underwear and back again to the woman in the peach-colored hat.

As he struck the final chord, he let it linger.

Charlotte watched as the piano player rose from his seat, lifted a single long-stemmed red rose and met her eyes. His look was not a challenge nor reticence. It seemed to see into her and reflect a light. As he moved towards her, the crowd of shoppers parted. And as he reached her, he bowed with ancient gallantry and then handed her the rose.

"It's a good song," she said.

He looked into her eyes and smiled and said, "Yes, a very good song."

The shoppers, crowded around the first floor escalator applauded as the piano player left Nordstrom Department store. Some shoppers followed. One shopper, a woman with sea green eyes and a peach-colored hat, did not. She knew that the piano player would be fine now, no matter what awaited him. And she knew, too, that what awaited her, what had always awaited her and what had blessed her, were not gentlemen who bored her but life.

GETTING COMFORT

Mother never said it would be easy to be a woman and an *artiste* or for that matter a human being. She knew what she never talked about. She'd belly-danced her way through barroom after barroom in south San Jose for twelve years trying to make ends meet and take care of me and that hadn't been easy at all. San Jose had been a rough town in those days with the pickers from the orchards coming into town Saturday nights and drinking up a week's pay. Mom made good money Saturday nights, but it was a hard way to make a living. She never complained, though. She just wanted me to be as tough as the toughest part of town so I'd never have to worry.

So the day I got busted for my "Sensual-Sensuous All-Nude Sex Dance" at an adult bookstore and bar on El Camino Real on a city block in Palo Verde that was the only sleazy one in town, I remembered Mom's words: "Take care of your body, sure, but take extra care of your mind. It's your mind they want." Mom never told me who "they" were, but I knew anyway. They were the people who lived and worked on the other blocks in town—the people who drove by the adult bookstore and bar only if they had to and with their windows rolled up in their BMW's and Volvos, their air-conditioning turned on full blast and their eyes fixed on the traffic ahead of them. Some of them drove by again, of course, the men, and stopped and stayed.

I wasn't nude yet when the cops broke down the doors and broke everything in their path on their way to grab me. I couldn't see a thing. It was always dark anyway except for the spotlight because nobody ever wanted to be recognized or recognize anyone else. All I could hear at first were grunts and screams and crashes. Then I got grabbed by two beefy cops who dragged me out the back door. I didn't grab easy. I clawed the cops and screamed and kicked one in the shins.

The cops threw me into the back seat of a squad car—I mean threw me—I hit like a sack of cement against the door of the car, which was welded shut. Then one of them climbed in next to me. That's when I got scared. I wasn't nude, but all I had on was a red silk chemise and a G-string. It wasn't much protection.

And sure enough, not a block away from the bar and bookstore, the cop next to me, who had begun to twist his leather-covered Billy club in his hand so hard that it squeaked, reached over and stuck his hand in my crotch. I fought him but he pinned me down—all except my feet. I jammed a four-inch stiletto-heeled sandal into his big toe. He lost interest in my crotch. He grunted a loud "Fuck" and then jammed the butt end of his Billy club into my stomach and said, "That'll fix you, you cunt."

My eyes started to tear up, but I held back so the cop wouldn't know how bad I hurt. You could never show any sign of weakness with them—with anybody—so the tears just welled up but the cop didn't notice.

When they got me to the station, they turned me over to a matron, who was beefy, too, and she stuck her hand up my crotch, only she put a plastic glove on first and tried to pretend the whole thing disgusted her.

And then she said, "You ought to be ashamed of yourself," and I thought, but didn't say, "Well, look who's talking."

She gave me a blue prison uniform that looked like a wrinkled housedress and shoved me down the hall and into a cell. When she left, she slammed shut the six-inch steel door to the cell block so hard it sent an echo down the block and made the bars on my cell hum. I figured she did that on purpose.

The cell was bare except for a toilet with no lid and a bunch of dust balls floating underneath the bunks and around the base of the toilet. There didn't seem to be anybody else on the block except a drunken woman who kept muttering the same thing over and over again and something I couldn't make out anyway.

I tried to think of Mom then. I sat down on the lower bunk and tried to hear her say, "Take extra care of your mind." I mean, maybe I did dance nude in front of strangers, but I wasn't some goddamned whore. Well, forget that. Even a whore does it only when she has to.

None of us deserves to get raped. And I felt raped. And I wanted Mom to say, "No, they tried, but they didn't get to you."

But the longer I sat, the harder it got to take care of my mind. I started wondering why Freddie hadn't bailed me out. Freddie owned the sex shop. He'd said he had "connections." There'd never be any trouble and if there were he'd take care of it.

That was when I remembered I was supposed to get a phone call. I started to yell for the matron. She let me yell a good fifteen minutes before she came and took me down the hall to the phone. I called the sex shop. The phone was disconnected. Then I called the apartment. Five of us girls lived there with Freddie. The matron stood right next to me, staring at a wanted poster from the FBI.

Stella answered. She and I were close. We were both dancers. We did ballet exercises together. We were going to audition for the San Francisco Ballet someday. When one of us danced in the bar, the other would yell at the guys to give tips. And we'd cheer each other up when Freddie'd get mean or when one of our men would get mean. Anyway, we were close.

But when Stella answered and I asked her to help, she said no. Just that—no. I said there was money, she could bail me out at least. She said no again. They needed the money to get out of town.

"You're on your own, baby," she said and then she hung up.

The matron smiled an ugly smile. I wanted to slug her. My mind was mush after that.

* * *

The day Cecelia got busted for her Sensual-Sensuous All-Nude Sex Dance, Elsie Goldberg woke up with a headache. It was happening to her a lot, that she woke up with an aching head. She was almost getting used to it, but it worried her. Maybe you went to bed with a headache, but you weren't supposed to wake up with one unless you had a hangover. Elsie suspected she was hung-over, from life.

She shrugged the thought away and sat up and punched Herbert, her husband, in the ribs.

"Time to get up, toots," Elsie shouted. Elsie was Herbert's alarm clock. He could sleep through anything except Elsie's shout and shove. Elsie didn't mind being the alarm clock, but it bothered her that Herbert could sleep so soundly.

Herbert grunted. "Okay, okay."

Elsie got up and took a shower and washed her hair. Elsie's hair was long but frizzy. She had spent her childhood and teenage years trying to make it look neat. She'd tried short cuts, ironing, three-inch diameter rollers and setting gel. Nothing had worked. She'd long since given up. She washed it, let it dry and did her best with a few hairpins. She'd given up on trying to look neat in general. She'd also spent her childhood in ill-fitting clothes that somehow always seemed to have stains somewhere, and she'd gone through puberty growing breasts too large for her small bones, growing too tall, growing too muscular to be lady-like and meanwhile her hair had gotten more frizzy. And she'd done all that in Palo Verde, a town where teenagers had generally looked like escapees from Hitler's Lebensborn—straight blond hair, blue eyes, perfectly proportioned bodies—and, of course, perfectly proportioned minds.

Elsie became a rebel and then she felt better about being odd. But this morning, as Elsie's hair dried into an electrified mane, she noticed as she passed the bedroom mirror that the color of her hair was dull, as if it were fading from gold to parched yellow. It seemed to be fading day by day.

Her headache suddenly got worse and she wanted to stay in bed but she knew she couldn't. She knew she had clients waiting at the city jail that morning—drunks most likely, 80-year-old shoplifters, a prostitute or two, usually 18-year-old boys these days—and Elsie couldn't ignore her clients. She liked to get them out as fast as she could since most of them hadn't ever done much except annoy the "blue-gray puffheads" in the town, the people who cheated on their income tax to the tune of thousands and cheated on their spouses but thought shop-lifting a candy bar was despicable.

So Elsie went down to eat the breakfast Herbert had fixed and, when he asked her to please not leave bits of egg encrusted on her plate after she'd eaten since it was tough to get them off if they hardened and when he asked it as he always asked everything, gently chiding her for her oblivion to most of the things that went on around her, Elsie answered back, "So scrub the shit off. What's the matter? Your arm broken?"

"Hey," said Herbert softly. He was sitting in his bathrobe playing with a half-filled coffee cup. Elsie sat across from him fully dressed in a gray business suit with a stain on the lapel.

"What's going on?" he asked.

Somehow Herbert always knew when Elsie wasn't angry with him. It amazed her. Every bit of anger that came her way she felt she deserved.

"Sorry," said Elsie. "I'm in a mean mood."

"Have you thought anymore about it?" he asked. Adoption was what he meant. Elsie knew he wouldn't say it. They, or rather he, had been talking about it again.

"Oh Herbert," Elsie said, not angry now, just pleading. "Don't start. The day's already bad enough."

Herbert let it rest, and Elsie went off to work more disheveled than ever, but she gave Herbert a kiss before she went.

When Elsie had gone, Herbert cleaned up the breakfast dishes so the egg wouldn't stick and thought about Elsie. How long did it take to recover was what he asked himself. Elsie had charged out of the hospital two weeks after the baby had died and two weeks after the surgery that meant she couldn't have another. She had gone right back to work, and Herbert had believed, insanely he thought now, that she'd recovered. Since then, though she almost never complained, Herbert had watched the furrows in her forehead deepen and seem deepest just when she got up in the morning, and he had watched the luster of the wheat-colored hair go dull and her ability to cope with anything outside her work, which had never been particularly good, worsen.

Herbert didn't want to go to work that morning. He was a lawyer, too, but in private practice. He generally could pick his own hours, which usually amounted to ten or twelve a day anyway. This morning he had no meetings or clients that he knew of and so he didn't even call in and simply sat down with a second cup of coffee and a beauty magazine he'd bought the day before at the drug store. He wanted to read about hair. He wanted to do something about Elsie's hair.

He didn't mind the frizz and he didn't mind that it was wild and unkempt. In fact, he loved all that. In fact, he still believed that the day he'd been prosecuting a case and Elsie had walked in as the public defender and he'd thought, "Well, this'll be easy," was the day he had fallen in love with her. He'd been so entranced by the beauty of her hair—the way it caught the light and seemed golden and wild and wonderful—he'd almost fallen apart in court and had lost the case to Elsie. He'd fallen in love with her that day, but it took three months to get Elsie to go out on a date with him (Elsie was religious about conflict of interest.)

Herbert knew Elsie had begun fretting about her hair, and he was determined to set at least one thing right and so he'd begun to take an interest in hair care.

He looked through the beauty magazine and came upon an article on hair that advised the use of beer, honey, lemon juice, $50.00

bottles of follicle-stimulating moisturizer, egg whites, Crisco oil, and, if all else failed, a visit to a specialist. Herbert felt better. He washed out his cup so the coffee wouldn't stain the porcelain and went off to work.

* * *

The night in jail was a bummer. The drunk kept muttering, and the one blanket the matron gave me at midnight didn't keep me warm. The light burned all night, and the place began to smell like piss. Plus I figured I might be stuck in there for a good long while since there didn't seem to be anybody left to bail me out.

I'd had rough times before, though, lots of rough times. I figured if I made it through those, I could make it through anything.

The only thing I'd wanted out of life as a kid was to be a ballet dancer. Mom had taken me to my first ballet when I was six. They used to come through town every couple of years. I never forgot that first night. We saw *Sleeping Beauty*, and I'd never seen anything like it. For days afterwards, I saw in my daydreams Princess Aurora, all in white, balanced on the point of one foot, taking a rose from twelve different suitors. I thought about the Prince kissing Aurora and breaking the spell of the old witch, and everybody living happily ever after. I figured I could use a prince in South San Jose to take care of the tough guys in the schoolyard who stole my lunch and tripped me on my way to the bathroom. But mostly I remembered the music and how the dancers moved. I wouldn't have needed a story—just the music and the dancers.

It was the most beautiful thing I'd ever seen. In fact, I think it was the only beautiful thing I'd seen except for Mom in her costumes, and it was the most wonderful thing I'd ever felt—wanting to get up on that stage and dance, too—just wanting to move every time the music started. I begged Mom for ballet lessons. She couldn't afford them at first so she bought me a record of *Sleeping Beauty* and a book on ballet exercises. I couldn't read, but I liked looking at the pictures, and I played *Sleeping Beauty* four times each day for at least two years until Mom took pity on me or maybe on herself and sent me to ballet school.

Madame Padazinski ran the school, and she was a tough, skinny old lady who wore black leotards, black eye make-up and a silk bandana around her head and one around her waist. She used to hit us with a bamboo stick if our stomachs stuck out or our butts were in the wrong place. We were all scared to death of her, but we loved her. She had been a ballerina in Russia. We weren't sure exactly where that was but we figured it had to be more interesting than San Jose. Probably everybody wore silk there and bandanas of all sorts and talked in hoarse voices like Madame. I didn't just like Madame. I liked dancing. I liked everything about it. I never cared if I got sore. I never cared if something was too hard. I never seemed to get tired. As soon as Madame put *Sleeping Beauty* on the phonograph or anything else, all I wanted to do was move and keep moving. I danced with Madame for six years, and then one day she told Mom, in private, that I should audition at the ballet school in San Francisco.

I had something, maybe, something good. And that night Mom fixed me cracked crab and a green salad and an ice cream sundae for dessert and served me a little glass of wine and a big glass of milk and told me what Madame had said. Two weeks later Mom keeled over in the middle of a belly dance. She died ten hours later. A blood vessel had burst in her brain. I never got to see her till she was already dead.

Then I lived with Dad. He drank and was a pig. I cleaned up after him until I couldn't stand it anymore. Then I went to live with an aunt. I had to clean up after her, too, and she was a lot more picky. Neither one of them thought I was worth the price of ballet lessons. They didn't believe me about the audition or maybe they didn't want to.

I left my aunt's at sixteen and started dancing—only it wasn't the kind of dancing I'd planned on. And so at twenty-seven, I ended up doing my Sensual-Sensuous All-Nude Sex dance and I guess I sort of made it day by day by just ignoring it all and, of course, ignoring myself too in the bargain. I wasn't happy about that nor the life that went with it, but I couldn't figure out how to change it.

When the morning finally rolled around in the cell, and I knew that only because the night matron suddenly stopped snoring and the morning matron brought lukewarm coffee and a bowl of some sort of mush, I figured I'd just have to start ignoring all this, too.

The matron, when she came to take my breakfast tray, told me the lawyer, a public defender, would be seeing me in a few minutes and to get tidied up. I looked like a slob, she said.

Oh sure, I thought. To my mind P.D.'s were the scum of the legal profession, which was pretty scummy to start with. The P.D. would just have to see a slob and make the best of it.

* * *

Elsie's car broke down three blocks from the city jail. She hiked the three blocks with her briefcase and two law books, feeling guilty all the way because she'd once again neglected her car. The last time she'd taken it to the auto shop, the mechanic had told her not to bother to bring it back if she didn't have the oil changed regularly. Elsie couldn't remember how long ago that was but she hadn't had the oil changed since and figured the mechanic would now despise her. The sound the car had made when it stopped was terrible—almost like a human groan. Elsie couldn't forget that sound.

With sore feet and an ailing conscience, Elsie interviewed her first client. The woman was incoherent and wild-eyed. Elsie told the guard she'd have her sent to the county hospital. The guard told Elsie the county hospital had refused to take her. That had been the cops' first choice. Elsie was furious and said she'd sue on behalf of the woman against the hospital, against the doctors, and against the county. She'd take it to the Supreme Court. She'd go to the newspapers. Elsie was particularly upset because the woman had dull yellow hair. It was straight as a board, but dull.

Elsie called the administrator of the hospital and threatened dire consequences if the woman weren't admitted. Thirty minutes later, when Elsie was interviewing her next client, the woman was in an ambulance on her way to the county hospital.

* * *

So the P.D. showed up. It was a woman. That was a first for me. The guard took me into a closet of a room with two chairs and a table, a bare light bulb hanging from the ceiling and lots more dust balls.

I sat down and then she walked in and, even though my mind was still mush, I knew right off this woman wasn't going to be much help.

She had on a suit, gray I think, I don't remember too well, but what I do remember was the stain that ran down the right lapel—looked like berry juice maybe or red wine—anyway a dark stain. And she looked, in general, like she'd just gotten out of bed. There wasn't an inch of her clothing that didn't have a wrinkle in it. Her hair, pulled up into a bun, was sticking out all over the place and falling around her neck and ears, and her briefcase, some canvas job, was splitting at the seams.

She stuck out her hand and introduced herself.

"Elsie Goldberg," she said as she dropped a notepad and two books.

"Cecelia Kornitsky," I said.

"Yes, I know," she said. She crawled under the table to rescue the notepad and books.

"Look," she said, finally sitting down. "This whole thing's outrageous. Just outrageous."

"Uh—" I began.

"Would you like some coffee, huh? How 'bout some coffee?"

She told the guard to get us some coffee. The guard looked doubtful but went to get us the coffee. I got the feeling this wasn't generally done but that the guard didn't want trouble and Elsie looked to be trouble of some kind.

"So," she said. "You ready to fight this thing?" I'd been charged with obscene and vulgar behavior, a misdemeanor.

"What's the point," I said. "I'm guilty."

"The point is, guilty of what? What's obscene, toots? Did you know the D.A. gets himself off every night at the only massage parlor he's left open?"

"Yeah?"

"Yep."

I started laughing. I couldn't help myself. The D.A.? In a massage parlor? I knew the D.A. see, or had been sent to jail by him. He was one of those types you figured didn't even do it with his wife unless he wanted a kid. He looked to be so straight I figured you'd have to take a battering ram to his middle to get him to bend over. I also believed he'd just as soon ask for the death penalty as anything else for everyone he prosecuted.

"So the D.A.'s got a girlfriend?" I said.

"More like ten," said Elsie.

"Oh boy," I said. "But how does that help me?"

It had something to do with the definition of obscenity, she said, and the constitution. Anyway she'd work on it.

When she left I still wasn't sure how that'd help me but actually it had already helped me. All my life people had been telling me I was low, and I always had an inkling that if they knew so much about being low maybe they weren't all that high and mighty themselves. Mom was convinced of it. I guess she'd been right. I gathered fifty dust balls together and tossed the clump from hand to hand and made a dunk shot into the toilet.

* * *

When Herbert got to his office, which was furnished with contemporary teak desks and chairs and well-placed indoor shrubs, he noticed his secretary's hair for the first time. Her hair was long, dark brown and absolutely straight—and shiny.

Before she could finish giving Herbert his messages, he asked her, "How do you keep your hair so shiny?"

His secretary was a health nut. She was perfectly reasonable in other ways—bright, intelligent, funny, pleasant—but she believed with religious fervor in jogging, bean sprouts, wheat germ, lecithin, lots of vitamins and chiropractors. Herbert expected an elaborate answer.

"Brushing," she said.

"Brushing?" he asked.

"Yes, one hundred strokes a night. It's supposed to bring out the oils or something."

That made Herbert happy. He envisioned brushing Elsie's hair for one hundred strokes.

"So you like it," his secretary asked, running one hand through the long brown strands and then shaking her head a bit.

Herbert ignored that and went straight into his office. Herbert's secretary had a crush on him. Herbert knew it but it caused him neither discomfort nor pleasure. Other women—besides Elsie—were just more people to deal with to Herbert's mind. He was absolutely oblivious to them as women. Even in a movie theatre when he saw an actress in a nude scene, the only thing he felt was a desire to be in bed with Elsie. It was not a conscious decision on his part; it was just the way he was. He'd been married to her for seven years and nothing seemed boring or routine with that.

* * *

Elsie had a tough time making it through the rest of the morning. She interviewed a twenty-two-year-old boy who looked fifteen and had gotten arrested for soliciting a male undercover cop and who'd previously been knifed by a customer. She ordered a visit to the doctor because the kid confessed to her, with a red face, that he had purple sores on his penis.

Then she interviewed a forty-five-year-old man who was a laid-off autoworker. He'd never been arrested in his life. He owned a house, which he was losing, two cars, both of which he was losing, and was married to a wife who was threatening divorce. His four kids still liked him, but he didn't like himself much and so he'd gotten drunk and torn apart a friendly neighborhood bar that had stained glass windows and an antique oak counter and cane-backed chairs.

But those stories weren't what made it hard for Elsie to get through the morning. It was Cecelia, the Sensuous-Sensual All-Nude Sex dancer. Cecelia had looked so pale and frail and beaten up that she almost looked like a corpse. Elsie had seen death before. She didn't want to see it again. She wanted to force Cecelia to fight. But she didn't know how to do that, and she wasn't up for the banter and cynicism of a city hall lunch with the other P.D.'s and the D.A. and his staff, so she took a cab to the school where she volunteered time. The school was named the "Casa Verde Residential Home," and it was no ordinary school. It was the permanent residence of one hundred mentally retarded children. The school staff didn't call the children retarded; they called them "mentally disabled." Elsie thought "mentally disabled" was just as bad and anyway she figured it wasn't what you called them but how you did it that made it derogatory anyway.

Elsie was no expert on mentally retarded kids. She simply liked playing with them. She knew they felt as out of place in the tree-lined suburb filled with kids who went to Harvard and Stanford as Elsie had, though for different reasons.

When she walked into the "Rec" room of the school that the staff had taken pains to make cheerful with bright paint and cushions and bulletin boards filled with drawings made by the residents, twenty children rushed for Elsie and clung to her hands and her legs and her clothing and twenty voices cried "Elfie" or "Elsie" or "Ellie" or "Momma." The two staff members gave a nod to Elsie and smiled.

And so for an hour Elsie finger-painted and cut up strips of yellow and blue and green paper and built small houses with toothpicks and glue and played with fifteen or twenty children, some of whom would never figure out what two plus two was, some of whom drooled constantly and had to be wiped off every now and then, some of whom had foreheads that were flat and eyes that slanted, and some of whom kept a hand resting on Elsie's shoulder for the entire hour because they were terrified when they couldn't touch someone. Elsie always wondered if the children were having as good a time as she was.

* * *

After sitting in my cell for a couple of hours, I began to be less sure about this P.D. I mean maybe she had a line on Fenton, the D.A., but this stuff about the Constitution worried me—I mean it had never helped me much in the past so I figured it probably wouldn't do me much good now. Plus the fact that the P.D. not only looked like more of a slob than I did but she looked worn out, too. I couldn't put my finger on why I thought this was so. I just knew she looked an awful lot like Mom did just before she died. I mean tired—like a worn rug that had had the dust beat out of it too much.

I was gonna see her again at two for the arraignment. I was supposed to plead not guilty. That'd mean a trial which I wasn't all that happy about, but the P.D. had said the "blue-gray puffheads" in town needed to find out what "decency" was.

At one-thirty, the matron brought me a gray wool dress (it was the middle of summer) with a little white collar, a pair of black pumps two sizes too big and a comb. All this was supposed to make me look presentable in court. At one forty-five, I was handcuffed to a teenager who'd shoplifted a bracelet at a dime store, and we were driven to the city hall in a squad car. This time the cops stayed up front and ignored us. At city hall I waited three hours in another cell with lots of dust balls and two metal benches for my name to come up.

Finally it did, and I was led into a stall in the courtroom with a matron standing two inches behind me. The P.D. asked the judge for a word with her client. She came up to me and took my elbow with her hand and said in a whisper, "Don't worry. Fenton is pissed about the plea. But everything'll be fine."

Oh sure, I thought. The last thing I needed was for Fenton to be pissed.

The P.D. asked for the charges to be dropped, which the judge refused after a short but what looked to be angry conference between himself, the P.D. and the D.A. And then bail was set, which the P.D. protested and the D.A. supported by reading my record out loud, which was long but was all minor scrapes with the law, although some of them had landed me in jail doing time. The P.D. protested again, and I actually began to be impressed. I mean this woman may have been sloppy in some ways, but her mind sure wasn't. I'd been in court plenty of times and never really understood much, but I could always sense when somebody knew what she was doing. The P.D. knew what she was doing.

The judge and the D.A. made remarks about me, which were nasty, and about the P.D., which were almost nasty and seemed to be some sort of threat. And, all the while, the P.D. just smiled and kept right on defending me as calm and cool as she could be.

When I pled not guilty, the D.A. gave me a look like he'd see me in prison for life if it was the last thing he did, and the P.D. hissed across the tables that separated them, "Cut that crap out, Fenton."

The P.D. told me to sit tight, and she'd see me again the next day and in the meanwhile she'd try to do something about the bail.

"Don't let the puffheads get you down," she said. She sounded like Mom then. I said, "Sure" and turned away so she couldn't see my face.

When I was on my way back to the jail, I still felt pretty good. I mean it was the first time in my life that I stood before a judge and said, "not guilty." And even though I felt guilty as hell or maybe just ashamed, it felt good to stand up and say no. I mean you have to understand what it's like to stand in a Salvation Army dress and gunboats for shoes in front of a judge who has a diamond ring on his finger the size of an apple and a district attorney who wears a different $800 suit each day of the month. Okay, so maybe I'm exaggerating. But I figured those guys had it made; they were respected, respectable, and here I was some little jerk who took her clothes off in front of slobbering men because I hadn't figured out any other way to make a living. And so maybe I wasn't much, but I didn't think I deserved to be crucified for that. Saying "no" felt good.

But then I went back to jail.

* * *

Between bites of Herbert's linguini with clam sauce and the big green salad, Elsie told Herbert about Cecilia, about how frail she was, about how worn-out she looked, about how unfair the charges against her were, and about how tough Elsie believed Cecilia was in spite of it all. Elsie often told Herbert about her cases, and he frequently had useful advice. But Elsie wasn't looking for advice that night. Herbert didn't offer any and asked questions instead. And, as they sat in the candlelit dining room sipping brandy after the dinner and not talking at all at that point, Elsie began to relax in a way she had not in months. Her muscles began to feel like liquid and her body eased itself into the curves of the soft, upholstered dining room chair and suddenly she wanted to be caressed, something she had also not felt in months, and as she sat and sipped the brandy and watched the flames of the candles flicker in unseen, unfelt gusts of air, she hoped Herbert would simply know that.

And apparently he did because he got up slowly and took Elsie's hand and said, "Let's go to bed."

They blew out the candles and walked hand in hand up the staircase and down the hall to the bedroom. Elsie held Herbert's hand in a hard grip. Nothing had felt so good to her in some time. His hand was square and strong and slightly damp with sweat. And she wanted to hold onto it and not let it go.

But when they got to the bedroom, and Elsie saw herself in the oval mirror over her dressing table, she removed her hand from Herbert's immediately. She had expected to look as she always looked on a night like this, like a girl much younger than herself, with bright eyes and smooth skin and wild, lustrous hair. But when she looked in the mirror this evening, she saw an old woman.

She sat down at the dressing table and started cleaning out one of the drawers. Her drawers were no neater than the rest of her. She started piling the jumble of odds and ends on top of her dresser, a blue button, a sales tag from a dress she had bought months before, a worn Emory board, one half of a pair of gold earrings.

"Stop that," Herbert said.

It was then that Elsie noticed the brush, a stiff natural-bristled brush with a tortoise shell handle.

"Herbert, did you buy this?" she asked.

"Yes," he said. "For you. Well, for me, too."

He stood behind her at the dressing table and began to remove the hairpins from her hair, letting it fall around her shoulders. Then he picked up the brush and began brushing Elsie's hair.

"No don't," Elsie said. It hurt. Her hair was not tangled; the brush didn't catch and tug at her scalp. It simply hurt.

"Please," said Herbert. "I want to."

"You can't. I can't." Elsie pulled free of Herbert and fled to the bathroom where she undressed and covered herself in a heavy flannel bathrobe.

* * *

Herbert sat down at the dressing table and turned the tortoise shell brush over and over in his hand and then pulled out the yellow hairs that had been caught in it one by one. They were so brittle he imagined they'd crack if bent.

At dinner he had been pleased. Elsie's eyes and even her hair had seemed to glitter in the candlelight. The story she had told about the nude sex dancer she had told with animation and feeling. And the way her body had looked easy, almost languid in the dining room chair, and the way she had taken his hand with no protest and held onto it and the feelings that had rushed through him at that moment, all of that had made him believe perhaps he could set some things right.

And before dinner, all day, he had looked forward to brushing her hair. He had imagined each of the hundred strokes.

But he should have known, he supposed, because he had seen it at dinner but ignored it—Elsie's too bright eyes, the animation and anger for someone other than herself, the dangerous hope of saving somebody who had no wish to be saved.

Herbert wanted to climb into bed and climb into it with Elsie. He wanted to undress her and wrap his arms around her. He wanted to swallow her up in himself just for that night.

He climbed into bed alone and carefully kept to one side when Elsie climbed in later.

* * *

I woke up from a sound sleep to a loud bang and a high-powered flashlight in my eyes.

"Not guilty, huh? You little cunt."

There was another bang. I jumped.

"Stand up and be counted," the guard growled.

I stood up, shivering. The floor was cold and damp, and I didn't know what was coming. The flashlight was blinding me.

Something wet and cold hit hard against my face. I almost fell over.

"I want you to clean up this pigsty now," the guard screamed.

What had hit me was a dishrag. And I should have taken it and done what the guard wanted done. But Mom had always told me to take care of my mind, and, if you let someone mess with you, you let them mess with your mind. So I said no.

"No?!" the guard screamed. She shoved a billy club into my ribs. I groaned and fell over. My head hit the side of the bunk, and I sank down on the floor. I couldn't catch my breath. It hurt to breathe and it hurt not to breathe. I felt warm liquid running down the side of my head. I waited for the next blow. It didn't come.

"Okay," the guard said. "Next time, listen to me."

She was breathing hard. I still couldn't see.

"An inmate got you in the shower. Remember that."

"Yeah, right," I said. I spit on the floor, but she'd already left.

I crawled into the bunk and held the dishrag to my head because it was cool. I thought about Mom then. Mom and I had been a team nobody could touch. I thought about her belly dancing, the few times she had let me see it, about the slow parts especially, those were my favorites, when her muscles would move like waves and she'd have a smile on her face that you knew had nothing to do with the catcalls or the weed smoke or the blue lights but had to do with those waves, with the motion itself, with the pleasure she took in the motion. And I tried not to think of the money, the dollar bills, stuffed into her crotch at the end of her dance and the smile on her face that would turn brittle and hard like a piece of sour lemon candy.

And then I thought about my own dancing. First, the Christmas pageant when I was eight. I was the head angel and had my own dance and a gold halo to set me apart from the others who were just plain angels. I practiced my part every day all day long for a month. I practiced in the school bathroom, in the bedroom Mom and I shared, and while I was waiting for the bus. Even so I was nervous as hell the day of the pageant and threw up two times before I got on stage. But then I got on stage and it was perfect. I goofed up a few things but even that seemed to work. I got three curtains calls. I thought that night, as Mom rubbed my blistered feet, that I would never ever stop dancing.

I heard Mom as clear as anything all of a sudden. "Take extra care of your mind, honey," she said and then I knew I'd never let anybody get to me, even if they beat me to death trying.

* * *

Elsie woke up with another headache but figured she'd just have to learn to live with it. She was about to punch Herbert and yell at him to get up, but she stopped herself. She sat up and looked at him instead. In the night he had turned towards her but not touched her as far as she knew.

He was really a very handsome man she thought—dark haired, dark skinned, surprisingly rugged looking for someone who had never lived outside a city. And he loved her. It had astounded her the first time he told her that. It astounded her at times still. She knew he was trying to help, and she wished she could let him. She studied him for a full thirty minutes. Then she leaned over and kissed him on the forehead.

"Hmmm," he said.

She kissed him on the mouth.

"Herbert, are you awake?" she asked.

"No," he said.

He hadn't moved.

"Herbert, time to get up," she yelled. She punched him in the ribs.

"Oh God, is it seven already?" he groaned, lifting only his head.

"Seven-thirty," she said.

He looked at her.

"I overslept," she said.

"I see," he said and smiled.

Elsie turned away and got up to shower and dress. On the bathroom sink she found a bottle of honey-lemon shampoo with a fashion designer's name on it and the price tag removed. She used the shampoo. It smelled very nice and made a heavy lather, but later, as she looked in the hallway mirror after breakfast, she thought the shampoo had not helped much. She went back and washed the egg off her plate anyway.

Herbert dropped her off at the county jail that morning. As she stepped out of the car, the first and only thing she noticed were the women on their way into City Hall. She noticed hair—long straight hair with blunt-edged cuts, strawberry blond hair, black, black hair, stringy hair that needed washing and then she noticed clothes—high-heeled shoes that wobbled when they hit uneven ground, sensible wedge-soled shoes, form-fitting sandals, gray suits with white silk blouses, pants with pleats at the waist and blazers with Italian cuts, summer knit shirts that showed big breasts and small breasts and breasts that hung low and breasts that sat high, stockinged legs and bare legs, fat ankles, slim calves, painted lips, plucked eyebrows, bitten nails.

It was a kaleidoscope Elsie couldn't make whole. She felt dizzy. She saw herself in pieces; then she saw only pieces of everything. The guard told Elsie about the "attack" on Cecilia, adding that it was her opinion that these "dames" shouldn't be babied, that was exactly what was wrong with them. They'd been spoiled. The guard didn't fool Elsie, but Elsie kept her mouth shut.

When Cecilia walked into the interview room, Elsie didn't see pieces of her, she saw her whole—and dead. It didn't seem possible that Cecelia could have looked worse than she had the day before, but she did. She looked more frail and more pale and had an ugly welt on the side of her head. Elsie couldn't stand it. She was going to get her out.

She phoned Herbert and asked him.

He said, "Sure, but be careful."

Elsie didn't want to be careful. She wanted to slay dragons if that was what it would take.

* * *

Herbert had noticed after standing in the shower for ten minutes that morning that the shampoo he had bought was stuck in the soap dish and had been used. He started singing to himself at that point. He was glad it had been used and that it was stuck in the soap dish so he could see that it had.

And at breakfast, when he and Elsie had said little to each other, he had thought that there just might be the beginnings of a shine on the tufts of her hair that sprung out from underneath hairpins, though he supposed that was stupid since the shampoo had been used only once.

But when he got to work and opened the door to his office and saw his secretary bent over a pile of papers she'd dropped and when he saw her long legs below a black linen skirt that had ridden up and smooth, tanned elbows and forearms below the cuffs of a white raw silk blouse, Herbert knew how badly he needed to touch Elsie's body. And it struck him that at some point maybe any body would do.

When Elsie called later in the morning, Herbert's secretary was sitting in his office, pencil in hand, in the middle of transcribing a letter Herbert was dictating.

"I'm gonna bail her out and take her home," Elsie had said.

"Let's talk about this," Herbert said.

"Okay, talk," Elsie said.

"No, I mean tonight. Let's think about it."

"The guard beat her up, Herbert. While we're thinking, she may get beaten again."

"And you're going to save her?" Herbert asked.

"Okay, okay," she said. "I just want her to sleep in clean sheets. Have a good meal. I want to give her a little something to go on, Herbert."

"Okay, Elsie," he said. "But be careful."

Herbert said all this in front of his secretary. He should have asked her to leave, but he didn't. Her presence obliged him to try, unsuccessfully, to obscure the fact that he and his wife were having a disagreement. He also had to mask his fear, for Elsie, which he did successfully since it materialized only as a sudden strong tug at the base of his abdomen and to mask his anger, at Elsie and for himself, which he also did successfully since the anger appeared as an unspoken thought, "I need a little something to go on myself."

When he hung up the phone, he said, "Elsie," and laughed to try to cover up everything.

"How is she?" asked his secretary, who knew Elsie only slightly.

"Oh, as crazy as ever," Herbert said, which was unlike him, and he immediately hated himself for having said it.

And then he felt guilty—all afternoon. And he wanted to talk to someone, and it would have been logical to talk to one of his two partners who were both very good friends. But he didn't. He wanted to talk to a woman about a woman. He actually considered asking his secretary out for a drink, a short, casual drink. Then he thought he was losing his mind.

He drove home by himself instead and stopped by the grocery store on the way and bought curry powder, chicken, white rice and peanuts and coconuts, raisins and cilantro, a twenty-six-dollar bottle of Napa Valley Chardonnay and a bouquet of yellow daisies, which was stupid because, although they were Elsie's favorites, he and Elsie had so many fresh flowers they didn't know what to do with them as it was.

* * *

The guard told me the P.D. would be by to see me at noon. I didn't care and I said I didn't want to see her. She came anyway and I saw her in the same bare room with the same bare light bulb and the dust balls.

She knew, about the guard. She didn't say anything, but I knew she knew.

All she said was, "We'll get you out of here."

I didn't believe her. She looked so worn out and disorganized, I figured she probably couldn't brush her own teeth let alone defend somebody in court. The only thing different than the day before was that she'd washed her hair. That was obvious because she had a lot of hair, I mean it stood out all over the place, and it looked clean and fluffier than the day before. But she had on the same suit with the berry juice stain and, all in all, even in the best of spirits, I would have had a tough time trusting this woman.

Two hours later I was on the street with the P.D. pulling me along the sidewalk to a cab.

"Who paid the bail?" I asked.

"Friends," she said. "Don't worry about it."

"I'll worry," I said. "I don't need any more friends."

"Okay, I did," she said. "Just stay in town so I can get it back."

Well, that was a first—a P.D. posting bail.

"What makes you think I won't run?"

"You won't."

"But what—"

"You won't, that's all."

She seemed so sure, I believed her.

We climbed in the cab.

"My car broke down," she said and then added, "You know anything about cars?"

"No," I answered, which wasn't true. I knew plenty. My Dad, who had lived with Mom for a year and hung around for about ten years after she kicked him out, was a mechanic. He had taught me the trade. But I didn't want to think about Elsie's car.

I was too busy looking at the town I'd been in for ten years and never seen. Oh, I'd seen the bars and the Taco Tio and McDonald's and I'd seen the all night coffee shops and the discount department stores, but I hadn't seen the antique shops with big wood canopy beds in their show windows and the French restaurants, all named after women, whose dinners probably would have cost me a week's pay, and all the fancy foreign cars that had those personal license plates like "I DOCTOR". Or maybe I'd seen them but hadn't wanted to notice.

"Look at this," I said.

"Yeah, this town ain't much for the likes of you and me," the P.D. said as if she knew exactly what I meant.

"So why are you here?" I asked.

"Same reason you are, I imagine. I grew up here and got work here. Besides, I enjoy stickin' it to them once in a while."

"Them?" I asked.

"The puffheads with the blue-gray hair. You gotta get to them before they get to you. By the way," she said, "Call me Elsie, okay?"

"Okay," I said.

"We'll go to your place, pick up your stuff and then we'll go home," she added.

"Home?"

"My place. You're staying with me."

"Oh no," I said.

"It's done. Don't argue," she said. She said it like a teacher would or a judge or the President.

"Okay," I said.

We went to the apartment, which had been stripped, even the furniture. Stella had taken some of my clothes and all the ballet records. I wanted to get out of there fast. I took what was left and a cardboard box of stuff I'd saved of Mom's and we headed for Elsie's.

Elsie lived in a big old house with her husband. The house was as neat as a pin except for her study, which overflowed like her briefcase. But the rest of the house was clean and tidy and smelled of furniture polish and 409—nice smells, at least to me.

"Neat, huh?" Elsie asked after she had given me a tour of the first floor.

"Yes," I said and then wished I hadn't. I sounded too surprised. I was beginning to like Elsie. I didn't want to be rude.

She laughed. That was nice. It was the first time I'd seen her laugh. She didn't look tired when she laughed.

"My husband does it," she said.

Her husband kept house, she explained. He couldn't stand "clutter" so he dumped anything he didn't recognize, and that was plenty, into Elsie's study. Sometimes Elsie didn't recognize it either, but it stayed in the study for six months to a year until she decided what to do with it.

"I can't abandon anything," she said.

I didn't believe her.

She took me upstairs to a room with a big bed in it covered with a blue quilt in calico print. The room had dormer windows that looked out into the backyard, a big backyard full of all kinds of flowers and a huge elm tree.

Elsie got me a fresh towel and fresh clothes (some of hers; they were clean but wrinkled) and pointed me in the direction of the bathroom.

I took a long, long shower and tried to wash off the dirt. I smelled like piss and had dust balls caught in my hair. I washed my body with soap, and I washed my hair with some fancy shampoo Elsie had, and I actually started to feel clean. But when I got back to "my" room and saw the fresh flowers and the white sheets and the polished wood floor, I couldn't even sit down. It was just too neat, too clean. I had to get out of there.

I put on the clothes they'd given me at the jail and took my handbag I'd rescued from the apartment and tried to sneak out the back door of the house. I didn't sneak quietly. I was in too much of a hurry. I kept stumbling and banging against things. I got to the back porch.

"Going somewhere?" It was Elsie.

I stopped.

"I wasn't running," I said. "I wasn't running."

"Well, not from bail anyway," she said.

"No," I said. "But I gotta go. I just gotta go."

"So don't go," she said. She took my arm. I tried to pull it away. Nobody touched me, ever. She held on anyway and took my other arm, too. I tried to fight her. Elsie, who didn't look strong enough to lift a five-pound bag of sugar, *was* strong. She held on tight as I tried to pull away from her. I couldn't stand it, not because her grip on my arms hurt me. It actually felt nice and warm and strong, too nice and warm and strong.

"I think I'm gonna be sick," I said. I felt dizzy, weak, shaky, all of a sudden.

"Don't," she said. "Just come on in and have some tea. We'll talk."

We didn't talk. We didn't have tea. We drank beer, some foreign stuff that was the best I'd ever tasted, and we just sat. Elsie hummed a tune in between taking sips. The tune was sweet, like a lullaby.

I asked her what it was.

"I don't know," she said. "Something my mother sang."

Elsie was smiling—not at me—she was smiling inside. It was a smile Mom had had sometimes.

I started to calm down a bit. Then I started to calm down so much I thought I was gonna fall asleep, sitting straight up in the chair in Elsie's kitchen. She told me to take a nap. She didn't have to convince me.

When I got to the room, which still made me nervous, I turned down the quilt and lay on top of the blanket. I fell asleep before I even realized I was about to. When I woke up, which turned out to be two hours later, I felt as if I'd rested for a year. I went downstairs to find Elsie and tell her I felt better. I found her in the kitchen with her husband.

* * *

When Herbert walked in the kitchen door, he heard Elsie humming to herself and then saw her in the utility room going through a box of clothes a neighbor wanted donated to the Casa Verde Residential School. Herbert stood and watched. The clothes were castoffs of the neighbor's teenage daughter and looked brand new. Elsie held up a bright blue dress with white polka dots and inspected a dark stain on one sleeve. She tossed the dress aside and pulled out a pair of red cotton pants. These she examined front and back and then carefully folded them and set them to one side.

Herbert walked back into the kitchen and slammed a cupboard door and yelled, "Anybody home?"

"In here," said Elsie, but she walked into the kitchen. "I was just looking for some clothes for Cecilia."

"Cecilia?"

"My client. The one I—"

Just then Cecilia walked into the room. When Herbert saw her, he could have been as hard-hearted and selfish as he was capable and still not have been able to turn her away.

Elsie's "client" was a waif. She was skinny and bony and looked bruised. It was unthinkable to him that Elsie could have done any differently. He welcomed Cecilia to his home.

And then he remembered the flowers and the dinner and the plans he had for dinner, and he decided that all that had been a good idea because now it could be a celebration of sorts, a welcoming to someone who look as if she needed to be welcomed somewhere. But when he handed Elsie the flowers and her brown eyes darkened and when he said they should eat in the dining room, because that was how he had envisioned dinner, and her eyes darkened to black, he got uneasy. He guessed that Elsie expected a repetition of the night before, perhaps that he would want to brush her hair, which he did indeed want to do. So he was careful not to touch her and to keep the dinner conversation pleasant and light, although he still insisted on the dining room and candlelight because he couldn't deny himself everything.

And he began to believe that his plans had been just right, for himself, for Elsie and for Cecilia, until Elsie mentioned something about a "jealous wife." He didn't hear her exact words at first since his mind was numbed by wine and his after-dinner cigar, but he heard them very distinctly ten seconds after she spoke them. It was then that he was forced to admit to himself his own reasons for all his plans.

He said nothing after that because he knew if he said anything, it would be to confess, to all sorts of things, and that would solve nothing and help no one. And he knew he didn't want to be alone with Elsie, not right then, and so he sought another plan and heard himself say, "Let's go for a drive," and was relieved when Elsie and Cecilia seemed to think it was a good idea.

* * *

Elsie introduced me to her husband, Herbert, as a "guest," and he said "Howdy" and "Welcome" as if it were as natural as the sun coming up each day that I was there and just as nice. And then he plopped down a bag of groceries and his briefcase and said he'd bought the fixings for "curry". I didn't know what that was. Elsie said fine, she'd fix dinner. Herbert said no he would, and I said, no, I could fix it if they told me how. And then Elsie said no too loudly and Herbert said, "Jesus, this is my treat." And then he handed Elsie some flowers he'd had hidden behind his back. He looked embarrassed.

"Just what we need," said Elsie. She didn't smile.

We all fixed dinner together, and we ate it in the dining room by candlelight, and Herbert and Elsie were very nice to me and they were very nice to each other, too, but something was going on, something I couldn't quite figure out, something about the way Elsie kept looking at Herbert, first when he gave her the flowers and then when he wanted to eat in the dining room and finally when he wanted to light candles, and something about the way Herbert avoided all those looks.

And then Elsie said after we'd done eating, "We don't usually eat like this. It's usually in the kitchen with something we throw together in fifteen minutes."

I nodded and Herbert laughed and said, "Elsie doesn't want to give you the wrong impression. We're not exactly elegant types."

And Elsie said to me, "When your husband insists on something like this, you're supposed to get worried, be a jealous wife." She laughed as if to say the idea was ridiculous, but the laugh sounded dead.

And Herbert looked pale all of a sudden and said, I guess trying to be funny himself, "So are you worried?"

And then they just stopped saying anything after that until Herbert said, "So you've been in jail, huh?"

And I said, "Yeah."

And he said, "So you need open space. Let's go for a drive. Okay, hon'?"

"Great idea," Elsie said.

I didn't know I needed open space. I thought I needed a closet to hide in. But we went for a drive anyway.

We headed north on the freeway. I had never been north on the freeway. The sun had just set in the west, and the sky was orange and pink and purple and the air was warm and the road almost deserted.

Elsie and Herbert didn't speak so I didn't either and, because of the quiet and the warm night and the safety, though I didn't realize that that was what I felt, I began to remember a time when I'd been small, maybe eight, maybe ten, and Mom had wanted to visit her cousin in Los Angeles and Dad had agreed to drive us down. Because it had been summer, like it was now, we left in the evening and drove through the night, and the night had been warm and Dad had driven south at a steady, quiet pace and Mom had hummed on and off but nobody had said anything. Mom and Dad had brought a pillow so I could sleep, but I didn't want to sleep, and I had sat all night with a water jug by my side in case the radiator blew, and I had soaked up every sound and every bit of warmth and steadiness and I knew Mom and Dad were doing the same, and I had felt safe.

This time, though, Herbert was heading north and then east, into the salt marshes near the bay.

We stopped and walked around for a while. It was cool but not cold.

"I think I want to fight it," I said to Elsie all of a sudden. I meant the charges against me. I hadn't been too sure about pleading not guilty and about the trial and all. Better to take the rap and get it over with. But now I felt like I wanted to fight it. Maybe.

Elise laughed, a big full laugh, and she gave me a bear hug and said, "Someday you'll be able to shout that, toots."

I didn't mind the hug. Maybe I even liked it.

And Herbert yelled into the breeze and the marsh so the seagulls could hear a mile away, "I'm gonna fight like hell."

And we all laughed. And then Elsie took Herbert's hand and squeezed it, and it looked as if the salt air were stinging her eyes.

* * *

Elsie had felt relieved at the idea of a drive, just relieved, nothing more, as if there'd been a stay of execution of some sort. But during the drive she had begun to feel more. First, simply an easing of the ache in her head that had returned at dinner and then the warmth of the evening breeze against her face and the sting of the damp salt air. And then she remembered two evenings that had occurred five years apart. The first was her wedding night when Herbert had said sex in a hotel room would be anti-climactic since they had already done that a number of times and so they had driven to Pescadero beach, a small strip of sand on an otherwise rocky coastline, and clambered down the wet, slippery slope onto the dry sand in the half-moon light. And what she remembered about lying on the beach and making love with Herbert was the feel of the sand as it cradled her body and the night fog that had cooled their hot skin and, as Herbert had buried his head between her breasts and then her thighs, the smell of the salty seaweed and the wet sand and the winter sea and the smell of Herbert and the smell of herself on Herbert. And Elsie had laughed into his ear later when the two were wrapped together in a blanket and said, "Herbert, we're in the middle of a cliché. A hotel room would have been more exotic."

And then a park ranger had found them and lectured them for ten minutes while they stood on the beach naked and then threatened to arrest them.

They got away free. And Herbert said in the car on the way back, "That was no cliché."

And Elsie said, "Only if we'd been arrested."

And then, five years later, when she had told Herbert she was pregnant. They were both sitting in bed in cotton nightclothes. It had been summer and Herbert was reading and Elsie was pretending to read but was actually trying to find a way to tell him that she was pregnant. Not that he wouldn't be pleased; he would be very, very pleased. And if he were, it would seem real then and begin to matter. Elsie was afraid to have it matter.

"Herbert, put down your book," she had said.

"Uh oh, this sounds serious. What'd I do, hon'?"

"You got me pregnant," Elsie said into her open book.

There weren't the obligatory delays of disbelief like "Are you sure?" or "No, really?"

No. Herbert, a subtle man, jumped straight to his feet and did a dance around Elsie's supine body, whooping as he went—sort of a fertility rite that was no longer necessary.

And then he stopped and said, "Oh my god, I jiggled you."

He had looked genuinely alarmed until Elsie had started to laugh. And then he had made Elsie pull up her nightdress, and he had lain next to her and simply rested his head on her abdomen and said, "Oh—well—yes," as if he could feel the life Elsie hadn't yet felt.

He fell asleep with his head on Elsie's abdomen, and Elsie had sat up most of the night terrified that it now mattered too much, more than she had even anticipated, and wishing that Herbert could hold her belly non-stop for nine months.

So when Elsie and Herbert and Cecilia had walked out into the salt marshes and Elsie had smelled again the odor of salt and sea and when she heard Herbert yell into the wind to comfort Cecilia, the two memories were suddenly clear and fresh, and so she took Herbert's hand and squeezed it because it was the only way she knew how to tell him what she had remembered.

* * *

I'd felt better on the drive, but when we got back to Elsie's house, I felt panicky again like I wanted to run. These people, Elsie and Herbert, they were getting to me, like maybe they wanted something. Of course, they wanted something. Everybody did. I decided to leave. I made it as far as the kitchen and had a glass of water. There was beer—the good foreign stuff—but I wouldn't allow myself that. I sat there and felt like two bouncers had a hold on me, one pulling me out the back door and another pulling me upstairs, but not to "my" room with the dormer windows and the clean sheets, to Elsie's room. For one second, I saw myself creeping into her room and up to her side of the bed and sitting down on the floor and tapping her hand and knowing she'd wake up immediately and say, "Did you have a bad dream?"

And then I could tell her about my bad dream.

The pull towards the back door got stronger.

"Can't sleep?" It was Elsie. The woman had better radar than the U.S. Air Force.

"No," I said.

"How 'bout tea?" She put water on to heat without waiting for me to answer. Her hand was shaking when she did it. In fact, she seemed to be trembling all over.

"So what's up?" she asked. I wondered the same thing, but I didn't know how to answer it for myself so I shrugged.

"What did you want to be when you were a kid?" she asked, sitting down across from me at the table.

I told her about ballet. I told her about the audition and Mom's death. Now it was too late, I said.

"Listen," she said. She reached across the table and took one of my hands in hers. "You deserve clean sheets."

I snatched my hand back and stood up from the table and backed away from her.

"Don't do this," I said, although I didn't know what I meant.

"Okay, sorry," she said immediately, as if she understood perfectly. "Would a blanket on the couch in my study be better?"

I said it would. We went to the study and she cleared off her couch and found a spare blanket and pillow and went back upstairs.

As soon as she left me, I turned the light back on and wandered around her study. I guess the room was actually pretty big, but it looked cramped because it had so much stuff in it. It had big fat law books and books about American Indians and books about Black people and a book about a mother on welfare, a stack of twenty-year-old *Life* magazines, a huge fish tank with ten healthy goldfish and one whose fin had rotted away, forcing him to swim sideways, a statue of two people kissing with one of the arms broken off, three coffee cups missing handles, four single high-heeled pumps without their pairs, an unopened jar of nectarine jam that looked like it might be moldy on top, a framed picture of Herbert in a bathing suit with a crack in the glass from end to end and an unopened package of children's alphabet blocks, and, ballet records, all my favorites. There was no phonograph so I couldn't play them, but just knowing that they were there made me feel better and I lay down on Elsie's couch and slept like a hundred-ton redwood log and dreamt dreams I didn't remember in the morning.

* * *

Herbert didn't sleep like a redwood log. He hardly slept at all. On the drive back from the salt marshes, all Herbert could think about was wanting to make love to Elsie. He'd remembered their wedding night in salt air. He wanted to make love to her, but he knew that was hopeless, even in regular air. They'd barely touched each other for months and not for Herbert not having tried. He'd been able to put up with it, been able to give Elsie time, but now he felt he had no more time. All the way home, he remembered the feel of Elsie's flesh, the feel of her breasts and buttocks under his kneading hands and the wet and the warmth of her that made him feel as if his lungs would burst, as if maybe he'd die or something, if Elsie weren't there for him to burst into. He had felt that always. Marriage and routine had not diminished it in the least.

And so when they had gotten home and put Cecilia to bed, though Herbert had intended to go slowly, perhaps just to brush Elsie's hair and shampoo it and not even do that if she were reluctant, he instead followed her into the bedroom and locked her in an embrace from behind.

"Let me go," she had said calmly.

"No," he had said. He had begun kissing her neck and, while holding her shoulder with one hand, had held a breast with the other.

"Herbert, for God's sake stop. Don't do this."

But he hadn't stopped. He had caressed her as she fought him until she had whispered, "It'll be rape, Herbert."

Then he stopped. He released her and walked out of the bedroom and down the hall to his study. The study had been a second-floor bedroom. He kept a bottle of whiskey and a shot glass there though he rarely drank any. Tonight he tried to get drunk. It only made him sick. Then he tried to sleep and slept only briefly and dreamt that his secretary peaked out and smiled at him from behind doors and pillars in a parking garage and that, when he pursued her, she disappeared and, in each spot where she had been, she left behind a small pool of blood. He woke up from the dreams believing he was losing his mind and stayed awake the rest of the night to keep tabs on it.

* * *

Elsie woke me up at eight and said she was off to work but she'd come for me in a taxi around noon. Her car was still on the road where she'd left it. She wanted to show me something, she said. There was food in the refrigerator, and I could have the run of the house. Herbert was taking a shower and would be down soon.

She looked gray, even her hair.

"You look tired," I said.

She turned away.

"I am tired," she said.

"Maybe you should rest," I said.

"That'd be the worst thing," she said.

She left and I went into the kitchen and found a pot of coffee and some Danish. Herbert walked in and sat down and said, "Jesus."

"What's wrong?" I asked.

"Everything," he said. "The plumbing, for one. You either get scalded or frozen."

"Oh," I said.

"You know anything about plumbing?" he asked.

"No," I said.

"Oh," he said and then, "I wish something could be fixed."

"What about Elsie's car?" I asked.

"What about it?"

"Well, maybe I could fix it. Do you have any tools?"

Herbert had tools, good ones he'd never used. Could I really fix Elsie's car, he wanted to know. Of course I could. He said he'd have the car towed home. He looked a little more cheerful then. And I felt better, too, because I needed to pay my way somehow. I didn't want to owe anybody anything.

Elsie's car arrived an hour after Herbert left for work. I started on it right away. There was dirty oil three inches thick over everything. I figured there must be a leak, plus the oil hadn't been changed since the car had been bought probably, plus Elsie obviously didn't know about tune-ups, either when to get them or that you needed to get them at all. I did what I could and that was actually quite a lot since Herbert's tools were good, seeing as how they'd never been used, and all Elsie's car really needed was a tune-up and an oil change and a new gasket. And getting really dirty with real dirt and spending the morning in the garage and being absolutely alone was nice. And it was peculiar because I didn't think about much. I mean you'd think I'd have at least worried about the charges against me, if not about what in the hell I was gonna do from there on in. Or you'd think I might have thought about the past, the old, old past or the shit I'd been through the last couple of days. But I just didn't. I worried about leaky gaskets and burnt out spark plugs and it made me—well—happy—sort of.

I completely forgot about the time. Elsie arrived at noon in a taxi and found me covered with oil and just putting away the tools.

"Jesus, what have you been doing!" she said. She was smiling.

"Fixing your car," I said. "It runs now."

"You're kidding!" she said.

I climbed in and started the engine.

She shook her head and laughed. "It's a miracle."

I was happy, like a kid. I blushed, couldn't help it.

"How'd you get it here?" she asked.

"Herbert had it towed."

Elsie stopped smiling then.

"Get cleaned up, toots," she said. "We should be off."

I asked her where she was taking me.

To the Casa Verde Residential School, she said.

* * *

The night before, Elsie hadn't slept like a redwood log. She was so numb in a way that she thought she should have been able to sleep. But she had simply sat, absolutely still, on her side of the big canopied bed and thought about drifting away, wishing the bed would simply float up through the ceiling and up into the clouds. Elsie imagined that if clouds were substantial enough for a person to rest herself on that being on a cloud might possibly be the quietest place a person could be. And she kept that thought.

It was only later when she heard Cecilia in the hallway and then on the staircase and when she went down and had a cup of tea with her and heard the tale of Cecilia's childhood that Elsie remembered gravity—people could sink through clouds and fall—air temperature—you'd freeze at 20,000 feet—and jet stream winds—it would be noisy. And she was forced to realize that there was no safety to be found, maybe just a little comfort. It was then that she decided to take Cecilia to the Casa Verde Residential School where comfort was a staple.

But the next day, when she ushered Cecilia into the Rec room at the school and forty children rushed up and grabbed onto both of them and cried "Who dis? Who dis?" and she said, "Cecilia," which none of them could pronounce, she realized immediately that she might have made a mistake.

Cecilia was backing away from the children and attempting to pull loose her arms, onto which twenty tiny hands, some with flattened, almost knuckleless fingers, grabbed.

But Elsie decided they should stay, mostly because she wanted to. And she showed Cecilia the finger-painting supplies and began to finger-paint herself and helped half-a-dozen children through two dozen brilliantly colored, wild paintings of common objects painted in uncommon ways. And then she saw Cecilia sitting still and watching from two tables away a tiny malformed girl who sat in front of a sheet of paper full of green paint and ran one perfectly formed finger around and around and around in a circle as she hummed a single note. This tiny girl never asked to be touched and didn't want it when she was.

After an hour, Elsie told Cecilia they should go.

"Sorry," Elsie said when they'd climbed in her newly tuned car. "Bad idea."

She felt bad. She'd been selfish, she thought. It meant a lot to her, the Casa Verde School, and she had thought, hoped ... Well she'd been wrong.

But Cecilia said, "No, not exactly. It's just that they're so—I mean they want, expect so much."

Cecilia looked away, and Elsie said nothing more. Maybe there wasn't even comfort to be found.

* * *

Herbert began looking for comfort of his own at exactly the hour Cecilia and Elsie went to the Casa Verde Residential School. Herbert, and his secretary, went to Chez Collette, an over-priced French restaurant that served miniscule meals in a decorative way. Herbert hadn't intended the lunch. His secretary had received a rose at mid-morning from a florist's shop and explained to Herbert, who saw the delivery man come in, that it was her thirtieth birthday. She had said she felt "over the hill," and Herbert had said, "Why, nothing of the sort," and then asked her to lunch.

And now he sat across from her and picked at his ground veal in puff pastry, gulped down a sixteen-dollar bottle of Cabernet Sauvignon from a California town he'd never heard of and listened to his secretary discuss her plans for paralegal training.

"I tried to rape my wife last night," was what he wanted to say.

"I hope you know what a help you've been to me," was what he did say.

"Really?" she said. "I didn't know. I mean—" She stopped.

"Go on," said Herbert. He was surprised at her surprise. He had assumed she knew. She *was* a help to him, had always been. He had found little to criticize.

"Well, you never said it, directly I mean. Sometimes I felt like an extra set of legal codes."

Herbert took a big gulp of wine, gagged, coughed and spewed a spray of wine droplets and bits of food into his lap, his plate, the tablecloth and onto one of his secretary's hands which held a wine glass.

"Mr. Goldberg, are you all right?"

The secretary grabbed Herbert's hand with one of her own and rubbed it.

"No," he gasped. His eyes teared up. He couldn't speak, but he let his secretary hold his hand.

"I'm a bastard," he said finally.

"No, you're not," his secretary said too loudly. Waiters and other patrons had begun to stare. "No, you're not," she whispered. "I—" she began and stopped.

Herbert felt as if he still might choke, as if he knew nothing about being nice to women, let alone loving them, and as if, in the next moment, he would ask his secretary to accompany him to a small hotel, where discretion and privacy came with room service, and ask her to allow him to make love to her.

He didn't choke; he did know something about women; and he did ask his secretary to go to the hotel. She said yes.

In a room that, unfortunately, had a large canopied bed as well as two large palm ferns, a bowl of fresh fruit, and a bidet in the bathroom, Herbert took his secretary in his arms. Her body was bony and thin and small breasted and felt nothing like Elsie's, and her hair was long and silky and fine. He asked her to finish her sentence. She refused. But she didn't refuse his tongue or his hand that lifted her skirt and moved up the backside of her leg. Herbert was cautious and methodical but his breath came out in hard bursts and his heart pounded. Then it occurred to him that his secretary was any body, that any body would have done. He felt ill, too ill to stand, to ill to sit, to ill to say anything. He fled to the bathroom.

When he returned, his secretary had gone.

* * *

I felt peculiar after the trip to that school. I mean the kids were so weird, like the ones the kids at my school used to tease and throw things at. I didn't like that then. I had felt sorry for them. I wasn't even sure they understood what was happening. But after a visit to the Casa Verde School, I figured maybe they had known what was happening. It was too awful to admit, though, because I'd never tried to stop the kids in school. So I decided the children at Casa Verde were just weird, but it didn't help much because I felt weird myself.

There wasn't much to do at Elsie's house. They didn't have a television set and you can only listen to a radio for so long and there wasn't any housework to do because Herbert kept everything tidy. But then I remembered the ballet records.

I went upstairs and found a leotard I'd rescued from the apartment and then went back downstairs and found the stereo and put on *Sleeping Beauty* and started to dance. Now mind you, I wasn't any ballerina. I hadn't seen the inside of a ballet school in fifteen years, but when I was alone, in a leotard, with some space and some music, I didn't care that I wasn't a ballerina, that I didn't really know what to do, because I felt like I did know. It was as if, I mean especially that afternoon, especially when I heard Aurora's theme, it was as if the music sort of oozed into my body and told it what to do and led me around the living room as if I had a partner. But then the strangest thing happened, because I actually felt as if I did have a partner and it wasn't a man in tights; it was that girl, I mean the girl I'd seen at Casa Verde, the little tiny thing all bent up, who couldn't have danced if she tried. That stopped me cold.

I turned off the stereo and went into the kitchen and was gonna have a beer and a cigarette, but I must have hit the wrong button because the *Nutcracker Suite* plopped down and began to play and I had to go back and dance. There were times when I just couldn't get my fill of it. I had to keep going until I dropped. So I danced and forgot about the bent girl from Casa Verde and the mean kids at school and just kept dancing until I got my fill. That's when I noticed Elsie standing at the living room door, staring at me.

* * *

Elsie got bad news when she returned to her office from Casa Verde. The D.A.'s "evidence" on Cecilia had arrived. The evidence was twenty-four eight-by-ten black and white glossy photographs of Cecilia on stage. They'd been taken before the bust and during the bust. Elsie hadn't bothered to imagine exactly what Cecilia had to do to earn her living. Now she didn't have to imagine. Elsie believed Cecilia's "friend," Freddie, should be castrated and sent up for life and the men who patronized the bar publicly humiliated.

The D.A. stopped by "just to make sure" Elsie had gotten the photographs. Elsie had plans for him, too. She had a friend on the local paper. He was keeping an eye out. But the time wasn't right. So Elsie, who kept a small likeness of the D.A. in the form of a doll in her desk drawer, took out the doll and stuck a pin directly below the belt of the little man in the three-piece suit. The doll had been crafted at the Casa Verde Residential School with the aid of a staff member who knew the D.A. Sometimes these acts of restrained violence made Elsie feel better. This time it didn't.

She drove her newly tuned car home, trying to figure out a way to tell Cecilia about the "evidence," and then deciding not to tell her at all, for awhile—especially when she saw Cecilia dancing. She'd heard the music immediately when she'd come in the back door of the house, and she peaked into the living room to see what was up and then she'd stood for a full fifteen minutes at the door. It wasn't exactly fair, she knew, to watch a private moment, and she knew this was a private moment for Cecilia, but she couldn't help herself watch the child of twenty-seven, who had looked so dead, come alive. There was color in her skin, muscle in her body and something else—something Elsie knew had been there but hadn't seen—something substantial that would make this child fight like hell. And that made Elsie feel a pain that closed on her heart like a vise.

The music stopped and Cecilia stopped and turned and looked at Elsie.

"You got it, toots," was all Elsie could manage to say. "You got it."

And she and Cecilia had looked directly at each other for a long moment, and Elsie knew that they'd each exposed a spot in themselves nobody else had ever seen.

Then she turned and went upstairs to change.

* * *

Elsie and I cooked dinner together. Herbert was late getting home. She and I were cutting melon cubes for the fruit salad when I asked her if she wanted to see something. She said sure, so I went upstairs and got a photograph of Mom from the box of stuff I'd saved and took it back down to show her. I don't know why I wanted to do that.

The photograph was a close-up of Mom's face while she'd been dancing. She had bangles dangling down her forehead and a veil around her face. She looked mysterious—you could only see her eyes—but she looked happy. In that photograph, she was taking care of her mind and it was my favorite.

I gave it to Elsie and she sat down at the kitchen table and studied it. Then she looked at me.

I turned away and looked out the kitchen window and said, "It's just a picture."

And she said, "She's beautiful, and so are you. I wish you knew that."

I looked around at Elsie.

"She *is* beautiful," she said.

"Well, she's dead," I said.

"Cecilia, don't," she said.

"I killed her," I said.

She looked up from the photograph.

"Killed her?" she asked.

"Yeah. I went to see her dance. I wasn't supposed to do that. She was ashamed, I guess. She had some kind of attack when she saw me in the bar. She just keeled over and died."

I'd never told anybody that. I didn't know why I was telling Elsie. I wished I hadn't. I wanted to run again.

"Cecilia," she said. "You can't blame—"

"I killed her. I can live with it," I said. "It's no big deal, so don't—"

"No, I won't," said Elsie, just like she'd done before, just backed off like she could read my mind.

We went back to the melon cubes.

Then, for some reason and without looking at her, I said, "Elsie, you'd make a good mother."

She dropped the bowl of melon chunks. It shattered, scattering bits of broken glass and watermelon and cantaloupe and casaba from one end of the kitchen to the other.

"Oh shit,' she said. "Oh shit." And then she looked up at me and smiled but it was the saddest smile I'd ever seen. "I'm very glad you think so," she said.

"I'm sorry," I said. "I—"

"A mop, toots," she said. "We need a mop."

And I got a mop and we started cleaning up, but I didn't say anything after that and Elsie didn't either because I think we were both scared.

And then Herbert walked in and said, "What happened?" He looked scared, too.

"Slippery fingers," Elsie said.

That was it. Nothing more. We ate the fruit salad and the rest of the dinner and everybody was very polite to everybody else.

* * *

It had occurred to Herbert, as he sat in his office with the blinds shut and the door locked after he'd returned from the hotel, that he really was a bastard, in addition to which his instincts were awful. He was either too indirect or too direct or direct in the wrong direction. He wondered if there were some sort of education he'd missed. He wanted to find his secretary and say to her, "Look, I'm your friend and your boss is a creep. Don't give him a second thought." His instinct was to do just that. He didn't. He wanted to go home and tell Elsie or perhaps scream at her, "I'm in love with you, see. I'm insanely in love with you. I can't help it. It's out of my hands. So help me." He was quite sure he wasn't going to do that either.

And when he had gone home he was absolutely sure he wasn't going to do that. "Slippery fingers," didn't explain the look on his wife's face and the look on Cecilia's face and the look that passed between the two of them. There was some sort of intimacy between the two he wasn't allowed to share. He felt shut out. At dinner he felt there were two extra guests, Herbert The Guilty and Herbert The Insane. Herbert himself didn't want to sit at the big oak table and eat dinner. He wanted to crawl under it, cover himself up with a blanket and hide out. Let the extra guests eat dinner.

He offered to wash the dishes and did so alone while Elsie helped Cecilia try on the clothes of the neighbor's daughter. Then he locked himself up in his second-floor study and tried to compose a letter to his secretary. He tried many times. Crushed papers piled up in his wastebasket and on the floor.

There was a knock on the door, and Elsie walked in with a manila envelope under one arm. Herbert laid his arm across his latest attempt at a letter. He hoped Elsie didn't notice.

She sat down on the couch and said, "I've got a problem."

Herbert was amazed and pleased. She'd come to him with a problem. His heart sped up a few beats.

Elsie handed him the manila envelope. He opened it and pulled out what was inside. He only looked at the first two photographs. Even that was too much. Cecilia was too young, too much a child, to have lived this life. Herbert was too much of a male, too close to the perverts who watched the child, to want to see any more.

"I've got to show them to her, Herbert. I don't know how."

Herbert became a lawyer then, because that meant objectivity and distance, at least in theory.

"They'll be damaging," he said.

"I know," Elsie said. "I don't know how much she can take."

"No, I meant in court."

"But what about now? Right now? How am I going to tell her?"

"Just tell her," he said, knowing full well he couldn't do the same and knowing too that it was the last thing he'd wish on Cecilia.

* * *

I was trying on some clothes Elsie found for me when she came into my room and asked me to come down to her study. She looked tired again, really tired—not sleepy, not like she needed to go to bed—more like she needed a year or more of peace and quiet and sunshine.

"I'm your lawyer now, okay?" she said when we'd gotten to her study and she'd sat behind her desk and I'd sat in a chair across from her. That scared me. I looked at a black vase on her desk that had oriental looking flowers painted on it and a big chip out of it at the rim. I didn't want to look at Elsie.

"They had photographs," she said. She handed them to me and I took a look. I had never seen a photograph of myself doing—well doing what I did. Of course, it came as no surprise that the smile on my face was a brittle as Mom's hard-candy smile. But I'd never taken a close look at what I did, and, when I saw it in black and white in glossy prints, I didn't want to take a look at all. I started to shake, hard shakes, as if I had a tropical disease or something. I couldn't stop.

"Now, whoa," Elsie said. "Now whoa. That's just the bad part. There's—"

I didn't let her finish. I stood up and shoved everything off the top of her desk into her lap and all over the floor. The vase broke, the cups missing handles shattered, books fell with a thud.

"Fuck you," I said. "Just fuck you."

Elsie came around the desk and tried to touch me, just on the forearm, just a little touch, but it was too much for me.

I almost slugged her.

"Okay, okay," she said, blinking and backing away from me. "Okay, now. I'll leave you alone, see? I'm gonna leave you here, all alone. But don't go running off, Cecilia. Just don't run."

She did leave me alone, and I didn't run. There was no place left to run. I guess I'd finally run into myself. I paced around the room for a while, kicking bits of china and pieces of paper about. Then I put everything back on Elsie's desk and put the pieces of china and paper into the wastebasket, and then I sat down and hated myself. I actively and meanly hated myself by making myself remember every mistake and every awful thing I'd ever done in my life, which was plenty. And then I thought that the least I could do for Elsie was to disappear.

And I was about to do that when Herbert knocked on the door and opened it a crack and asked, "How you doin?"

Just like that, as if I'd been sick or something and he was checking on me.

"Is Elsie okay?" I asked, figuring it was she who needed the care.

"May I come in?" Herbert asked.

I nodded.

He pushed aside a stack of manila folders stuffed with papers and sat down on the couch.

"Elsie's not so good," he said. "It's just that she didn't know how to tell you, about the photographs."

I stared at a hole in the carpet and bit my lip. I couldn't look at Herbert. I knew then he'd seen the pictures, too.

"She just didn't know how to tell you," he said again.

I'd smashed Elsie's desk and she was worried about me. It didn't make sense. Nothing made sense. I stared at a piece of broken china in the wastebasket and said, "What does she want, Herbert? What does she want from me?"

"She wants you to fight—them—not her."

I sat down and shook my head. I don't know why I did that. I wasn't saying no exactly.

"Elsie lost a baby, seven months ago. It only lived eight hours," he said.

I sat absolutely still. I wasn't sure I wanted to hear this.

"Elsie acts tough," he went on. "She *is* tough. She's a one-woman armored tank against her 'blue-gray puff-heads' ... but she's as raw inside as you or I. She doesn't want to own you, Cecilia. She just wants you to thrive."

"I want to see her," I said.

"In the morning," Herbert said. "You both need some rest."

And then he made me sit still while he made up a bed on Elsie's couch and brought me a beer and a pack of cigarettes and left me saying, "Have good dreams. That's an order."

I didn't expect to have good dreams, even if it were an order. I knew exactly what kinds of dreams I was gonna have.

* * *.

Elsie had walked into her bedroom after her talk with Cecilia, had sat down at her dressing table and had not moved for ten minutes. She stared at herself in the mirror. What she saw seemed unspeakable to her. Her hair looked the color of dead wood. She felt she should never leave the room.

Herbert came in after ten minutes and touched her shoulder. Then Elsie did move, just slightly, just to get free of his touch.

"How did it go?" he asked.

She shrugged.

"I didn't know what to do. I still don't. About anything."

"I'll go down and talk to her," Herbert had said.

That was fine with Elsie. She didn't want to move. She didn't want to talk to Herbert. She stared into the mirror so hard she stopped seeing anything.

When Herbert came back, she couldn't see him either, but she heard him and then felt him.

First he said, "Cecilia'll be okay. Don't worry."

Elsie said nothing.

Then he said, "Stop this, Elsie. For God's sake, stop this."

And Elsie said nothing.

So finally, he took her by the shoulders and forced her to turn towards him and screamed at her, very loudly, "I'm in love with you. I am insanely madly in love with you. See? Get it? I'm in love with you and I can't help it. So help me."

For the first time in months, Elsie saw Herbert's face, saw his eyes that had been blue but now seemed blackened and sunk into his face as if into a skull, and saw his lips that had always felt soft to her but were now contorted into a hard grimace and she saw the tears that ran in rivulets over the stubble of his after-five beard.

And Elsie groaned and then cried out and got up suddenly and staggered towards the door, but she had to bend over before she got there because she felt as if a knife had ripped down the front of her and so she staggered the few steps to the bed and fell on her knees bedside it. She heard Herbert say, "Oh, Elsie."

"Don't touch me!" she screamed. "Don't you touch me," but she knew at the same time that she'd probably disintegrate if Herbert didn't touch her.

She pulled a pillow off the bed and cradled it and squeezed it between her arms and her breasts and then she remembered.

The birth had been easy even though it was her first. It was a little too early but the doctors hadn't been worried. But when the baby'd been born, Caroline they'd named her, and had given a faint croak instead of a full-bodied cry, the doctors' and nurses' smiles had disappeared immediately, as had Caroline, who was carried off to an intensive care nursery. Difficulty breathing, everybody had said. Nothing to worry about. And then Elsie had begun bleeding and there was plenty to worry about. The doctors removed her womb; there was no alternative they said. Several hours later, the nurses brought her her baby, her dead baby.

Elsie was lying in the ward with two other women who'd just given birth to pink, chubby eight-pound babies. The nurses drew the curtain around Elsie when they brought the baby in. And Elsie took Caroline in her arms—a tiny bundle of bruised-looking skin, a small head and frail arms and legs, a tiny, absolutely still, bundle. And Elsie had held the bundle to her breasts and tried to comfort Caroline and herself as well. But the bundle was too small, too insubstantial.

Elsie had told the nurses to take the bundle away, and, when Caroline was buried the next day, Elsie buried the feel of the bundle along with her.

And now with the pillow, Elsie tried to bring Caroline back to life but only brought back the feel of the still, silent bundle. And so she held the down-filled pillow in her arms and wept for what she'd never gotten to hold and would never get to hold.

Some time later, Elsie couldn't have said whether it was minutes or an hour or many hours, she felt Herbert sit down next to her and then she felt his arms go around her and she thought it was the best thing she had ever felt in her life and she curled into Herbert's body and rested there.

* * *

I didn't have good dreams and I didn't sleep. At first I lay on the couch and thought about Elsie. It was like being pulled by the two bouncers again. I didn't understand how I could want so much to have someone take care of me and be so angry at the person at the same time, and I got so upset, the only thing I could think of was to either really tear Elsie's study apart, break everything, or leave, just leave, just run.

And then I started hearing shouts and cries from upstairs. I couldn't understand what either of them was saying but it scared me and I wanted to scream, too. I said to myself, "Momma, I can't take care of my mind anymore."

And I thought I'd see her smiling, like she always did when I was upset, and hear her say, "Don't let them get to you, Cecilia. You can take care of your mind. You can always take care of your mind."

But I didn't see her smile. I saw her face, the night she died.

I'd seen her face when I had sneaked into the bar where she danced, to watch her for the first and last time. I'd come in the front door but nobody had seen me because they were too busy watching Mom. And I'd stood at the back and looked through the haze of the smoke and the darkened room lit only by blue Christmas tree lights and saw Mom who was lit up by a red spotlight. I'd watched and thought it was the most wonderful thing I'd seen. Better than the ballet. Mom in gold bangles and filmy red cloth, shimmying and swaying and teasing, not the men, but her own body. And Mom was smiling and laughing, and the music, the beat of the small leathered-covered drums, speeding up and Mom's belly and her body shimmying so fast it was almost a blur and Mom laughing out loud and the drum beat not loud but pounding faster and faster. And then, suddenly, it stopped or slowed, slowed to almost nothing, and Mom moved in a slow circle to the front of the stage and the music was soft now but the men's voices weren't. And their hands weren't soft either as they tore at Mom's skirt. I screamed and ran towards the stage and fought the men who tried to stop me. A flashlight had suddenly shown on me and Mom and I saw each other at exactly the same moment. I saw her face, her eyes, with a look of horror in them, and I saw her lips move though I couldn't hear what she said and then I saw her stagger and fall and I tried to get to her, pulling hard at the arms that held me back, and kicking and screaming and biting, but I couldn't get free.

I was carried home, which was only a block away, and told to wait for my mother. I waited all night. Dad came at six a.m. and told me she was dead. She'd died in the night. He told me it wasn't my fault. I didn't believe him. I wanted to see her. I saw her, in a coffin two days later, her face surrounded by pale blue satin that made it look pasty and painted with makeup that was as gaudy as a clown's. There wasn't any expression on it and so I decided she was mad at me, as mad as she'd ever been.

And I saw that face again that night in Elsie's study and I started to cry and kept crying and begged Mom to forgive me and realized suddenly I'd wanted that since I was twelve years old and realized, too, that I was never going to get it.

I sat on Elsie's couch and cried so hard my chest began to ache. But even then I couldn't stop.

* * *

Elsie lay in Herbert's arms. They'd each showered and dressed in nightclothes and then they'd climbed into bed and lain right next to each other with their bodies touching from their shoulders to their feet. Herbert had put his arm around Elsie, and Elsie had thought about how soft the bed seemed, how soft the pillow felt, and how soft Herbert felt, how quiet the room, the house and her own mind were and she had said into the still and the darkness, "I didn't want to lose you, too."

And Herbert had said, "I know," and had pulled her tightly against him. And Elsie had kept lying there, wide awake, and still and calm.

But then she heard a sound, or sounds, coming from below—a dog perhaps, whimpering in the garden.

"Herbert, are you awake?" she said.

"Yes," he said.

"Do you hear that?" she asked.

"Yes," he said.

"Cecilia?" she asked.

"Yes," he said.

Elsie got up and put on a robe and made her way downstairs in the dark. She was sure it would be a mistake to turn the lights on.

She didn't turn the light on in the study either when she arrived at its door and when the whimpering was no longer indistinct and no longer animal but very clear and very human.

She found the couch and found Cecilia and took the thin, frail woman into her arms and listened to a story of yet another death, and she felt the body that was so thin it seemed to have no substance tremble and twist in her arms in spasms of pain and guilt and heard the child in that body cry out.

"I killed her. I killed her."

And Elsie forgave the child in the only way she knew how.

"I love you, Cecilia," she said. "Like my own."

There were more tears after that but the body in Elsie's arms relaxed and seemed to gain some substance and then Cecilia said, "I don't want to go to sleep tonight," and Elsie realized she didn't want to either and so she said, "Let's have some tea, toots."

After they'd brewed the tea, Cecilia said, "What about Herbert?"

And Elsie said, "Let's take everything upstairs."

Herbert and Elsie and Cecilia sat up the rest of the night drinking tea and talking about themselves. Cecilia talked about ballet and her mother; Elsie talked about the "puffheads" and being pregnant; and Herbert talked about his and Elsie's wedding. At dawn, Elsie said she and Cecilia would have to get themselves put together because they were due in court at ten and Herbert said to Cecilia, "What would you advise for Elsie's hair?" And Elsie touched her hair and frowned. And Cecilia said, "Beer and egg." And Elsie said, "Do you really think that'll work?" And Cecilia said, "I'm sure of it." And Herbert said, "Oh good." And so Cecilia mixed up a froth of beer and egg and ladled spoonfuls over Elsie's head while Elsie bent over the bathroom sink and Herbert washed her hair. And the bathroom got steamy and hot and intoxicating and nobody wanted to leave.

* * *

Elsie and I went off to court at ten. She had some scheme to get my charges dropped, although I had my doubts.

We fixed ourselves up some and Elsie's hair shone like it was lit up. And even though I'd ironed her clothes for her, they still looked wrinkled and worn, and I was too skinny for the neighbor's kid's clothes so they hung on me like a potato sack. We were "presentable," Elsie said, but I didn't think we were gonna impress anybody. I didn't care, though, because I figured nothing could stop us now.

Elsie walked into that courtroom as if she really were an armored tank, with her hair spewing out from her bun in big golden tufts providing camouflage. And she held my elbow in such a tight grip, I felt as if I were in a steel-plated side car, all safe and sound.

The D.A. and the judge walked in and were fooled by the camouflage. The judge sniffed and sat down. The D.A. plucked a piece of lint off his suit coat.

"Don't worry, toots," Elsie said. "Remember who they are."

Elsie had reminded me of the D.A.'s visits to the massage parlor and then she'd told me the judge had contracted V.D. ten times in the last year, according to his personal doctor, who had a loose tongue when he was drunk.

After some formalities, Elsie made her motion and the judge said forget it, only not so politely, so Elsie got a little testy and then the D.A. got a little testy and said I was a "vulgar little parasite" which got me testy and Elsie very testy and then the judge got red in the face and said, "One more word out of you, counselor, and I'll hold you in contempt."

Elsie slammed her notebook down on the big wood table we were sitting at and took a deep breath and I thought she was gonna blow it so I blew it instead and said, "Don't you lay a hand on her, you pervert."

And for a second, only a second, but a very nice second for Elsie and me, for that second the D.A. and the judge looked really scared, I mean *really*, because, of course, they *were* perverts and they knew it and they thought we knew it.

But then the judge cleared his throat with a disgusting gurgle and said, "Motion denied," and set a date for the trial.

Elsie waited until we got out of the courtroom to mutter "Fuck you," and then she patted my shoulder and smiled at me and said we still had a chance and then she turned away to get a drink of water but when she bent over the fountain, she didn't drink any. And then she said we needed a breather and, when she was done interviewing her clients, we should go to Casa Verde and play with the kids. For some reason that really did sound like a breather to me.

* * *

On his way to work, in the middle of thinking about Elsie's hair, Herbert suddenly remembered his secretary. His last glimpse of Elsie's hair had been as she sailed out the front door with Cecilia in tow—it was golden, alive, almost billowing. That memory was replaced by dread and guilt. He hoped that maybe his secretary wouldn't come in and then hated himself for hoping that. And he almost thought he'd be sick again until he remembered, at the doorstep to his office, that maybe his instincts were better than he had thought.

And so, when he walked in and saw his secretary sitting at her desk, pretending she was absorbed with her work, he asked her to come into his office, which she did, although reluctantly.

He sat down in his chair and his secretary sat opposite him, studying the floor.

"Look," he said. "I'm your friend, and your boss is a creep. Don't give him the time of day."

His secretary, Susan, laughed a little, then stopped and then looked at the floor again and said, "I don't think you're a creep."

"Maybe not entirely," Herbert said. "But I've been a creep with you. As your friend, I'd advise you to forget your boss immediately and find somebody who has the time and the energy to tell you every day how intelligent and smart and special you are. Meanwhile your boss will try to stop being a jerk and remember to tell you once in awhile too, okay?"

It was okay with Susan. She looked relieved in a way. Herbert suddenly wanted to take her to lunch and get to know the woman who had sat outside his office for five years. But he knew that would be a mistake. Maybe he'd have lunch with Elsie and Cecilia and find out what happened in court.

* * *

Elsie hadn't been sure that Cecilia would want to go to Casa Verde. She was surprised when Cecilia agreed immediately. She was even more surprised when, just as they were about to leave the courthouse, Cecilia asked if they could stop by the house and take Elsie's ballet records with them.

Herbert was going to meet them there. That had surprised Elsie, too. Herbert had never gone to Casa Verde, but on the phone he had seemed almost eager.

He was waiting at the front door of the school. Elsie thought she'd never been so happy to see anyone. Cecilia looked pleased to see Herbert, too. The three of them walked into the Rec room with its pale green walls and brilliantly colored paintings, and they were immediately surrounded, grabbed, cuddled and petted by the forty misshapen children who laughed and grinned and tried to say Herbert which came out "Hoober" and "Burrr" and "Herbo." Elsie saw Cecilia cuddle and pat the children and then gently free herself and speak to one of the staff. The woman smiled and nodded and took Cecilia by the arm to the phonograph.

As Elsie tried to hug twenty children at once and as she saw Herbert, with a silly grin on his face, trying to do the same, Aurora's theme began playing and forty energetic children fell silent and still, and Elsie and those forty children and Herbert, too, watched Cecilia cross the room and take the small bent girl by the hands and begin to dance with her. It was almost as if the bent body unbent and the arms and legs became as fluid and supple as they should have been. Everybody began to dance. Elsie and Herbert danced with each other. It was then that Elsie felt as if she had plenty of bundles to hold on to.

* * *

I go to Casa Verde every day now. I'm a staff member. I teach dance – jazz, ballet, modern. I'm taking classes so I can keep up with the kids. I still live with Elsie and Herbert, but I plan to move out on my own soon, well some time. I've got the money now, but I can't get organized. I'm too busy. I got convicted, but my case is being appealed through the courts. Elsie says it might make it to the Supreme Court. That'd be something.

Anyway, it still isn't easy to be a woman and an *artiste* or a human being, for that matter, but I really feel like all three now and that makes it easier, not easy, but easier.

THE GOLDEN RULE

Raymond Arguen posted his last sticker on a street lamp at the intersection of El Monte Road and the expressway. The sticker read, "STOP ORGANIZED CRIME, IMPEACH THE PRESIDENT." As Raymond reached up to smooth the sticker, the elbow of his suit jacket gave way. This didn't upset him; the suit was old and worn and didn't fit him anyway. As he pedaled home on his bicycle, he made a mental note to visit the Goodwill the next day to look for a new one.

Home for Raymond was a room at the back of Lila Gish's garage. Ms. Gish was sixty-six years old and a very kind and fair landlord.

In his kitchen, Raymond sautéed canned new potatoes in margarine while he looked at a magazine he had bought the day before at the Goodwill, a fifteen-year-old *People*. He was looking at the pictures, particularly the photographs of men. He studied how they stood and what they wore. One picture pleased him a great deal. It was a photograph of a young man wearing a loose fitting white suit and a pale blue T-shirt underneath. The man did not wear socks, but a pair of sunglasses hung from the neck of his T-shirt.

Raymond shoved his potatoes onto a chipped fake Wedgwood plate and sat down to eat. Since his finances and his beliefs forced him to be frugal, he was always hungry. He had been looking forward to dinner since 10 a.m. But someone was knocking on his door.

"Raymond, I'm very sorry to bother you," Ms. Gish said. She was wrapped in a purple silk kimono covered with embroidered birds of paradise.

"No bother," Raymond said. "I've just made dinner. Would you care to join me?"

Lila peeked past him into the room and then shook her head. "Actually I was going to invite *you* to dinner, tomorrow."

"Well, thank you!"

"My grandson, Wesley, will be visiting. I don't think you've met him."

Raymond shook his head, but said, "I'll be there." Lila nodded and left.

Actually Raymond knew all about Wesley—the young man in the framed photograph on Ms. Gish's piano—the rugby player, the law student, the Young Republican, the tall, tan, blond young man who wore loose fitting suits and T-shirts. Wesley was ten years younger than Raymond, but Raymond had nevertheless imagined himself and the boy as fast friends.

Raymond returned to his plate of potatoes and realized with a start that Ms. Gish couldn't have joined him for dinner even if she had wanted to. He had only one chair.

The next morning at 7 a.m., Raymond ate breakfast and made a list of what he would need at the Goodwill—a chair and something special to wear to Ms. Gish's dinner. At 7:15 a.m., he was on his bicycle, riding through a still sleeping neighborhood of three-bedroom, all-electric kitchen homes with wall-to-wall carpeting. He was posting up flyers calling for the imprisonment of the CEO's and the chairmen of the board of all Fortune 500 companies. Those who had hired Raymond to post the flyers believed these individuals to be guilty of intractable greed.

Raymond was not an anarchist nor a revolutionary. He had no desire to destroy the modest three-bedroom homes he passed by on his bicycle. Raymond's political theories amounted to nothing more than the Golden Rule, though he referred to it as the self-evident rule. It had come as the bitterest of disappointments to him as he passed through childhood and into adulthood that a rule so self-evident was so routinely and widely ignored. The world had come to seem highly untrustworthy to him. Yet, he persisted. Posting leaflets for causes he believed in was his contribution to making the world a little more trustworthy.

He made a stop at the AWIP office where the members of "Abolish War, Invent Peace" paid him twenty-five dollars for posting two thousand flyers announcing the upcoming AWIP dance. Then he pedaled off to the Goodwill.

At the entrance he began passing out leaflets despite the fact that he had twenty-five dollars in his pocket and every intention of spending it. Duty always came first with him. He passed out leaflets for an hour and a half, and, just when he was planning to quit, a stout man with a florid face suddenly stuck an AWIP leaflet in his face and screamed, "YOU COMMIE PINKO FAGGOT OF A JEW MAMA'S BOY, GO BACK TO NEW YORK WHERE YOU BELONG."

"I'm not a communist, nor a homosexual, nor am I of the Jewish persuasion," Raymond replied, calmly and politely.

"You're a Democrat? They're all pinko, too," said the man.

"No," Raymond said.

"No what?" the man said.

"No, I'm not a Democrat."

"You're a *Republican?!*" the man asked, dumbfounded.

Raymond could have said no. He could have tried to explain. But Raymond believed that the kind thing to do was to leave this man with something to think about, since Raymond himself always enjoyed being left with something to think about. He smiled and said nothing.

"Well I'll be," the man said, walking away and shaking his head. "I'll be."

Raymond entered the Goodwill and headed for the racks of suits. He found a pale blue suit for ten dollars. It was baggy enough to please him, but the trousers had bell-bottom legs. He wished he could have asked the man in the photograph in *People* magazine if the suit would do.

"No, you don't want that." It was the man with the florid face. "You want to get yourself good quality—none of this pansy stuff." The man handed Raymond a suit made from yellow and green plaid wool. "Try it on," he said. Raymond knew that the suit wouldn't do, but he tried on the jacket just to please.

"Nice," the man said.

"I don't think so," Raymond said.

The man shook his head and walked away. "A *Republican,*" he muttered as he went.

Raymond took a chance and bought the pale blue suit. He also found himself a lavender T-shirt and a sturdy metal chair, and, for a dollar, he bought himself the first pair of sunglasses he had ever owned.

He pedaled home with the chair balanced between his back and the rim of the rear wheel of his bicycle. It worried him a great deal that he had not had the money to purchase a pair of shoes. He had only the shoes on his feet, black wing tips, which might or might not look good without socks, to say nothing of how they would look with bell bottom trousers.

Once back in his room, he set the chair down at his table and stood back. Now he could invite someone in.

Raymond lay down on his bed for a rest. He was not due at Lila's for another two hours. He wondered what he might say to Wesley. Raymond knew nothing of rugby, little of the law—despite the fact that he had been arrested a time or two for posting posters in the wrong place—and he didn't know all that much about the Republican party either, except that they had never asked him to post up a single thing.

The fact that he had so little in common with Wesley began to worry Raymond. And then a thought struck him that set his mind at ease. He would re-read the *People* magazine and memorize items of note. Everyone seemed to like gossip, for reasons he didn't quite understand, but he was fully prepared to be a good sport about it.

He fixed himself a glass of grape juice and a bologna sandwich and studied the magazine carefully. After a time, he set it aside to dress. He turned his back to the mirror as he did so. He did not want to see his creation piece by piece; he wanted to see it whole. He realized almost immediately that he had miscalculated a bit. The "bell-bottoms" were also "hip-huggers," but they did not hug his hips. He cinched the trousers around his waist with a belt and buttoned shut the jacket. As a final gesture, he hung the sunglasses from the neck of his T-shirt. Then he wheeled around to look in the mirror.

The effect was not exactly what he had intended.

Wesley roared into Aunt Lila's driveway and slammed on the brakes. Stops on a dime, he said to himself. As he got out of his brand new MG, he patted the hood.

"Yoohooooo." Aunt Lila was calling. Batty as ever, Wesley thought. Look at that get-up. *Purple* panty hose. No wonder Pop doesn't want anything to do with her.

Wesley walked up the brick path, threw his arms around his aunt and planted a kiss on her cheek.

"Boy, you're getting stronger every day," Aunt Lila said.

Wesley showed her his biceps. She felt them and whistled. "My kind of man."

Wesley laughed. Batty yeah, but all right.

"Do come in," Aunt Lila said.

She held open her screen door and ushered Wesley into her living room, which was stuffed with satin pillows, crocheted doilies and figurines of ballet dancers and kitty cats, and a dozen framed photographs of Clark Gable, some of them signed, "To Lila with All My Love."

Whoa, who is *this?* Wesley asked himself. And look at *that* get-up. Ichabod Crane in drag. Wesley had to stifle a laugh.

Ichabod Crane stuck out his hand. "Raymond Arguen," he said.

"Uh, Wesley, Wesley Smith." Arguen's hand felt like a chicken wing. Wesley had never shaken a hand so bony and thin.

"Sherry?" Aunt Lila asked.

"No, no thanks," Wesley said.

"Maybe Wesley would care for a beer," Arguen said.

"Well, if you're having one," Wesley said. He smiled. Arguen smiled back. Even his teeth look skinny, Wesley thought.

"No, I'm not having one," Arguen said. "But you should have one if you like."

"Oh, okay, sure," Wesley said.

"I'll get it for you, honey," Aunt Lila said.

"It's just that I think everybody should have what they want, within reason," Arguen said.

"Right," Wesley said. Was this guy serious?

"And you play rugby?" Arguen said.

Wesley started. "Yes, I do. Do you like the game?"

"I don't know," Arguen said. "But I'm prepared to like it."

To Wesley's relief, Aunt Lila returned. She handed him a beer in a glass and set a crocheted coaster on the table beside his elbow. Remaining by his side and assuming a dramatic three-quarter turn pose, she stuck a cigarette in a silver and ivory holder and held the holder to her lips until Wesley had lit it for her. Aunt Lila took a deep drag and sighed.

"In just a moment we will dine," she said. *"Coq au vin,"* she added. "Your favorite, Wesley, and Raymond is partial to it, too, aren't you Raymond?"

Arguen nodded and looked at Wesley. "In what field of law are you interested?" he asked.

"Corporate. Well, anything that'll make me money," Wesley said and laughed.

"Do you think that's important?"

"What?" Wesley asked.

"Money," Arguen said.

Wesley laughed again. "You must be joking," he said. Wasn't the guy joking?

"Boys, let's dine," Aunt Lila said. "Come help me put things on the table."

Wesley and Arguen helped Aunt Lila carry in the food and wine to the ten foot mahogany dining table where they were obliged to sit down directly across from one another, since Aunt Lila had sat herself down at the head.

"So Wesley, tell me about the new movies," Aunt Lila said, as she served him half a chicken.

"Let me see. Oh, there's a great one about a beautiful lady who goes to Africa with her husband—she doesn't love him—and he goes off hunting and leaves her alone and she has to fight tigers, or was it lions? Anyway she has to take care of this big plantation all by herself and then she meets—"

"Ooh, don't tell me!" Aunt Lila cried. "Let me guess. She meets a big game hunter!"

"That's right," Wesley said. That's nice, he thought. It's so easy to keep Aunt Lila happy. That wasn't true of most people these days. You had to buy them a Porsche or a compact disc player to keep them happy.

"Elizabeth Taylor may get married again," Arguen said.

"Yeah?" Wesley said.

"To whom?" Aunt Lila said. "Tell us."

"Robert, uh, no, uh, Peter? No, uh—" Arguen stuttered.

"George? George Hamilton?" Wesley offered.

"No. No, I'm sorry. I seem to have forgotten."

"No need to apologize," Aunt Lila said. "Here, have another chicken wing."

They ate in silence for a few minutes. Aunt Lila filled their wine glasses. Wesley took a gulp.

"I always thought Elizabeth should have stuck with Richard," Aunt Lila said.

"That's it!" Arguen said. "Richard Burton! She's going to marry Richard Burton again!"

"But he's *dead,*" Wesley said before he could stop himself.

Arguen choked on the chicken wing and turned red. He gagged and coughed and then stood up.

"If you'll excuse me," he said.

"Oh, sit down, Raymond. Have a glass of water. Wesley dear, fetch Raymond some water."

Wesley raced for the kitchen. He took his time finding a glass and filling it from the tap. When he returned to the dining room Arguen was gone.

"The poor dear boy," Aunt Lila said.

"What's wrong with him?" Wesley asked. He had had about enough of Arguen.

"He's a bit shy," Aunt Lila said. "A bit too much on the serious side."

Wesley picked at the bones that remained of his half of a chicken. He found a sliver of white meat and popped it into his mouth.

"Go talk to him," Aunt Lila said.

"Me?"

"Wesley, be nice."

Wesley found Arguen crouched over in a bed of petunias in the back yard. He was shredding a purple flower. His face was red and covered with tears.

"Hey, Raymond," Wesley said. "Come back inside. Have a beer. Or have a sherry. Whatever you want."

"No, thank you," Arguen said.

Wesley felt like an idiot. He knelt down next to Arguen.

"Listen, it was just a mistake. No big deal. I only happen to know because I watch so much television."

"Thank you," Arguen said.

"So you'll come inside?" Wesley asked.

"No, thank you," Arguen said.

Wesley stood up. "You sure?" he asked.

Arguen looked Wesley straight in the eye and shook his head.

Well, the guy has dignity, Wesley thought as he turned back to the house. I'll say that for him. But what does that get you? Jeez, it's every man for himself these days. Dignity went out with the Bible.

At Aunt Lila's back door, Wesley suddenly felt cold and shivered. He opened the door and shouted to his aunt, "Hey, how about some of your fancy coffee to warm me up!"

"Nothing I'd like better, dear, than to warm you up." Aunt Lila giggled like a girl. "Is Raymond with you?"

O COME LET US ADORE

It was Christmas Eve at the Palo Verde Shopping Mall, and the display windows beckoned with still-life scenes of elegantly dressed couples and children surrounded by extravagant toys. But Sarah could not find a place to park. Curbs, sidewalks and handicapped spaces were all full. Even plots of shrubbery had been mowed down by Mercedes sedans and shiny black Range Rovers. Cars moved through the asphalt lot in fits and starts, threading their way up one aisle and down another. Sarah crept along in her brand new baby blue BMW, an early gift from her husband. The sleek green Jaguar following her edged up close to the rear bumper of her brand new car.

Sarah had planned to visit the stationery store that turned its upstairs loft into a wonderland of green, gold, silver and red ornaments each year. She had been going to that same store for more than three decades, first as a child led by her mother, then as a mother herself with her two sons in tow. Now her sons were home watching football on TV with their father. But Sarah didn't mind going alone.

She turned on the BMW's Blaupunkt radio, and a children's chorus sang out, *O come, all ye faithful, Joyful and triumphant* ... Her heart fluttered. Christmas, she thought. She sang along, *Above thy deep and dreamless* ... On "sleep," she jammed on the brakes to avoid hitting a tomato red Porsche Carrera. The Jaguar slid to a screeching halt less than a foot behind her. Horns began to beep and blare.

O come ye, O come ye to Bethlehem ...

The Porsche Carrera began to move again. Sarah followed. She passed by display windows that lit up fine china and beaded silk dresses. The windows seemed to hold the promise of a safe elegant present and an ever brighter future. Sarah wanted to park and move into the realm of promise, but all remaining plots of vacant earth, asphalt and concrete were guarded by traffic cops in khaki who stood impassively as angry drivers shouted obscenities at them.

The hopes and fears of all the years ...

Sarah began to panic. Her brand new baby blue car felt like a trap, or maybe a prison. But suddenly she saw a neighbor, Lydia Hamilton, staggering across the parking lot weighed down by shopping bags. Sarah frantically honked her horn. Lydia looked up, smiled, and staggered over.

"My dear!" she exclaimed. "You don't look well."

Sarah wanted to burst into tears and weep on Lydia's shoulder.

"Oh, I'm fine," was all she said. "I just can't find a parking space."

"It's *murder*," Lydia exclaimed. "Just *murder!*"

Sarah's hands began to tremble on the steering wheel. Her mouth quivered.

"I tell you what," Lydia said, "you just follow me and park in my space."

The chorus of sweet voices sang another song, *Word of the Father, now in flesh appearing, O come let us adore him; O come let us adore him* ... Sarah's eyes filled. She was being silly, she knew it, but she was happy. Up ahead, Lydia set her shopping bags down beside a lemon yellow Mercedes 560SL sedan.

When Sarah had succeeded in inching her way forward to the sedan, she stopped but the Jaguar didn't. Sarah felt a sickening jolt as the sleek green nose of the Jaguar, carried forward by the inexorable momentum of a 4.2 liter engine, crashed through the trunk of her car and buried itself in the baby blue leather of the back seat. Meanwhile, the snub nose of her own BMW sank neatly and deeply into the rear end of the tomato red Porsche Carrera. Sarah's pocketbook flew to the floor and landed upside down. Stunned, Sarah sat and stared at two securely wrapped tampons that lay unharmed on the baby blue rubber mat.

When she had collected herself a bit and realized that she was shaken but not hurt, Sarah got out of her car prepared to direct her anger and indignation at the driver behind her. But the owner of the Jaguar, a fastidiously coiffed matron whose hairdo sat slightly askew on her head, had been rear-ended herself, as had the person behind her. Attempts were made to sort out exactly who had hit whom first, but the accidents appeared to have had no beginning and no end. There were shoppers standing by their cars arguing and fuming three aisles over on either side.

Sarah lost track of the arguments. She was too busy staring at her car, a $40,000 *objet d'art* of Bavarian engineering, which had taken the hit every bit as well as a Ford Pinto might have. The prophylactic rubber bumpers were now inlaid in the auto body itself. Traffic cops arrived and began yelling at shoppers to get back in their cars and move on. Shoppers yelled back. The traffic cops became nervous and belligerent. Sarah saw a young officer accost two perfectly reasonable, well-dressed middle-aged men, who were in the process of exchanging information about insurance carriers. The cop ripped the men's notepads right out of their hands and ordered them, as if at gun point, into their smashed German-made automobiles.

Sarah scurried into her car and tried to start the engine.

It's beginning to look a lot like Christmas ...

The radio remained in perfect working order. So, to Sarah's amazement, did the engine.

The Porsche Carrera slipped from the grasp of the BMW's front-end as smoothly as a bag of giblets from a Christmas turkey, and the sudden massive union of metal, rubber and chrome dissolved into a vehicular snake. *Soon the bells will start, And the thing that will make them ring is the carol that you sing,* Rosemary Clooney sang.

Sarah followed the line of dented bumpers and crushed front-ends. Her only desire now was to go home—to a warm fire, a hot bath, a nice glass of wine, and to her husband and sons. There would be no more trying to park, no more endless switchbacks on level ground. The shopping mall had lost its allure. Sarah couldn't remember what her husband and sons looked like.

At the exit the tomato red Porsche Carrera made a U-turn. *He's going back in?* Sarah wondered. She was amazed that anyone, under the circumstances, would make such a choice.

A traffic cop awaited Sarah. She could see herself in his sunglasses. Her hair was awry and her make-up smudged.

"You'll have to turn back," the traffic cop said.

"What?" Sarah asked. She strained to see through the mirrors into the man's eyes.

"I said, you'll have to turn back in."

"No!" Sarah gasped. "No, I want to leave."

"You can't leave," the cop said.

"Of course I can leave," Sarah said. "I mean, why not?"

"Here's a little something to make your stay more pleasant." The cop held out a thick roll of bills he had just pulled out of a metal box beside his feet. "Ten thousand dollars," he said and smiled.

"But," Sarah said, thinking *ten thousand dollars?* "But I think I'll just go home."

"Get this straight, lady," the cop said, resting his hand on the butt of a pistol strapped to his hip. "You can't go home. Nobody goes home. You gotta turn back in."

Long lay the world in sin and error pining ...

A famous tenor voice sang Sarah's favorite carol. She turned back in. Her speed ranged from two miles per hour, to five, to a dead stop. Her neck felt stiff, her shoulders ached, her throat was raw with thirst. As the sun set, the sky lit up in pinks and golds. Christmas lights glittered in the dusk. The tenor's voice filled the cool air inside Sarah's battered car.

A thrill of hope, the weary soul rejoices ...

And then it happened. Sarah found a parking space. She parked automatically, without even thinking about it.

Fall on your knees, Oh hear the angels voices.

Oh night divine, Oh night ...

As Sarah walked steadily towards the windows that beckoned but no longer tantalized, shoppers passed her, boxes piled so high in their arms that Sarah could not see their faces. Lydia, dragging a new load of shopping bags, lurched towards her.

"How much have you spent?" Lydia called out gaily.

"Nothing yet," Sarah said.

"Nothing?!" Lydia screeched. *"Nothing?* You better get going. They'll give you another ten thousand next time around."

In the shopping mall proper, there were hundreds, perhaps thousands, of shoppers elbowing each other and hurtling past and over each other. At the entrance to Neiman-Marcus, a huge wedge of people sardined themselves through double glass doors. Sarah let herself be sucked into the wedge and thrust through the doors, which shattered behind her and left a dozen shoppers cut and bloody. Inside, Sarah watched mothers and fathers, sisters and brothers, and uncles and aunts, armed with coat hangers and display umbrellas, fight each other off for silk ties, gold earrings, and alligator handbags. A woman in Italian high-heeled pumps and a silk dress made a swan dive into the center of the jewelry counter to get her hands on a string of baroque pearls. A child in designer overalls sat and cried beneath a department store mannequin that had been denuded. The mannequin smiled pleasantly.

Sarah was hungry and thirsty. She went into the gourmet food shop and flipped the lid off an imported raspberry soda, unscrewed the top of a mushroom garlic pasta sauce, sat down on the floor and began to eat and drink. The in-house sound system blared overhead:

Away in a manger, no crib for a bed ...

Thin strong fingers grabbed Sarah's wrist. She tried to wrench free.

"Ma'am, let's have no more of that," said a young man dressed in an immaculate gray suit and pink shirt.

"What's wrong?" Sarah asked, and then added, "Leave me alone."

"You haven't paid for what you are consuming," the young man said politely.

"Here," Sarah said, thrusting the roll of bills at him. "Is that enough?"

He smiled. "More than enough, ma'am. I'll just take a hundred." He pulled off a single bill.

"No, take it all," Sarah said.

"I'm sorry. I can't do that. It's against the rules."

"But I don't want it."

"But it's your responsibility," the young man said very gently.

Bless all the dear children in Thy tender care,

And take us to heaven to live with Thee there.

When the man had left, Sarah shop-lifted a two-ounce jar of beluga caviar, a bottle of Château Mouton-Rothschild and a box of individually-wrapped salted wafers. Armed with provisions, she headed for Woolworth.

In the dime store, the crowds of shoppers were dense and agitated. Sarah concentrated her efforts on the "dollar" tables in which nobody else seemed particularly interested. As other eager but dazed shoppers carried crates of Kodak 35 mm film and Scott paper towels (marked down twenty-nine cents) to the cash register, Sarah quietly pilfered a large canvas handbag in which she placed tiny yellow stick-on pads, a miniature tool set, a plastic tomato slicer, a pair of knit baby booties, a tin box of bandages, a framed photograph of Joe Montana, a set of four bright red plastic soup bowls and glasses to match, a cloth Christmas corsage made with ribbons and plastic pine cones covered with painted snow, a 99¢ knife with a wood-grained Formica handle and a bottle of hand lotion with no name-brand recognition.

A soothing silky voice crooned from a speaker in the ceiling:

Toyland, Toyland,

Little girl and boy land ...

"Hand it over, now."

A large beefy man in a polo shirt and jeans grabbed Sarah's arm and squeezed.

"No!" Sarah said.

The man squeezed harder. Sarah handed over her canvas bag. At the cash register a young woman with nine purple fingernails and one gold one rang up the total: $37.92.

"Pay up," the dick said.

"No," Sarah said.

"No?" the dick said. "Why not? You got the dough."

"Arrest me," Sarah said. Her husband would bail her out. That would be the end to it.

"Fine by me," the dick said, "but it's a capital offense."

"I'd get the death penalty for shop-lifting at *dollar days?*" Sarah gasped.

"No, not for shop-lifting. For refusing to pay once you get caught." The dick shrugged. "It's kinda un-American, lady."

Childhood's joyland,

Mystic, merry Toyland!

Once you pass its borders,

You can ne'er return again.

Sarah paid her bill. Outside Woolworth, she slumped against a wall and sat down. It was dark and cold. Her legs ached. Her stomach was cramping. If she were at home, she would be fixing dinner, but she couldn't remember what her kitchen looked like. Would a tomato slicer come in handy there or not? she wondered. She pinned the plastic pine cone Christmas corsage to her blazer and applied the nameless hand lotion. Then she sat back and listened to Elvis sing with husky longing while she swilled Château Mouton-Rothschild from a brown paper bag:

I'll have a blue Christmas without you.

I'll be so blue just thinking about you.

A young man dressed in janitor's coveralls walked by, keys jangling in his hand. His dark brown face was scarred by a jagged tear that ran from his left temple to the base of his chin.

"Are you leaving?" Sarah asked.

"Yes, *señora,*" the young man said.

"Will they let you out?"

"*Sí, claro,* of course," the young man said. "I just work here."

Sarah's heart leapt with hope.

"Will you take me with you?"

"No," the young man said. "I'm sorry, but that is not permitted."

"In the trunk of your car," Sarah said, staggering to her feet. "You could take me out in your trunk."

The young man shook his head. "I'm sorry, but they check trunks."

"I'll pay you," Sarah begged. "I've got ten thousand dollars. Right here." She thrust the bills at the young man.

"I'm sorry, *señora*," the young man said again. "I don't need money. I've already paid. Perhaps you didn't notice." He walked away, the keys still jangling in his hand.

Sarah sank down against the wall. Elvis caressed the night and the longing.

Decorations of red on a green Christmas tree
Won't be the same, dear, if you're not here with me ...

Sarah wondered if it were possible to spend $9,862.08 on ornaments and strands of tinsel. She got up immediately and headed towards the stationery store.

The first level had been stripped of nearly everything except accountants' ledgers and guest books for weddings. There were only a few shoppers. A fit, handsome man sat in the middle of an aisle mumbling "but I am a *neurosurgeon*" while he methodically ate chocolate-covered cherry candies, wrappers and all. The elegant matron who owned the squashed Jaguar browsed through a rack of Halloween masks. She chose a Michael Jackson likeness, covered her head with it, left cash at the abandoned register and walked out of the store.

At the foot of the steps to the loft, Lydia Hamilton, surrounded by a dozen shopping bags, lay unconscious, or perhaps dead. She clutched to her chest an out-dated calendar which featured photographs of award-winning pies. As Sarah ascended the stairs, she wondered if rigor mortis had set in.

The loft was untouched. The room sparkled with glass, foil and gold. Sarah saw tiny wooden Santa Clauses, angels made from cornhusks, strands of multicolored tinsel, globes covered with rhinestones and fake pearls and silver braid, hand-painted eggs with intricate baroque designs, and small clay nativity scenes from Mexico. So much to choose from, Sarah thought, so much one could buy.

She didn't have the energy, or perhaps the inclination, to select which items she preferred so she began to take one of each and then two of each and ten or more of each. She made a huge pile on the floor, a mound of stationery store ornamental artifacts. When she believed that she was done, she surveyed the mound, which sparkled and glittered in the fluorescent light, and she was satisfied.

She crawled carefully into the middle of it and covered herself with ornaments. "He maketh me to lie down in green pastures," she murmured. Then she listened to a single, clear contralto voice that sang out through the random static of the stationery store's antiquated speaker:

I'll be home for Christmas
You can plan on me ...

The mushroom garlic sauce and the wine had given Sarah indigestion. She burped loudly and violently. A bright red globe, decorated with green braid and silver sequins, rolled off her abdomen and smashed onto the floor. Sarah burped again more gently and sighed. Then she rested.

Christmas Eve will find me
Where the love-light gleams.
I'll be home for Christmas,
If only in my dreams ...

A JOURNEY, NOT A CATACLYSM

I met Robert Whitman at the Recycle Bookstore. He had a passion, I learned later, for cast-off books. And his passion was not for well-read dog-eared copies of classics or bestsellers. Robert liked books that had never been read, never been reprinted, had never made it into paperback—*The 1959 Pillsbury Cook-Off Winners Recipes,* for example.

The day I met him, I was standing in line ready to buy a pristine edition of the seven-record set of Elvis Presley's greatest hits (the cellophane wrapper was still intact). I was also trying to hide what I intended to buy. I'd even gone so far as to pick up a quarto-sized book of Georgia O'Keefe paintings and place it on top of the fat record album. The book was big but not b<u>i</u>g enough. Robert, who was standing directly in front of me in line, turned back and said, "Oh, so you like Elvis Presley," just as if we were on a date and getting to know one another.

"It's for my son," I said. Robert smiled.

"And this is for my daughter." He held out a copy of *The Best Jokes of 1972*. I laughed.

"And this is for my wife," he said, holding out a tidy paperback entitled, *How to Dress and Undress for Your Husband.* It was covered with a blurred photograph of a model in a pale blue pillbox hat and suit to match. The model bore a disturbing resemblance to Jacqueline Kennedy Onassis.

"It has visual aids," Robert said.

"So you're married," I said, not having meant to.

This time Robert laughed. We were at the counter.

"Wrap this up for me in gift wrap," Robert said to the clerk. The clerk said the store didn't carry gift wrap. Robert paid for his books. I paid for my records. Robert watched me do it.

"Shall we polish this off with Diet Pepsi?" he asked. I nodded.

We walked down to the University Creamery, a coffee shop that had stayed open twenty-four hours a day, seven days a week for thirty years and in this way had avoided the unpleasantness of ever having to sweep or mop its floors or replace the upholstery in its booths.

We ordered Diet Pepsi. Robert choked on his first gulp.

"I gather you don't drink this regularl," I said. It was meant as a joke, but Robert frowned, gazed across the restaurant and said, "I don't think I do much of anything regularly. There's something sinister about time clocks, calendars, schedules, of any sort."

"But people tend to like structure," I said, stupidly.

"One of life's little pleasures is a weekly minder," Robert said.

I sipped my Pepsi. Robert shredded a paper napkin.

"So tell me about you," he said suddenly, as if he'd already revealed a number of confidences about himself. "You're not married?"

"No," I said, "but I'm attached."

"Ah," he said. "Attached."

I waited for him to continue. He didn't.

"What do you mean, *ah attached?"* I asked.

"What do *you* mean?" he asked. "You said it as if it were some disease you've contracted."

This time I choked on the Diet Pepsi. "Well ... " I said.

"Sorry," he said. He looked as if he meant it. "I tell you what, let's go listen to Elvis Presley."

I said no. It was getting late. Stephen would be home by now wondering what had happened to me. It was his afternoon off. And I had work to do. I did graphics and copy on a computer, freelance. I currently had a job for a group proposing that the wild squirrel population in town be preserved at any cost, despite fears of plague, pestilence and landscaped garden destruction. My only other job at the moment was for a cooperative grocery chain that wanted to change its image from counter-culture to nouveau riche.

"Well, take my card anyway," Robert said.

I took it and went home. I left his card—a simple one with just his full name and phone number, no title, no profession—and the Elvis Presley records in my car.

Stephen was sitting in the living room drinking orange spice tea and listening to Albonini's *Adagio in G Minor, s*omewhat funereal music for five-thirty on a spring afternoon but that was Stephen. He smiled when I came in.

"What have you been up to?" he asked.

"Shopping," I said.

"Buy anything?" he asked.

"No," I lied. There was a considerable inequity in Stephen's and my salaries which meant that he paid most of the bills. He wouldn't have been pleased about twenty-seven fifty for the seven-album set of Elvis and it wouldn't have just been the money.

I got a glass of wine and sat down next to Stephen. He was leaning back in his chair, relaxing, eyes closed, hands limp on the arms of the easy chair.

Stephen relaxed a lot. He was a cardiologist, and his patients invariably died on him. Stephen was convinced that they died due to bad habits and a failure to relax. He never accused them of this; he didn't condemn or judge them to their faces or even privately. He was, in fact, a compassionate physician who believed, in spite of his patients' bad habits, that he owed them the very best he had to offer. He got to know his patients, their hopes, dreams and failures, their troubles with sex, their favorite books, the names and species of their pets, and he'd sit with relatives and pat hands and explain things in detail and for hours on end.

But when they died, he was convinced that they had wilfully committed suicide.

So Stephen regularly, compulsively and obsessively relaxed, in addition to which he didn't smoke, drink to excess, or eat red meat. His intention was to avoid the same fate as his patients. Oddly enough, faced with so much death, Stephen persisted in denying his own mortality. Oddly enough, and with so much relaxation, he suffered from a recurrent ulcer.

"How does a weekend at Pajaro Dunes sound?" he asked, eyes closed, brows smooth, breaths deep and regular.

"Fine," I said.

We always went to Pajaro Dunes, to relax. Pajaro Dunes was beginning to bore the hell out of me. We rented the same condominium each time. We walked on the same beach. We even seemed to eat the same food and read the same books. But I was aware that the weekend might have been a bid by Stephen for a revival of our somewhat strained "attachment." We'd spent our first sleep-over date at Pajaro, and it had been anything but boring

"Fine?" Stephen said, sitting up and frowning. "You don't sound very enthusiastic."

"It's just that we always go to the Dunes," I said. "Couldn't we go someplace else?"

"I like it," Stephen said.

"So do I, but …"

"But what?"

"But…one of life's little pleasures is a weekend at Pajaro Dunes," I mumbled.

"What?" Stephen said.

"Nothing," I said. I smiled. I took Stephen's hands. His hands were large with big knuckles but were always clean and soft. He washed them at least ten times a day and applied lotion every time. His hands were nice to hold, nice to feel on my body and in my body, when it came to that, which it came to less and less often.

"When do we go?" I asked. I wasn't ready to reject outright a bid for a revival of our "attachment." If nothing else, Stephen was stability. He provided a structure to my life that I couldn't or wouldn't provide for myself. He was or had been more than stability in any case.

He squeezed my hand, crushed it actually. "Weekend after next."

We made dinner together that night—an omelette of tofu (Stephen didn't eat eggs), vegetables, tamari sauce, shrimp (Stephen's idea, they're full of cholesterol by the way; nobody ever reaches perfection and so much for immortality).

After dinner, Stephen worked on a case report he wanted to submit to a cardiology journal. The case was of a ninety-five-year-old man who smoked three packs a day, drank a six-pack of beer before dinner, walked ten miles back and forth to work (he was a night clerk in a hotel), ate steak and eggs at every meal, and had a fourteen-year-old daughter he'd sired. He came to see Stephen for chest pain. Turned out he'd strained the cartilage in his rib cage lifting hundred-pound weights at a gym.

I think Stephen was writing the report out of self-spite. The man had deeply depressed Stephen. That was about six months ago when our "attachment" had started to unclasp.

I holed myself up in the study with my personal computer, trying to anthropomorphize, both visually and verbally, the wild squirrel population. I lost interest after twenty minutes and turned to my-small-but-detailed pen and ink drawing of a quiet suburban town with tidy, sturdy two-story houses and large elms and oaks and wide streets, beneath which a subterranean world populated with large worms, squirrels the size of Paris rats, mutant locusts, naked men with giant penises, large busty women in SS uniforms, and children in camouflage outfits with machine guns over their shoulders were eating, shoveling, clawing, axing, and tunneling their way through the roots of elms and oaks and the foundations of refurbished Victorian houses and dragging their prey back to dead-end tunnels where they were left to rot. Meanwhile the men, women and children were engaging in erotic, unseemly and unlawful sexual acts. My drawing wasn't exactly original, but it gave me a great deal of pleasure to draw it. Too much pleasure I thought.

By bedtime, as was frequently the case, Stephen and I had spent the evening building a chasm between us which even sex, or maybe especially sex, couldn't get us across.

The next morning, Stephen asked if I could take his car in for him for an oil change and lube and if he could borrow mine. He drove out the driveway at seven a.m. in my ten-year old Toyota. At seven-thirty a.m., I was still in my bathrobe, on my fifth cup of coffee, eagerly reading the nastier details of a scandal in Washington in the morning newspaper.

Stephen called. "Who's Robert Whitman?" he asked without saying hello.

"Who?" I said. "What?"

"Robert Whitman," Stephen said. "Don't play stupid. His card was in your car."

Oh my god, I thought, the *Elvis Presley records.*

"Some guy," I said, waiting for Stephen's full throttled anger, about the records.

"What guy?" Stephen said.

"Just some guy." I said. "I met him in the Recycle Bookstore."

I heard a beeper beep in the background. Stephen cursed.

"Listen," I said. "I'm sorry about the records. I know you don't like—"

"Records?" Stephen said. He sounded distracted. "Listen Julia—all *right,* I'm coming! Julia?"

"Yes?" I said.

"I've got to go." Stephen hung up.

I took Stephen's Jaguar to the British Motors repair shop. Robert was there, leaning in the window of a Rolls Royce, which looked as if it had been sandblasted. He wore a torn white T-shirt and jogging shorts. He was drenched in sweat and his T-shirt stuck to his body, outlining a nice chest. I took a look at his chest longer than monogamy should have allowed.

Robert suddenly pulled his head out of the window and turned and saw me.

"Oh, I'm glad you're here," he said, as if he had been expecting me. My face flushed. He didn't seem to take any notice.

"Is this yours?" I asked, meaning the Rolls.

"No, it's not mine," he said, "but it has the *potential* of being mine." He smiled.

"My lover found your card in my car," I said. Robert nodded and waited.

"He was upset, I think," I said.

"You aren't sure?" he asked.

"Well, yes, no—he was definitely upset."

"Would you care to join me for lunch?" Robert inquired.

"Sure," I said. I had work to do, a great deal of work—searching for the right words, the right *concept* to allure the consumers of high-end groceries to the cooperative market whose *chevre,* so my copy claimed, was at once the cheapest on the market and the very best that money could buy, or that the goat had had to give.

I followed Robert out to a nine-foot 1957 Kelly green Cadillac with white sidewall tires.

"This is yours?" I asked.

"Climb in babe," Robert said. "We're going for a spin."

We went for a spin, to Robert's house, listening to "Are You Lonesome Tonight" and "Don't Be Cruel" on the Cadillac's tape deck.

Robert's home was a small, extremely tidy-looking pale blue wood frame house with white shutters. Robert saw my hesitation when he and I had gotten out of the Cadillac.

"Come on," he said. "I am a very reliable man, not regular, but certainly reliable." He chuckled to himself.

The inside of the house was anything but tidy. The walls were lined with books, some on bookshelves, some in stacks, the floor and furniture strewn with magazines and newspapers as well as an odd assortment of objects—a Madras suit jacket circa 1960, ceramic saltshakers in the shape of a dog and kitty cat, a water jug with a picture of Mickey Mouse on its side, a moth-eaten beret, what appeared to be an ivory cigarette holder and a tarnished silver cigarette case, a Lone Ranger and Tanto lunch box, an architect's drawing of a glass and concrete structure 24 stories high. The room looked like a rummage sale.

I didn't notice until later, weeks later, the Persian carpet with the deep pile, and the carefully restored Edwardian era leather furniture.

Robert told me to take a seat, that he'd take a quick shower and then get lunch. "I won't be a second."

I removed a pile of books including *The Jayne Mansfield Story*, as told by Jane Mansfield to somebody else, from an easy chair and sat down in it or rather was swallowed up by it. I gazed around at the collection of dog-eared books and bric-a-brac and thought about Robert in the shower. Since Stephen and I, five years before, had begun to live together, I hadn't been alone in a house with a man taking a shower, except, of course, for Stephen. It was exciting. Because it was exciting, I felt guilty.

Robert walked in in a clean T-shirt and jeans, with two plates, two glasses and a bottle of wine in his hands. He placed the food and drink on the only empty square foot of space in the room, a section of a large round coffee table that filled the center of the room and was littered as well.

"You like sushi?" he asked

"Yes," I said.

He poured the wine and handed me a plate full of rice delicacies covered with raw abalone, shrimp, and thin strips of lean meat. I did notice that the wine was good and probably expensive.

"One of life's little pleasures," he said, "is eating raw meat."

I laughed.

"So how's your *attachment?*" Robert asked, as he took a glass of wine and cleared off the seat of another easy chair with one grand shove.

"Well, we don't generally eat meat," I said. "Stephen's a cardiologist. He thinks it kills you."

"Does he?" Robert said. "Now that's interesting."

"It is?" I said.

"Mildly," Robert said. "Go on."

I thought a minute. Once you start betraying, is there an end to it?

"Do you smoke?" I asked. Robert looked at me.

"Yes, occasionally I do. I like a puff now and then."

"I smoke in the backyard, when Stephen's on business trips," I said.

"I see," Robert said, nodding. "You've got a secret life."

"Not much of one." I said.

Robert nodded again but said nothing. He ate his suchi and sipped his wine. I was acutely aware of his chest, so much so that I couldn't really eat. Guilt is an infallible appetite suppressant.

"Stephen is really a very nice man," I said. "And I do love him." Robert nodded and kept eating.

"It's just that—"

"Just that?" Robert said.

"Nothing," I said. I wanted to go home suddenly. I wanted to go home and call Stephen and say, take the afternoon off, come away with me, anywhere, just come away with me.

"Want to know the best joke of 1973?" Robert said.

I laughed. "Okay," I said. "What's the best joke of 1973?"

"What do you get when you cross Rasputin with a TV repair man?"

"I don't know," I said.

"Richard Nixon," Robert said. I laughed. Robert laughed so hard tears formed in his eyes.

"It's a stupid joke, Robert," I said.

"I know," he said. "That's why it's so funny." He started laughing all over again.

I said I had to leave. He drove me back to the repair shop. As I began to get out of the Cadillac, he reached behind the seat and pulled out *How to Dress and Undress for Your Husband.*

"I want you to have this," he said.

I took it, thanked him, and then said, "Why don't you come for dinner some time. You can meet Stephen."

"I'd be delighted," he said. "You have my card."

His *card,* I thought, driving back home, deciding maybe I wasn't cut out for love, maybe I wasn't cut out for life. I decided to be especially nice to Stephen. I hid Robert's book in my study.

I worked hard the rest of the afternoon and early evening. I created mouth-watering computer graphics of goat cheese, wine, crystal glasses, and high-priced romance, all of which, I suggested in my copy, could be had for a pittance. I waited for Stephen. He didn't come home. I gave up on the cooperative market's future and went to my drawing. I drew a Rolls Royce that was being melted from beneath by a blow torch and whose molten metal was oozing down beneath the surface of the earth. The creature who held the blow torch was a satyr.

Stephen came home at 11:30 p.m.. He looked haggard and unhappy. He dumped his briefcase by the easy chair and sank into it. He asked me to fix him some tea. I did.

One of Stephen's patients had died—a sixteen-year girl, on the waiting list for a heart transplant. She had been ill all her life.

Stephen and his colleagues had taken extraordinary measures to save her.

"I just keep thinking, there must have been something we could have done," Stephen said. I didn't say anything. It wasn't possible at times like these to jolly or comfort or cajole Stephen.

"Medicine is a pathetic profession," he said. "It's so limited ... I sometimes wonder what we are all *doing.*"

Stephen didn't really think he had failed his patient. I knew that. Even he may have known that. He had failed himself.

"Could we invite Diane over for dinner?" Stephen asked suddenly. "It's her ten-year anniversary on the job."

"Of course," I said.

"Is there somebody else we could invite, too?" Stephen asked. "I mean she's single. Is there somebody else?"

Diane, Stephen's administrative assistant, was a young mother raising a ten-year-old boy on her own. I began thinking of our friends. They were all in one manner or another attached or else they didn't deserve Diane.

"Who's Robert Whitman?" Stephen asked.

I choked on my tea. "Oh," I said, "We could invite him."

"Who is he?"

"He's—he lives and works here in town," I said. Who was he, indeed? I didn't even know what he did for a living.

Stephen reluctantly agreed. He was too dejected to put up much of a fight.

In bed later, he suddenly turned to me and asked, "Who did you buy those Elvis Presley records for?"

"Me," I said. "I like him."

"Oh," Stephen said. "I thought it was a gift. I didn't know, that you liked him I mean. You like him?"

"Go to sleep," I said.

Stephen groaned in his sleep all night long. I lay awake and thought about my drawing, my secret supply of records, and Robert. Did Stephen have secrets? Another woman? Unlikely. Stephen's secrets were the things he kept from himself. And what purpose did our secrets serve? What were we longing for? Why did we long for anything? Ninety-nine percent of the hungry, solitary, embattled world would presumably consider us extravagantly fortunate.

I called Robert the next day and invited him for dinner three days hence. He agreed immediately.

I spent the afternoon of the day cooking an anchovy and roasted tomato pasta sauce from scratch and cleaning house. The pasta sauce went fine. The house didn't. It suddenly looked boring and predictable to me. Just what Robert would expect. And why did I care what he'd expect? I wanted to hang up my drawing. Over the fireplace maybe. I didn't.

Diane arrived first and before Stephen. We sat and chatted. She made an effort to be cheerful, but life was clearly wearing her down.

Robert arrived, beaming, in a cashmere sweater, white shirt open at the neck and corduroy slacks. He was carrying a *case* of Pouilly-Fuissé wine. He set the case down and said, "You look wonderful."

I could have said the same myself, of him. But just then Stephen came walking up the brick path to the front door.

"Robert, this is Stephen. Stephen, Robert," I said.

The two men shook hands, warily I thought. I introduced Diane and Robert. We all sat down with Pouilly-Fuissé-filled wine glasses.

"So what do you do, Robert?" Stephen asked. He was more predictable than our house.

Robert laughed. "A little bit of everything. I rescue things, I guess."

"Wildlife?" Diane asked.

"No, I'm afraid not, at least not wild *animals*," Robert said with a slight bow in Diane's direction. "Stephen, Julia tells me you're a cardiologist."

Stephen gave me a dirty look. "Yes, I am," he said.

"I don't envy you," Robert said.

Diane looked at Stephen. I smiled into my napkin. Stephen looked at Robert, as if he expected to see a smirk or hear some platitude. He didn't. Robert was serious.

"Who *do* you envy?" Stephen asked.

"No one, with the possible exception of my grandmother who is safely tucked away in a nursing home, thought by the family to have lost all her senses."

Stephen laughed.

"I know exactly what you mean," he said. Then he turned red, looked at Diane, avoided looking at me, and said, "Julia and I are going to Pajaro Dunes next weekend," to nobody in particular.

Diane said, "How nice."

I said, to Diane, "To a condominium. *If* we can get it. We rent the same one, every time we go."

"There's nothing better than going to a place you know," Stephen said.

"Right," I muttered.

"I don't know," Diane said. "I've been stuck in one place for so long. I think I'd settle for anything that was different, good or bad."

"Here, here," I said.

"You haven't called the agent yet?" Stephen asked.

"No," I said.

"Jesus, Julia, it's crowded this time of year. We won't—"

Robert cleared his throat. It was a studied expectoration of phlegm. "Julia, why don't we listen to Elvis."

I laughed and blushed.

Diane said, "Elvis, God, I haven't listened to him in twenty-five years. I used t*o lov*e him. I *necked* to Elvis Presley." It was Diane's turn to blush.

"I think we can do without Elvis," Stephen said.

"No one can do without the King," Robert said. "It has been a great loss. Julia, go ahead. Stephen, have another glass of wine."

I put the first album of the seven-album set on the phonograph.

Well, since my baby left, I've found a new place to dwell. Well it's down at the end of lonely street at Heartbreak Hotel ...

Robert extended a hand to Diane.

"I wish I had Bobbie socks," she said.

She and Robert bebopped around the living room. Stephen shook his head and took a gulp of wine. I watched Robert and Diane. Bobbie socks ... there were more memories than that, not all of them good, but there were feelings, too. As I watched Robert twirl Diane on the dance floor, our carefully polished hardwood, I remembered forbidden possibilities and the unknown.

Don't be cruel, to a heart that's true. I don't want no other love. Baby, it's just you I'm thinking of.

Diane sat down laughing and out of breath. Robert grabbed my hand. "No," I said, but I didn't resist. Stephen poured himself another glass of wine.

Dont be cruel, ooh ooh ooh ... 1956 ... a sweaty hand in mine, a stranger's body twirling me underneath his arm. I laughed out loud. Robert grinned and sang, *"to a heart that's true, don't be cruel, ooh ooh ooh, to a heart that's true ..."*

Would the next dance be *slow*? Would the stranger put his arm around me? Would we dance cheek-to-cheek?

Hold me close, hold me tight, let me thrill with delight, let me know where I stand from the start ...

It was a slow dance. The stranger was restrained. Nevertheless, Stephen cut in, staggering ever so slightly.

I want you, I need you, I—I—I love you, with all my hear-ar-ar-art...

Stephen crunched me to him and muttered, "This is ridiculous. It's just dumb."

Cheek-to-cheek we slid around the dance floor. Robert and Diane clapped and then joined us.

"I thought I could live without romance," Robert sang out. *"Until you came to me ..."*

Stephen body's felt wonderful and smelled wonderful—slightly of aftershave and sweat. I closed my arms around him. I could feel his arousal.

"But now I know that I would gone on, loving you eter-er-nally," I sang.

"You know the *word*s," Stephen said to my cheek.

"Yes, Stephen," I said into his ear, "I know the words." I let my breath linger. Stephen pulled away from me slightly, hoping perhaps I wouldn't notice. (Didn't I always notice, even in 1956?) He danced me over to the dining table and took a gulp of wine. "What else do you know?" he asked.

Well, it's one for the money, two for the show, three to get ready, now go cat go, but don't you, step on my blue suede shoes ...

I grabbed Stephen's hand and started jitter-bugging.

"Enough," he said. Diane, too, gave up. We sat down at the dining table. Robert was grinning.

"Are we too old for this?" he asked.

"I was too old for this in '56," Stephen said.

"God, I haven't done this in years," Diane said, gasping for breath. "I feel like a new woman." She laughed and drank wine.

"You *are* a new woman," Robert said. "Nobody ever stays the same after the King."

"Baloney," Stephen said, but he gave Robert a strange grin.

I went for champagne. We'd chilled two bottles for Diane. I noticed we'd already drunk four bottles of wine. I returned to the dining room. The phonograph had just clicked off.

We toasted Diane.

"To a noble woman," Robert said.

"How would you know?" Diane asked, laughing.

Robert, with a smile, "One can tell these things immediately."

"To ten years of administrative bliss." Stephen said. I choked. Diane groaned. Stephen apologized. We drank. Diane toasted herself.

"To ten years of loyal servitude," she said and then gasped and looked at Stephen. Stephen apologized.

After four bottles of wine and two bottles of champagne, Robert said, "I have a house at Pajaro Dunes. Why don't we all go to Pajaro Dunes?"

"Fine idea," Stephen said.

"I'd have to bring my son." Diane said.

"Bring your son," Robert said. "Everyone is welcome."

"Excuse me," I said.

I went to the bathroom and ran cold water over a washcloth. In the mirror I saw a pale, stricken face. I wondered whose it was. I left and went to the kitchen to make coffee. The clock on the electric range said 1 a.m. I put water in a pot and set it on the range to heat. Then I heard a groan and a shuffling of feet and chairs.

In the dining room, Stephen was slumped over the table, clutching at his stomach. "I'm going to be sick," he said.

Robert pulled Stephen to his feet and said, "Where's the bathroom?"

"Over there," I said.

"Perhaps I should go," Diane whispered to me.

"Yes," I said. "Have some coffee first." I watched Robert drag Stephen into the hall.

"I've only had two glasses of wine," Diane said. You mean the three of us drank the rest, I wondered silently.

"Will Stephen be all right?" Diane asked.

"Yes, fine," I said. "It's just his ulcer."

Diane left. I went to the bathroom and found Stephen hunched over the commode, retching, while Robert gently rubbed his back.

"Is there anything I can do?" I asked.

"Get his bathrobe maybe," Robert said. "He didn't quite make it to the toilet."

Stephen stopped retching and sat down hard in front of the commode. "Ugh," he said.

"Honey, are you all right?" I asked.

Stephen laughed weakly. "That remains to be seen," he said.

"Do you want me to call Hendricks?"

"No," he said. "Hendricks, he'd kill me." Stephen shivered.

"I'll get his bathrobe," I said to Robert.

Upstairs, in the bedroom, I suddenly felt ill myself and had to steady myself against the door jamb. I got Stephen's robe and returned to the bathroom. Robert was running a hot shower. Stephen was wiping his face with a washcloth.

"Feel any better?" I asked.

Stephen smiled. "Not much."

Robert reached out for the bathrobe and said to Stephen, "Climb in. This will perk you up in no time."

I stood in the doorway. Stephen began to undress. Robert helped him. Stephen didn't seem self-conscious. Neither did Robert. I did. I watched Robert help Stephen step out of his boxer shorts as Stephen clutched his arm. Robert nearly lifted him into the shower stall and closed the glass door.

Robert looked at me and smiled. "He'll be fine," he said.

"How would you know?" I said. "You don't know anything about ulcers."

"True, but I don't think this is an ulcer."

I left them to it. I finished making the coffee and took a cup into the living room and sat down without turning on the lights. The coffee didn't seem to sober me up. It just made my heart flutter and my hands shake. I wondered if I should call Stephen's gastroenterologist. I wondered if I should be in the bathroom with him. I wondered, given his irritation in times past with my attempts at ministrations, why he preferred Robert's help now. I wondered why I wanted to go back to the bathroom.

Someone came into the living room. I hadn't heard footsteps. The intruder switched on the light.

"He's in bed," Robert said.

"Turn the light off," I groaned.

Robert dimmed the lights. "I'm going," he said.

"You can't," I said. "You've had too much to drink. Have some coffee first."

"I didn't have much to drink, Julia," he said. "Only a glass of wine and one of champagne."

So it was the two of us, I thought.

"Well," I said. "In that case—"

"I meant what I said about the house, at Pajaro Dunes. You're welcome to come next weekend."

"I have to ask Stephen," I said.

The next morning, Saturday, Stephen got a call from the hospital at 8 a.m.

"How will I face them?" he asked as he weaved through the bedroom pulling on the clothes he had worn the night before, which were encrusted with dried vomit.

"Face Diane?" I asked.

"Anybody," he said. "Everybody," he added.

I helped him into fresh clothes and made him a pot of coffee, and, when all that seemed to fail, I called the hospital and said he was ill and that they would have to get someone else.

We both got back into bed. Stephen was ill all day. We didn't fully sober up until Sunday afternoon, about the time Robert called.

Stephen answered the phone. "Well fine," he said. "Well, better … Well, let me ask Julia."

He turned to me. "Should we go to Robert's beach house instead of the condo?"

I shrugged. "We may have trouble getting the condo."

Stephen turned back to the phone. "All right, Robert. We'll join you." Stephen hung up. "He says, don't forget the King."

Stephen managed to "face" Diane Monday morning with a minimum of embarrassment. She seemed to have enjoyed herself and inquired only as to the condition of Stephen's ulcer. She declined, however, the invitation to Pajaro Dunes. We didn't hear from Robert that week, and I didn't see him even though I went to the Recycle Bookstore, twice, without buying anything, and drove by the British Motors repair shop once, wishing Stephen's jaguar would break a rod.

I finished the ad for the cooperative market. They were pleased with it. They recommended me to the local battered women's organization, the members of which were in search of a new look for their newsletter, an appeal to a wider audience. Normally, an assignment of this sort would have delighted and absorbed me. I barely touched it. I returned again and again to my drawing. I drew a two-story fake Tudor house (much like my own) in which a couple slept, while beneath the foundation of their home, a fiendish wild-haired woman hunched over an alchemist's pot funneled vapors into the heating ducts of the fake Tudor house. Though my drawing was in black ink, I imagined the vapors in purple and blue-black. I imagined them poisonous but not fatal—merely dulling to the mind, to the senses—not a narcotic that produced blissful indifference, but a drug that reduced life to a state of putrefied indifference.

Stephen, after having maintained his composure with Diane and after having managed to pass several days at the hospital without the death of a single patient, regained his professional confidence and spent long hours at work. In the evenings, however, he did not relax. He did not meditate, breathe deeply or jog ten miles. His stomach hurt, he said, but he continued to refuse to see his gastroenterologist. He returned to his case report—the man who'd defied death and been dealt merely a severe case of sore ribs.

When Stephen wasn't around, I took a peek at his case report. Despite Stephen's attempt at scientific objectivity, the report had an angry tone to it, indignation really.

Neither Stephen nor I spoke of the dinner, and neither of us spoke of the upcoming weekend. Stephen slept fitfully at night; I slept not at all. Frequently I crept back to my drawing or read *How to Dress and Undress for Your Husband.* This book, while perhaps suffering from the attitudes of a generation ago and perhaps not even having found a loyal following in that generation, nevertheless interested me a great deal. It was the attention to subtlety and detail on the author's part that struck me most. Successful seduction was a series of small moments lived to their fullest, used and enjoyed for all they were worth. Dressing and undressing for your husband wasn't for your husband alone as it turned out. The author (a woman, her picture was on the back cover of the paperback, a bottle blond in a hideous red suit) suggested that as the wife undressed for her husband, lifted her stocking-covered leg languidly to the edge of the bed, tensed its muscles and then proceeded to release the stocking from its garter and help it to slide ever so slowly down her leg, that she herself feel the stocking slither over her bare flesh, that she herself admire the long shapely leg, and feel herself that last breathless moment as she eased the stocking off her toes and dropped it to the floor. Sex, the author said (cautioned?) is not a cataclysm, it is a journey.

Stephen and I left for Pajaro Dunes Friday just after noon. Robert said he was tied up until five and would join us for dinner. He'd bring dinner. We brought fixings for breakfast and lunches and a plastic gallon jug of Maalox for Stephen. I brought my pens and ink and my drawing and the King.

We arrived at the Dunes just after one and found Robert's house—a spectacular redwood A-frame on stilts with steep staircases up to the entrance and deck. After we'd carted up the groceries and our suitcases, we stopped to take a look around.

The house was a rectangle with a huge living room, huge stone fireplace, open-countered kitchen and one very large bedroom and wall-to-wall, floor-to-ceiling windows. It was nothing at all like Robert's home in town. It was austere to the point of bareness. There were few furnishings and what there were were in beiges and muted earth tones. The house and its furnishings drew you outside of itself, to the beach and the Pacific and to the slough along the fields of artichokes and strawberries and to the mountains beyond.

"My God," Stephen said, as we stood in the bedroom looking out. I embraced him from behind. He took my hands and wrapped my arms around himself. "I think I needed this," he said and laughed.

I freed my hands and began unbuttoning his shirt.

"Where are we supposed to sleep?" he asked.

There were large divans in the living room. I hadn't considered it a problem.

"Lie down, stupid," I said. I shoved him on the bed and climbed on top of him.

"But if Robert," Stephen began.

In the middle of Robert's huge bed, surrounded by the best that nature had to offer, Stephen and I made love—stiffly, awkwardly, self-consciously. Stephen, at least, found something in it to give him pleasure, of a sort. I didn't.

It was dusk when we woke up from a nap. We could make out lights on the Santa Cruz and Monterey coasts. The sun was edging below the horizon in brilliant streams of orange and magenta.

We weren't entirely finished dressing when Robert arrived.

"Hello, hello," he shouted as he came in. "I see you've been spending your time wisely," he added when he found us in the bedroom.

"Sorry," Stephen said.

"No need," Robert said. "How's the ulcer?"

"Fine," Stephen said.

"Say that like you mean it," Robert said.

"What about dinner?" I asked.

"Okay, not so fine," Stephen said.

Robert nodded. "So you're hungry, Julia. I shouldn't wonder."

I laughed. "Robert, stop this."

"I've planned a light meal—consommé—homemade, a good crisp salad, bread, and Perrier. Plus dessert if anybody cares to eat it."

"That sounds good to me," Stephen said.

"Julia, you look disappointed," Robert said.

"It's just that—"

"Just that?" Stephen and Robert said simultaneously. They looked at one another and laughed.

"I'm hungry," I said. "I was hoping maybe for a little meat."

"You'll get that," Robert said, "but I was considering the gastric status of one of my guests."

We helped him fix dinner. It didn't take much time. We took it to the table, kept the lights down low, and watched the sky turn ten shades of blue to black.

"So what *do* you do?" Stephen asked.

"A little bit of everything really," Robert said. "I'm not being evasive. It's just that I don't have to do anything in particular."

"You've got money," Stephen said.

Robert laughed. "Quite a bit."

"I wish I had money," Stephen said.

"You wouldn't know what to do with yourself," I said. "Besides you do have money."

"If you really had money," Robert said, "you wouldn't want to be a cardiologist?"

"I think I'd rather not have the choice. Life isn't so bad anyway."

"My, what an enthusiastic recommendation for the human condition," Robert said.

"Maybe we're just spoiled," I said.

Robert gave me a direct look. "I saw your drawing," he said.

"How?! Where?" My hand froze on my glass of Perrier.

"What drawing?" Stephen asked.

"I don't think what I saw was born of decadence," Robert said.

"What drawing?" Stephen asked again, looking from Robert to me and back again.

"Just a drawing," I said. "Something I fool around with on my own time."

"You brought it?" Robert asked.

"No, yes."

"Well, may I see it for God's sake," Stephen said.

I went and got the drawing and returned to the living room. I stuck it in front of Stephen's nose and sat down, giving him a look that dared him to make a comment.

He stared at the drawing. Robert got up to look at it over Stephen's shoulder. Stephen said nothing. He didn't move, for a least sixty seconds. Then his eyes welled up with tears.

"I didn't know," he said. "I never knew."

"It's nothing," I said. "Nothing at all."

"It's a very remarkable drawing," Robert said. "More remarkable each time you look at it."

"You hate it so much?" Stephen asked. He didn't mean the drawing.

"Do you?" I asked.

Stephen shook his head. But he wasn't saying no.

"If you'll excuse me," I said. I went out onto the deck and watched the moon rise and dark clouds flow in from the north. I wanted a cigarette. I picked chips of sealant off the redwood deck. I looked back once, back into the dimly lit beach home with a fire burning and saw Stephen with his head in his hands bent over the dining table. Robert sat next to him, sipping Perrier. They didn't seem to be speaking.

When the wind came in with the dark clouds, I went inside. Robert made coffee (decaffeinated) and played the piano solos of Beethoven's Emperor Concerto for us on the stereo. *Adagio un poco mosso* ... it was not funereal music, but it was capable tearing out your heart. The three of us sat silently, warming our feet by the fire, looking out on dark ocean turned silver by moonlight breaking through the clouds, listening to the kind of perfection that for some brought exhilaration, joy, and wonder, but for us? Robert, eyes shut, seemed transported. Stephen stared into the night. I wanted to go visit Beethoven.

What was inside of you? I would have asked. Please tell me, I would have wept.

At the final chord, Robert stood up, turned off the stereo, and said, "Use my bed. I'll sleep here."

Stephen and I undressed, showered, and got in bed without speaking. We lay side by side without sleeping.

"Robert says he loves life," Stephen said suddenly. I said nothing. "Because Beethoven was once alive and so was Elvis Presley, that makes him love life."

I took Stephen's hand. The room seemed huge. Through the curtainless windows, the dark, now moonless night enveloped us in black empty space. We fell asleep hand in hand.

In the morning the three of us took a somber walk along the beach looking out at the gray waves and looking up at the heavy black clouds. A sea otter, a member of a nearly extinct species, swam up near the shore, dived into the foaming sea, and surfaced again. He rolled over on his back and began cracking a clam shell again his chest. He bobbed in the water and seemed untroubled by our close proximity and the close proximity of the waves that threatened to crash over him. We stood and watched as he dove and surfaced and rollicked in the water.

"One of life's little and many pleasures," Robert said. He smiled, to himself.

As we neared the beach house, the clouds let loose in a deluge. The wind rose and pounded rain drops against the windows and seemed to rock the house. We went inside. Stephen built a fire. I made coffee. We all sat down in the living room and began to watch the rain.

"Let's do something," Stephen said suddenly. "*Anything.*"

Robert put Elvis on the stereo.

Stephen groaned. "I don't consider that something," he said with a weak laugh.

Robert extended his hand to me.

"No," I said, as he dragged me to the center of the living room.

Don't, don't, don't, that's what you say
Each time I hold you this way

Robert pulled me into an embrace. I felt his arousal immediately. I looked over at Stephen. He was watching us.

If you think that this is just a game I'm playing
Il you think that I don't mean every word I say
Don't, don't, don't, feel that way

Stephen, cut in. He smelled faintly of salt and sweat.

This you can believe I will never leave you Heaven knows I won't

Stephen and I danced, close, cheek-to-cheek. When the song was over, I wrenched myself free and sat down in an easy chair by myself. Stephen sat down on the sofa next to Robert.

"Let's liven this up," Robert said.

"Stop it, Robert," I said, laughing

"Don't," Robert said and smiled.

"Hey," Stephen said, "I just remembered an Elvis song! *Such a Night*."

"How very convenient that I happen to have it right here," Robert said.

It was a night, ooh what a night it was, it really was such a night

"That's it!" Stephen said.

The moon was bright, oh how bright, it really was, it really was such a night
The night was alive with stars above
Ooh when she kissed me I had to fall in love.

Stephen sat on the couch and actually sang along. *"Oh it was a kiss, ohh what a kiss it was, it really was such a kiss.*

"Oh how she could kiss, oh what a kiss it was it really was such a kiss."

Robert and Stephen sang the chorus and laughed out loud. It was the first time in a long time I had heard Stephen laugh out loud. Maybe I had never heard Stephen laugh out loud.

Just the thought of her lips sets me afire

I reminisce and I'm filled with desire

Robert and Stephen sang to me, grinning, giggling, like two drunken teenagers.

"Dance, Julia," Robert shouted.

I laughed, but shook my head. Robert grabbed Stephen's hand. "Come on, we'll show her."

"No," Stephen said, but he didn't resist, not much anyway.

Such a night, Elvis sang out. And then, *Love me tender, love me sweet, never let me go ...*

Robert held Stephen in a sloppy embrace as they staggered around the living room.

You have made my life complete and I love you so ...

I looked out the window. The rain had let up. It was drizzling. "I'm going for a walk," I said. I left without looking back.

The beach was deserted. The sea otter had gone to look for more plentiful pastures of clam beds. The wind was icy. I walked into it and away from the beach house—from Stephen, from Robert, from life's little pleasures. I walked, staggered by my own cowardice, along a gray endless beach. And then I walked for some time and some miles just looking two feet in front of my feet through the fine gray sand. But eventually, I looked out at the bleak sea again. The horizon was obscured by the gray sameness of the water and sky. I realized that all this would come soon enough. I turned back.

At the house there was no one in the living room. In the bedroom, Robert and Stephen were lying next to each other, against large pillows, a sheet covering them to their waists. They hadn't heard me come in. I watched them. Stephen was looking out at the sea. Robert was looking at Stephen. Together like that, unclothed, they seemed younger, and vulnerable, so vulnerable that it scared me.

"I don't know," Stephen said to Robert. "Different, better maybe."

Then he turned and saw me. "Oh God, Julia!"

"It's all right," I said. I smiled.

"Would you care to join us?" Robert said.

"No!" Stephen said.

"Climb in," Robert said.

I climbed in and over Stephen and got under the covers, fully clothed, in between the two of them.

Stephen began to undress me. Robert helped him. They uncovered me bit by bit. I felt the texture of two different skins against my own—one soft and smooth, one rougher. They undressed me and then they made love to me.

Afterwards I fell sleep in their arms.

I woke at dusk. Stephen was sitting up in bed, looking out at the sea. He looked over at me, smiled and pointed. The sea otter had returned. It was rollicking in a gray-green sea. Robert was gone

"What did you mean, different?" I asked.

"I don't know. I didn't know then anyway."

"And now?" I asked.

"As if I just woke up."

The three of us never spent a weekend like that again. But when we returned to town, Stephen tore up his case report, and I stuck my drawing in a closet, turned my computer off and began to paint. Robert continued to rescue life's detritus, but he began to restore it as well. His debris ended up in the homes of nervous doctors and uneasy painters and in the hands of children for whom it was a delight and comfort. And, despite the fact that we were all doomed one day to be life's detritus, we found ways to survive, even thrive, in the company of each other, and with the incalculable aid of Beethoven and the King.

THE IMPORTANCE OF STARS IN THE SKY

"Harry, it's green," I said.

"Not for long," he said.

"The stoplight, Harry."

Harry ignored me. He was staring at a eucalyptus tree that had blown over in a late-winter early-spring storm the week before. It lay sprawled along the curb on the opposite side of the street.

There were a lot of eucalyptus in town and a lot had blown over in the storm. Someone had had the bright idea thirty years ago to plant them all over the place, in town and on the University campus nearby. It was just when the town had started growing, when aeronautical engineers and electrical engineers were moving in by the dozens, and somebody had forgotten that eucalyptus trees are notoriously unstable. So every winter since then they've been falling on cars and into streets and on top of all the nice one-story three-bedroom houses with all-electric kitchens that were built at the same time the trees were planted.

"I'm gonna make a U," Harry said. "I want to get a closer look."

"Please," I said. "I'm going to be late."

"So what," he said. "Those meetings are like soap operas. You could miss forty of them and not miss a thing."

"Stop it," I said.

"Sorry," he said immediately.

The meeting for which I was now going to be very late was a committee meeting of Citizens for Nonintervention in El Salvador, otherwise known as CITNES. Harry hated the group. Well, no, maybe that's too strong. Its existence upset him. The need for its existence upset him a lot.

"Look," he said. "It'll just take a minute."

"Okay," I said, but I knew it wouldn't.

We stopped at the curb and climbed out. I stood there looking at something that was to me a sort of interesting natural disaster. Harry stood looking at it as if the world had come to an end. He rubbed one long silvery leaf gently between his thumb and forefinger. You'd have thought it was a piece of Chinese silk.

"It's dying," he said. "It's already dying."

"I suppose so," I said, starting to get worried.

He knelt by the trunk.

"Twenty-five years old," he said. "Dead at twenty-five."

I believed him—about the twenty-five years, I mean. Harry knew a lot about trees. When he'd come back home to Iowa from Vietnam, he'd announced to his family that he was not going to be a lawyer as he had intended. He was not quite sure what he was going to do, but he was damn sure it'd have nothing to do with people. Then the town tree surgeon was injured, and Harry offered to help him out, and then Harry just stayed with trees. He'd learned a lot about them in the last thirteen years.

But for Harry, trees were more than a business. He never said so, but you could tell. On our second date, Harry and I drove 250 miles, the last ten on a dirt road, to see a 1500-year-old Juniper tree—a big, solid, magnificent tree—standing all alone on a Sierra Nevada ridge. When Harry saw it he cried, and I almost did, too. I loved Harry from that moment on.

And you could tell with the eucalyptus, too. Harry leaned over the twenty-five-year-old tree and ran his hand down its trunk as if he were making love to a woman. Harry never touched a human that way. But he had that look in his eyes, the look he got when he forgot where he was, when he'd burn his hand or cut himself without knowing it. So I said, "Harry, I have to go. Come on, I have to go." And I said it as if I were angry, you had to do that, to get him out of it.

And he said, "Okay, okay."

He drove me to the CITNES office, telling me on the way that he'd seen a good buy on floribunda rose bushes and asking me if we could plant some, at which point I reminded him of the size of our garden (ten by twelve feet). We lived in one quarter of an old brown-shingled house, built before the eucalyptus were planted. There were four houses just like it on the block, all buried behind huge trees. It had been my flat originally. Harry had moved in two years ago.

One day he had come to top a redwood tree in the front yard. He had moved to California from Iowa six months before because business was flagging, and he was getting edgy and because a Vietnam buddy in town told him we had a lot of trees and a lot of people who took their trees seriously. The buddy had been right. We had redwoods, maples, pines, elms, palms, cypresses, apricot trees, cherry trees, peach trees and, of course, the eucalyptus—in backyards, front yards, and lining almost every street. Some of us had money, and those who did wanted to spend it on their trees.

Harry and I talked the day he topped my redwood tree and then we talked some more. We seemed to hit it off, which took us by surprise because we were both stubborn about independence and love-shy, too, but for different reasons. We kept talking, though, and then Harry began moving in bit by bit. He'd leave behind a shirt or a book or a thick rope that he needed to do his job. Before either of us realized it, he was living with me fulltime, and, when we realized it, nothing was ever said, but I, at least, was pleased. Harry, with his large frame and love of flowers and trees, quietly filled up the huge silent spaces in my otherwise small flat.

When we got to the CITNES office that day, Harry said suddenly, "You can't do a fucking thing about El Salvador. If they want to go in, they will. They're already there."

Harry wasn't being mean. I knew that. In fact, he probably would have sold his mother into slavery not to believe what he had just said.

I patted his arm and said, "I think it's worth trying."

"Don't patronize me," he said.

"Okay," I said, "but don't stop me."

He laughed. "Who could stop you, Jan? A tank couldn't stop you. And anyway, the tank wouldn't want to."

He was right about that. I was stubborn, sometimes stupidly.

Harry pecked my cheek and drove off. I was meeting Mona, my friend Mona, at the office. She and I were the leaflet writing committee. We'd been together in Berkeley years back and were long-time patriots in the war against evil. But Mona was serious. Nothing had struck her funny in twenty years except the resignation of Richard Nixon.

The CITNES office was a room at the back of a garage, loaned out to us by a 70-year-old woman who had never recovered from the death of her first husband in World War II. Mona was sitting between battered bookshelves and fourteen cartons of "literature."

"Read this," she said without preamble as she handed me five pages of legal-sized, single-spaced typewritten text.

"Mona," I said. "Nobody's going to read this. It's longer than a front page article in *The New York Times*."

"Um," she said. "Had a fight with Harry?"

Mona disliked Harry.

"Harry and I are getting along fine," I said, which was mostly true.

"Sure," she said.

"Stop it, Mona."

"Okay, okay," she said. "I'm just thinking of you. It must be tough. I mean, he's so—cold."

"Stop it, Mona," I said again.

She stopped and apologized.

Harry wasn't cold, just distracted maybe, just distant, especially with Mona. It wasn't really her fault. It wasn't Harry's fault either. They just couldn't get along. One evening, for example, when the three of us had polished off a half gallon of cheap red wine and were lounging somewhat inebriatedly in Harry's and my living room, Mona asked, I suppose because we had reached some sort of intimacy uncommon to us before, "What was it like, really?" meaning the war.

Now that may seem like a tactless question, maybe even cruel. It did to me. But I understood why Mona had asked it. She and I had spent years—years and years—in a twenty-hour-a-day fight to stop a war about which we really knew nothing. Somehow it was important to know. I guess that, thirteen years later, Mona had finally worked up the courage to ask somebody who did know what they knew.

Harry sobered up in a second when he heard the question and rose up from the floor with one movement and said, "Eat a glass, Mona. Then you'll know."

After that, Mona and I stayed friends, but she wouldn't have much to do with Harry. She couldn't forgive him for the truth.

So in the office that day, I accepted Mona's apology and agreed to do a major paring job on her five-page polemic and didn't agree although didn't disagree to attend the CITNES fundraiser on the following day.

By the time I got home, Harry was home as well. He'd bought the rose bush so we planted it. It took a fair amount of work since rose bushes need a hole the size of a ditch for their roots. Once it was in the ground, Harry watered it carefully, looking very pleased with himself.

"Let's celebrate," he said. He disappeared into the flat and returned with a chilled bottle of white wine and two glasses. He'd been prepared. Harry filling up the silent spaces again. We sat on our small porch and looked at our rose bush, which was still in the bare root stage and was, at the moment, scrawny and unimposing. But Harry looked at it as if it were the paintings on the ceiling of the Sistine Chapel.

"You know, the floribundas used to be wild," Harry said. "So did the eucalyptus, at least in Australia ... they've civilized them," he added, almost with a sneer.

"Um," I said.

"If I had a big garden, I'd plant it with wild roses and eucalyptus trees."

"You wouldn't have many visitors," I said, laughing. "Wild roses are ferocious."

"That's the point," he said and he laughed, too.

We sat for a time in silence. A hummingbird buzzed by to sip from a feeder. Harry didn't notice. He was in his overgrown garden.

I wanted to ask him if I were included in the garden, but it seemed like such a rare moment of peace for him that, even though I wanted to and needed to ask, I didn't.

The light outside gradually grew dimmer and the evening air cooler, and we were just about to go in and have supper when we heard a knock on the front door.

It was Mona.

"You left my tome at the office," she said as she stood uneasily at the door.

"Come in," I said.

"Well thanks, no. I mean, I shouldn't."

"Come on in," said Harry from the kitchen. You could tell from his voice, as if the life had been drained out of it, that the mood was gone, whatever mood he'd been in.

"Have some wine," I said.

Mona came in and sat down. I got a fresh glass and poured her what was left of the wine from the open bottle.

"I collected forty dollars for CITNES today," she said. "Forty dollars, at Safeway no less."

In the kitchen, Harry mashed something in the food processor with such vigor that both Mona and I jumped.

"Why don't you have dinner?" I asked.

"No, best not to," Mona whispered.

"No, please," I begged. "I'll get some more wine."

I took Mona's glass and mine and went into the kitchen. "Harry," I hissed, "Make an effort."

He was taking zucchini out of the refrigerator. He glared at me and then slammed shut the refrigerator door so hard that the whole thing wobbled.

"Harry," I said. "I love Mona. I can't abandon her."

Harry's knees began to buckle under him, and he grabbed the sides of the refrigerator for support.

"Harry—"

"I'm okay," he said as he broke into a sweat.

I reached for Harry.

"Don't. Don't do anything."

"I'll tell Mona to go."

"No," he said. He sounded as if he were stifling a scream. He took a deep breath and turned from the refrigerator to me.

"No," he said again, more calmly. "You're right. I'll try. I will." He turned back to his zucchini and, with a perfectly steady hand, began cutting uneven, oddly-sized slices.

The three of us had dinner, and Mona, bless her heart, asked Harry if he could do anything with an old oak in her front yard that had lost a limb in the storm. And Harry was ready to help right then and would have if we hadn't reminded him that it was dark outside. Everything was fine and almost congenial until Mona asked, timidly, but asked nevertheless, "Harry, are you going to bring Jan to the CITNES party?"

Harry said "no" and rose immediately to clear the table though we weren't done eating.

I should have known. Mona couldn't help it. We were impossibly different. I wanted peace—at any price, or nearly any price—in my home. Mona wanted peace—at any price—in the world.

So Mona persisted.

"General Perez is going to be there. He was with the army. Now he's speaking out against the government. You should hear the stories, Harry. They're incredible."

"I know the stories, Mona," said Harry. "And they aren't stories."

"Sorry," said Mona. She had gotten the point.

But now Harry persisted.

"Have you ever been to a slaughter-house?" he asked.

"No, and I don't think I'd want to go," said Mona, hoping to stop what she had started.

"You should," Harry said. "The cow you ate for dinner screeched his way to death. That's a story. Nobody dies quietly."

That made Mona and I nearly lose our dinners. Harry did lose his dinner. But he waited until Mona had left, which was shortly, and then he closed himself up in the bathroom and retched for a long, long time. I sat on the porch listening to him and shivering under an April night sky that was full of stars. I wondered suddenly if there were stars in the sky over DaNang in 1968 or in Morazan province in 1985. I supposed that there were, but nobody took the time to notice.

But I heard Harry retch in a way that sounded as if he were being torn apart, and it seemed inconceivable then that there could have been stars.

But the retches stopped finally and Harry appeared on the porch, seemingly in one piece. He sat down and said, "Apologize to Mona for me, okay?"

I nodded. "I think maybe Mona should apologize to you," I said.

"It's not Mona who owes me an apology," he said, and he got up suddenly and knelt down by the rose bush. He began patting the soil around its small trunk and then took a bit of soil in his hand and rubbed it between his thumb and forefinger.

"Just right," he said.

"The moisture?" I asked, thinking he was talking to me. He wasn't.

"You'll do fine," he said. "We'll feed you. Help you grow." He smiled and I knew he was lost again.

But then he suddenly turned away from the bush and said, "Let's go inside. It's freezing. Let's build a fire."

He took my hand in his. It dwarfed my own. His hands were huge and strong but gentle when he wanted them to be.

A fire seemed stupid in April (it wasn't really freezing), but we built one anyway, and, once it had begun to warm us up, Harry began telling me about his mother, who was still a housewife in Iowa, and how, if he had felt bad as a kid, his mother would make a fire, even in ninety-degree weather, to cheer him up. And he remembered that at sixteen he had told his mother that he didn't need any more fires and how hurt she had been. But when he came back from Vietnam with the entire back side of his body blown off and after he had spent two years in a VA hospital having his body rebuilt, which was at best miserable and at worst painful beyond bearing, he went home and his mother built a lot of fires.

"Fires are natural," he said. "Trees to wood to ashes."

We went to bed that night contented, I think. At least Harry's grunt as he rolled away from me sounded content. I stroked the lumpy flesh of his back and buttocks for a while. He had been pieced together so that his back was like a quilt with bits of skin and muscle taken from elsewhere and stitched together.

He fell asleep immediately and I drifted into a half-wake, half-sleep dream in which Harry and I were walking along the boardwalks that crisscrossed the salt marshes near the bay. But we weren't walking leisurely; we were nearly running, and Harry kept checking the sky. He knew the danger, but I didn't. But I knew from the look on his face, that whatever it was, it was terrible. And then suddenly Harry screamed at me to duck, and I tried to but lost my balance and fell into the marsh and started to sink. I screamed, too, and in the same moment heard the drone and saw the planes, black planes with sinister beak-like noses, and Harry saw them, too, and he lay flat on the boardwalk and reached out to grab me. I held up an arm, but Harry grabbed me round the neck, with his powerful hands, and, as he pulled to free me from the clutches of the marsh grasses and mud, he began to choke me and the more he tried to save me, the closer he seemed to killing me. I couldn't breathe. I tried to scream again but couldn't.

Then I woke up and still couldn't breathe. Harry's hands *were* around my neck, and he was screaming, over and over again, "Why didn't you duck, why didn't you duck, you cock-sucking son-of-a-bitch." I tried frantically to pull Harry loose, but he was too strong. I couldn't budge him. So I kneed him in the groin. That woke him up.

He flung himself away from me, curled into a ball and groaned and groaned again. I clambered out of bed and stood shaking and gasping and crying at the foot of it. Harry groaned again.

"Jan?" he whispered.

"I'm here," I said.

"Was it you—was it you?"

"No—yes."

"Oh Gaaaaaawd."

I think Harry woke up the entire block.

"Don't," I said. I reached out and touched one of his feet, which was cold.

He jerked it free and said, "Go away—go away."

I left Harry. I sat the rest of the night on the living room couch with a cup of tea and a starlit sky to keep me company. I didn't hear a sound out of him all night. I don't know how he managed to survive the hours until dawn. I'm not sure how I did either, but it had something to do with those stars. That is, that I was seeing the light from stars that were already dead and seeing the light from stars that had just burst apart into millions of tiny meteors and that I was not seeing and would never see, nor would my grandchildren nor my great-grandchildren, the light of stars that had just been born. That knowledge made me feel like a mere speck of something. But it also made me think that at least I got to be a speck and got to watch it all, even things that had disappeared.

Harry emerged from the bedroom at dawn, walked past me without seeing me and disappeared into the kitchen. I heard the radio go on and the agricultural report start.

The agricultural report came on at 6:30 a.m. every Sunday morning. It was Harry's favorite radio show. Oroville Skidmore, an expert apparently, spent an hour telling his friends and neighbors when to plant tomatoes and artichokes, and the danger of cutting back fruit trees too severely, and when to pick Valencia oranges, and where to procure non-toxic spray for their rose bushes. And the friends and neighbors would call in with questions. Harry loved Oroville Skidmore. He had called in himself a time or two.

When I heard Oroville's gravelly voice that morning, it was the most reassuring sound I could have heard. If Oroville had time to worry about mildew on roses, surely the night before must have been just a bad dream and only that.

Harry came into the living room with two cups of coffee and a wan smile on his face.

"You okay?" he asked.

I nodded. "How about you?"

"I'll take you to the party," he said as he sat down. "After I find a place to live."

"What's wrong with here?" I asked.

"You know what's wrong. I almost killed you. Don't pretend differently," he said.

"Harry, I don't want you to move. Sleep on the couch until things get sorted out."

"Suppose things don't get sorted out?"

"They will."

Harry looked at me, hard, as if he thought by staring at me something would be revealed to him.

"Why?" he asked.

"Because I love you and I can't—" I stopped myself.

"Can't what?" he asked.

"Nothing," I said. Can't abandon you was what I had meant to say.

So he was to stay and sleep on the couch, and we would see if "things got sorted out."

That evening we went to the party, which was at Mona's big old Victorian house. Mona had decorated it with remnants of the "Sixties." As Harry and I came in, people were lounging on paisley covered pillows the size of Pontiacs, walking into bedraggled Boston ferns hung from the ceiling with massive macrame ropes, and avoiding looking at, with some difficulty, eleven four-by-eight foot posters of Chinese, women, Afro-Americans, Africans, South Americans, Central Americans and Vietnamese taking up arms against their oppressors, which were plastered on every available inch of wall space in Mona's large living room.

Harry headed immediately to the kitchen where there was "mountain red" wine and guacamole dip, and I circulated among acquaintances and friends. I lost track of Harry for awhile until Mona took me aside to tell me that he was getting happily drunk in the kitchen and appeared to be having a good time, which seemed unlikely, and I would have gone to investigate, but Mona just then called us all to order and announced that General Alfonso Perez Garcia would speak for a few minutes.

A remarkably small, meek-looking man with a salt and pepper mustache joined Mona at her side. He began to speak in halting English, for which he apologized, but his message got through to us—in graphic detail. He spoke of the methods of torture used by the military and government police, of which he was aware but in which he claimed not to be a participant. The tortures ranged from merely beating people with rubber hoses to pouring acid on their open wounds or hacking their limbs off piece by piece. Nobody ever talked, he said. Nobody. They screamed, but they didn't talk. That had given him pause. And what had given him further pause was when he incurred the wrath of his superior by sparing the life of the son of a neighbor, who also happened to be a guerrilla of some note, and was tortured himself. General Perez was missing a few fingers and all of his fingernails.

One day, after his torture but when he still maintained his rank, he spoke to an old woman who sold fresh rolls on a street corner. He had bought a roll from this woman every day of his life for fifteen years. He had never spoken to her until the day he decided to ask her what she thought of her country. Perez was in uniform. The old woman looked at the uniform and said, "You can kill me. I'll die soon anyway. But I'd join them if I could—the compañeros. I would join them for my children, for my grandchildren. You've robbed us—the Yanquis have robbed us. I've got nothing left but these hands and these feet."

General Perez had looked at her hands and her feet. They were twisted and swollen from age and arthritis.

Then the old woman had looked Perez right in the eyes and said, "But that is what will kill you. Hands and feet. You shouldn't have left us our hands and feet. You're strangling. You just don't feel it yet, but the hands and feet will crush the life out of you."

She had spat on the ground then and walked away.

General Perez quietly fled to the United States the next day.

I saw Harry out of the corner of my eye. His expression was unreadable.

Perez asked for questions. Nobody had any. We'd heard about all we wanted to know. But Harry had one.

"How do you live with yourself?" he asked.

Mona jumped up immediately.

"I think the General needs a rest now. I—"

"But—" Harry began.

"I'll answer that," said the General. "To live with what I did is not easy—not easy at all," he said easily.

General Perez' words had put a considerable pall over the festivities. Everyone headed immediately for the "mountain red" wine and even the General got slightly drunk, and so, although raw horror wasn't easy to ignore, we all began to have a reasonably good time—until the scream.

Although it was a wail that was more animal than human, I knew it was Mona's.

There was an immediate crush around the door to the kitchen and then a woman fled from the door and raced towards the bathroom with her hand held to her mouth as a man said "Jesus" and another whispered "God."

I walked calmly to the kitchen door and, when I got there, the crush of people suddenly parted, and I thought it was because Mona was in trouble (I could hear her sobs) and that people knew we were friends, but when I saw the kitchen, I knew differently.

There was blood—lots and lots of blood—on the floor, on the table, and all over Harry who sat absolutely still with one hand lying palm up and from which a remarkable amount of blood continued to gush forth. Mona stood across from him holding a bloody butcher knife, which she looked at suddenly and then flung into the sink with another wail.

"Call an ambulance," I said coolly.

Someone did. At least he said that he did.

I grabbed a wad of paper towels and tried to stem the flow of blood. Harry had tried to saw off his thumb. I could see muscle and bone and tendon. I pressed the paper towels into the wound, which made him groan but he didn't move. He didn't even flinch.

The ambulance never came so I drove Harry the two miles to the University hospital through stop signs and red lights, and Mona followed behind with her hand laid solidly on her horn.

Harry was stitched up. It took a long while. He had done quite a bit of damage. There was concern among the specialists who had gathered that he might lose the use of his thumb. Harry didn't care. He didn't even appear to notice. He looked as if he were more interested in watching the scenes being played out just behind his eyeballs.

But when his hand had been bandaged, he stood up without the slightest bit of difficulty and walked right out of the Emergency room.

I followed him. Mona started to follow me. I told her to stay put. She began to object, but I said no in a way that stopped her. Harry had headed straight across the campus. He walked on absolutely steady legs, which amazed and calmed me a bit. I kept following and realized that he was heading for a dense grove of eucalyptus. He walked into the middle of it and sat down. I followed him in and sat down a foot away from him. It was silent in the grove and Harry was silent. I couldn't even hear him breathing. It was dark, silent and peaceful, and above us the sky was filled with stars.

"Harry, honey," I said. "You can't be a tree."

"I know," he said.

"What is it?" I asked. "Is it one thing or all the things?"

"All the things," he said.

I said nothing.

"You should leave me," Harry added.

"No," I said. "I won't."

He said nothing.

"Harry," I said. "Look at all the stars."

He looked up then and sighed, and then he lay back on the down of dry leaves. I lay down next to him, and he wrapped his uninjured arm around me. We lay there looking up through the gentle, safe, silent eucalyptus and watched the stars move across the sky.

Harry's hand healed eventually, but the wound left a big scar and his thumb was permanently stiff. He did seem to cheer up a bit, though, as always, it was hard to tell. Our lives didn't change much, but I, at least, had come to know during that night under the eucalyptus when Harry held me and silently endured the throbbing in his wounded hand, that, as cruel at it was to have stars above the

Western Front or Hill 330 in a Vietnamese jungle, it was also essential, as essential as it was not to abandon the sight of them or the sight of anybody else.

THE COLLECTED CORRESPONDENCE OF JO LYNNE DUCKET AND EDWARD R. BECK

July 26th

Dear Ms. Ducket:

I am writing to tell you that I liked your book a lot. Your stories all seem to be about love, which is a subject that interests me. And we have something in common; I write too!

I was thinking, Ms. Ducket, that you might like to correspond. I realize that you didn't move to Northern California to be bothered, but I have an idea. I enclose a stamped self-addressed picture postcard of Tinkerbell at Disneyland (this is one of my favorites). Just check the boxes as you wish and drop it in the mailbox. No obligation. Looking forward to hearing from you.

Yours,

Ed Beck
General Delivery
Needles, California

Postmarked September 14th

___I do not wish to correspond.

___I wish to correspond.

Maybe

September 16th

Dear Ms. Ducket,

Thank you for your letter, well postcard. I think it's wise to think these things over. Nothing is safe these days, not even introductions. I read your book again. It was even better the second time around (which is more than I can say for love) (and not that it wasn't wonderful the first time around), but what depresses me (and this is not a criticism since my psychological state is hardly your responsibility) but if you take, for example, your characters, the Bradley's, after fifteen years of marriage, children and thousands of Sundays eating pancake breakfasts together, they're still at *introductions*.

What's really pathetic, Ms. Ducket, is the human capacity (well my capacity) to have a perfectly reasonable conversation with somebody in an elevator and then sound like an aphasic when I'm trying to talk to a woman friend.

Even so, I send along a picture postcard of the Glass Slipper Motel in downtown Needles (They have magic finger beds!) Looking forward to your response.

Ed Beck

Postmarked October 15th

I moved to "Northern California" because:

___ it is more dignified than "Southern California."

___ I like it.

___ to be alone.

_X_ Other (Please specify

October 18th

Dear Ms. Ducket:

I knew they were stupid questions. But introductions are always stupid. How can you say anything interesting or ask anything interesting when you don't have any idea what the other person would call interesting? And the pitiful thing is, Ms. Ducket, that's only the beginning.

So maybe it's stupid to want to correspond. But I do. To tell you the truth, I spent all my money on whiskey, and my woman friend threw me out (I don't blame her). So I bought a trailer and hauled it out to the Mojave so I could sober up. Spot, my dog, is very loyal and likes to drink, but he doesn't write books. I'm not drinking now which leaves a lot of time on my hands. If you'll continue to correspond, I promise I won't try to be interesting. You don't have to be interesting either (unless you want to be).

So I enclose a picture postcard of a Delta Airlines 747. (Do you have a mailbox, Ms. Ducket, or do you walk to the post office each day, have a soda at the fountain in the Rexall Drug and then walk home?) Oh sorry, just check the boxes. I don't expect anything more. I've always expected too much of people. Take for example my woman friend. No, nevermind. Hope to hear from you soon.

Yours, Ed Beck

Postmarked November 12th

When I write, I sit

___At my desk at the window looking out on the brown hills and the sea beyond.

___In an easy chair looking through an open door at the peonies and marigolds in the kitchen garden.

___In the local saloon, at the back, drinking a beer and watching the boys play pool.

X_Other (Please specify)

November 14th

Dear Ms. Ducket:

So you write at the kitchen table? It's Formica, isn't it—red with a chrome trim? Do you keep salt and pepper shakers on the table, and a little plastic bin for napkins? No, I'm not going to ask you that. I'm rationing myself. Do you drink black coffee and smoke cigarettes? No, I won't ask you that either. Do you—well probably not—what I mean is, I don't suppose you've ever been writing along, content and cozy, when suddenly, out of nowhere, comes the thought that not only are introductions stupid but that your writing, what you *do,* is nonsense, pointless, a void. I guess not, not someone like you.

I'm not drinking, not a drop. Spot had a bout of the DT's and my hands shake but we're planted here in our trailer steady as rocks. I have a kitchen, a bed, and conveniences even. Right now I'm sitting in my doorway, Spot's lying at my feet, and I can hear coyotes and see the moon. Hank Williams is on the radio: "The silence of a fallen star lights up a purple sky." God, he can sing.

I'm enclosing a picture postcard of John Wayne at the Grand Canyon. Too bad he didn't fall in when he had the opportunity (just kidding). Anyway, I want to know what music you like, sort of fill in the background details.

I'll be thinking about you picking this up at the post office and going to the Rexall for your soda (a cherry coke? vanilla cream?)

Yours, Ed Beck

Postmarked November 26th

Yes/No

My favorite songs are:

    <u>No</u>   Barry Manilow singing "Copacabana" (pitiful, say no)

    <u>Maybe</u>   Elvis singing, "Are You Lonesome Tonight" (say yes) (sorry)

    True/False

    <u>Maybe</u> I couldn't live without Patsy Cline singing, "I Fall to Pieces"

November 28th

Dear Ms. Ducket:

Great, I knew you couldn't live without Patsy Cline. I feel the same way about Hank. So I'm immortalizing him in my play (I'm writing again!)—the *true* Hank Williams story (what does Hollywood know)—a man who knew in his heart and soul just how silent a falling star is, just how lonesome a purple sky can be. Do you get lonely? I do. In fact, I'm celibate, not that that's of any particular interest except that for me that's unusual.

It was just that women, *some* women, told me I was deep. I liked that. But I'm about as deep as the Salton Sea (average depth more or less 20 feet, depending upon evaporation). My woman friend didn't think I was deep. She thought I was full of shit. She said she loved me for my other qualities. I don't know what she meant. I don't have any other qualities.

Do you think loneliness has anything to do with the void, Ms. Ducket, or is it the reverse? What I mean is, supposing that you were lonely (which I'm not suggesting is so), and the door to meaning yawned open over a large oily black vat and, in desperation, you turned away from the door and hooked up with a playwright who thought that he was deep. Would that be an improvement? I would like to think so, but, quite honestly, Ms. Ducket, I'm not sure any of us can help much with anyone else's large oily vat.

I wish I knew what you wear when you write. A silk kimono? Blue jeans and a red flannel shirt? A pink chenille bathrobe? Do you wear underwear underneath the bathrobe? Sorry, sorry, it's none of my business. But I can see the kitchen now and hear the music, but I can't see *you*.

I'm sorry. I apologize. I sound like a mental peeping tom. It's just that you're my heroine (I'm not saying that you're deep.) See, if you'd read my plays (which may not be the case, I realize) but if you had you'd realize that we are writing about the same thing—introductions! Hank was trying to get past them; so am I. Maybe you are too?

I'm sorry. This is all wrong. I'll just send along this picture postcard of the Empire State Building which they sell at the Model 6. Feel free to add something.

Yours,

Ed Beck

The postcard that was never returned:

I want to be alone because:

    ___an unfaithful man hurt me and I'm trying to recover.

    ___an unfaithful woman hurt me, etc.

    ___the human race is on a roller coaster ride to hell so I prefer to be alone and far away from deep people.

    ___Other (Please specify)

January 1st

Dear Ms. Ducket:

Happy New Year! I feel awful because I haven't heard from you. Did I ask too much? Did I ask *for* too much? Should we stick to introductions? Spot and I are drinking again. I'm sorry, but the winter has been bad—not the weather—the purple sky.

I've worried about you. I hate to think of you spending the winter in that little kitchen. I wonder if you have enough food and firewood. I wonder if you're all right during all those nights when the wind blows and the rain comes down in pellets. But maybe you're sitting in your pink chenille bathrobe by the wood stove, writing with your freshly sharpened Ticonderoga pencil and listening to Elvis sing, "It's Gonna Be a Blue, Blue Christmas Without You." No, maybe Bing Crosby, "White Christmas"? No, that isn't right either. Why can't I imagine this? Where are you Ms. Ducket?

Please send back this picture postcard of Santa Claus at the North Pole. I won't be unfaithful. I'll stop drinking.

Yours,
Ed Beck

Postmarked February 20th

Choose one:

I don't care to discuss the reasons why I did not return your postcard,

___and I don't care to correspond further.

___however, I wish to continue our correspondence.

I am currently at work on:

___a collection of short fiction.

___a novel.

nothing Other (please specify)

February 22nd

Dear Ms. Ducket:

You have made me a happy man! The falling stars sing in the purple sky. You aren't writing? Are you sure? I mean, what do you do then? I don't think you drink. It isn't like you. Did the critics hurt your feelings? But you don't care about the critics, do you? Is it that you, too, feel it is pointless, to write I mean? It *is* pointless, Ms. Ducket, but so is everything else. Just because it's pointless is no reason not to do it. Where would we be if Hank had "never seen a night so long, the time goes crawling by." I'm not exactly sure where we'd be, but wherever it is, I wouldn't want to be there.

Anyway, Ms. Ducket, the point is you just have to go right ahead and write. You know all this, but you are despairing. (Are you? I'm awfully sorry). Anyway, as my mother used to say, if you fall off a horse, you have to get right back on again. Since we didn't have a horse, this never made sense to me. But under the circumstances, Ms. Ducket, whatever the circumstances are, I think this is good advice.

Now what you should do is write, to me. I'm going to be tough. No postcard. But I'll give you a question. Try a word or two. Don't despair.

<u>When do you cry?</u>

Good luck. I'll take care of everything.

Yours, Ed Beck

*** *** ***

March 22nd

Dear Mr. Beck:

The wind blew ...

Sincerely,

Jo Lynne Ducket

March 24th

Dear Ms. Ducket:

You did it! The wind blew... Back to the Formica table, back to Ticonderoga pencils. Wonderful, Ms. Ducket. So it was a very grim day? The sky was clouded over? You were wearing a blue down jacket and a red stocking cap and the wind in your face made your nose run? A grim day, maybe lonely even?

In case it's of any interest, the wind blows here, too. Last night I was trying to write (to you) when all of a sudden a wind came up and took the door right off my trailer. I couldn't get it back on. Spot and I slept all night under the bed. Pretty exciting. Well, not exciting exactly. To tell you the truth, more miserable than anything else.

So your phrase, Ms. Ducket. The wind blew ... I guess this is when you cried. I'm very sorry. A person like you should not have to cry. John Wayne, may he rest in peace, should have to cry. I appreciate your honesty. You'd think I would have cried last night, but I didn't. I don't generally cry. I really never cry, hardly ever, well once in awhile. I cried when I couldn't envision you. That is of no interest whatsoever, but since we're being honest.

So, Ms. Ducket, you're on your way. Try a few more words. Don't get nervous.

Your question:

Do you feel safe?

Yours,

Ed Beck

*** *** ***

April 15th

Dear Mr. Beck:

… the shore grasses …

      Sincerely,

      Jo Lynne Ducket

April 17th

Dear Ms. Ducket:

Beautiful. Perfect. I'm so proud of you. And on twenty-weight bond. Very fancy.

So the wind blew the shore grasses. I'm sorry the world is so unsafe, Ms. Ducket. Look what happened to Patsy—wiped out in her prime. You could stay off airplanes, of course, but then again your food processor could dismember you on any given day. Staying alive isn't any too safe. For example, you're a writer and then—boom!—you can't write. There's no insurance against this kind of thing. Blue Cross doesn't cover it. Getting married doesn't help (although I wouldn't rule it out). Eating fiber doesn't do a thing.

I'm in no position to offer advice on the matter, but the thing to do, Ms. Ducket, is to calm down and keep writing. There's safety in words—not much I admit—but more than there is in a food processor. Finishing a sentence, for example. There it is, safe and sound. You go back a month from now and it hasn't left you, it hasn't cheated on you and it didn't die. It'll talk to you whenever you want and it'll go away when you want to be alone.

So calm down, Ms. Ducket. Me, I'm perfectly calm. Well, I'm calm when I drink anyway, not that I'm drinking, I'm not, which is why I'm not calm, which is why I am not writing much, really not at all. Spot's nervous, too. At night we jump at noises. That's why I don't have a food processor.

Your question, Ms. Ducket:

Do you think you could grow to love Spot?

    Yours,

    Ed Beck

*** *** ***

April 25th

Dear Mr. Beck:

... flat against the sand dunes.

Sincerely,

Jo Lynne Ducket

April 27th

Dear Ms. Ducket:

Oh, congratulations, applause, bouquets! Oh, Ms. Ducket, I'm humbled. I'm inspired! I could write a new play and buy a food processor. Okay, I admit a sentence doesn't seem like much up against a lethal blade or an airplane or weapons of war, but nevertheless, Ms. Ducket, sentences can sometimes spit in the eye of carcinogens and oncoming bullets.

I know you're happy now. You even hum while you write, maybe "Your Cheatin' Heart." Oh Ms. Ducket, hum something else. How about "Sweet Dreams of You"? Perfect.

I had thought it would be nice to have a cherry coke in the Rexall with you. But I guess not. You have much better things to do with your time now. But I still want to read another sentence. I don't really have a reason for this. I can't think of a point to it, but would you write me another sentence, anyway? Whatever you like.

Yours,

Ed Beck

*** *** ***

May 5th

Dear Mr. Beck,
    You can't sleep with a sentence.
        Sincerely,

           Jo Lynne Ducket
           Route 29, Box 492
           East of Gualala

May 8th

Dear Ms. Ducket:

I take your point. I'm on my way. (Two sentences, you might note that, while they may lack the requisite neural receptor sites for proper "sleep," are nevertheless capable of assisting in a seduction. (Anyway I hope so.)) Oh, I know what you're thinking—too many sentences. Okay, we'll sort this out when I get there. I'll pick you up a six-pack of cherry coke in Gualala before I head out on Route 29.

Yours sincerely,
Ed

P.S. I won't say a word. I promise. Not a word. Not a syllable. Not even an utterance. Well, maybe, technically an utterance. What I mean is…

IN MEMORIAM

Julia, dead at six months old

Isabel, dead at 18 months old

Janie or perhaps Jeanie, dead at four or five years old

Tommy, dead at six years old

Randy, dead at 13 years old

Tom, itinerant Afro-American male, unknown age at time of death.

All souls tortured and murdered and buried in the backyard hill. Los Altos, California, between 1947 and 1952

Made in the USA
Columbia, SC
23 April 2022